a beautiful kind of love

ELLIE WADE

Visit my website at www.elliewade.com

ISBN-13: 978-1508952190

To my mother, who has always been my biggest fan.
Thank you for loving and supporting me.
You taught me to value myself at an early age.
Because of you, I've always had the courage to be myself,
to fight for my dreams, and to live a meaningful life.
I love you.

❤

contents

Here's the thing. Life happens. What does that even mean? Well, it means just that.

Life.

Literally.

Just.

Happens.

It is in constant motion, going on, no matter the circumstances and regardless of the outcomes. Sometimes, things happen the way we want them to, and sometimes, they don't.

In actuality, we have little control over how things turn out in the end. It is impossible to know how the choices we make will change the course of our future, how a small break from a relationship might seal our fate, or how an inconsequential choice over something we deem temporary could become permanent.

You see, every action has a reaction, and that reaction has another, and so on and on. Therefore, once that action is put out into the universe, we have no control over the infinite amount of reactions that might occur, forever changing the future.

I don't know if I believe in soul mates, but I do know that someone is out there for everyone.

There is one person who fits so perfectly in my life, someone I love unconditionally—someone who makes me laugh until I cry, and someone who I'm so attracted to that my blood will race through my veins at his every touch.

Okay, that sounds a lot like the definition of a soul mate, so maybe I do believe in it. Perhaps though, people can have more than one, but I don't.

I have one, and his name is Jax Porter.

I have known Jax my whole life, and by extension, I have loved him with every breath I've taken throughout my entire existence. Our mothers have been best friends, and Jax and I were born a mere month apart. Ever since we could communicate through slobbery gurgles, we have been put in the position to be inseparable best friends.

So, one might think our story is sealed, our fate written.

Unfortunately, that's not how it works. Through this experience of life, we have many choices to make, and each one will lead us down another path.

I find myself at a destination that I never imagined, and to be honest, I am terrified of it.

Yet here I am.

Now, I have to figure out where to go from here.

prologue

age twelve

I turn my face, laughing, as a gush of water collides with my cheek. Wiping the wet drops from my eyes, I see Jax surfacing from his recent cannonball.

"That was a big one, right?" His smile is wide with enthusiasm.

"Yeah, it was okay," I tease. "I bet mine will be bigger!"

I swim toward the ladder of our pool, taking note that the normally bright blue liner underneath the rippling water is taking on more of a greenish hue than normal. I love our pool in the humid Michigan summers, but I hate cleaning it. I sigh inwardly, remembering that it's my week to vacuum the pool. *Yuck.* Maybe I can bribe my younger sister, Keeley, to do it for me. She is usually pretty easy to win over. Admittedly, she sucks slightly more than I do when it comes to cleaning our algae-happy pool, so perhaps that isn't such a good idea.

"Sure, *Little*. Give it your best shot!" Jax grins as he flexes his arm muscles, displaying his manly biceps.

I grab on to the ladder and pull myself up, shaking my head, with a big grin spread across my face. He always makes me laugh. He has been my best friend for as long as I can remember.

Our mothers have been best friends since they were young. They grew up as next-door neighbors, and because they were each the only child in their families, they were more like sisters. They were each pregnant at the same time with Jax and me. So, we have been thrown together since we were born—or at least a month after I was born since I am a month older than Jax.

"Hey, it's Lil, not Little!" I say in reference to Jax's love of switching my nickname as a joke. "And remember, 'Though she be but little, she is fierce.'" The framed Shakespeare quote has adorned my bedroom wall for several years. It was a birthday present from Jax's mom, Susie.

The Little jokes are just that—jokes. I'm not abnormally small for my age. Well, I was one of the smallest girls in the sixth grade, but I know that in a month, come seventh grade, I am going to shoot up. At least I hope I will.

Usually, my size doesn't bother me, but I was the last girl in my class to get my period, and that was embarrassing. I wear a training bra, but to be honest, I don't even need it. I've got nothing. My older sister, Amy, is fifteen, and she has had legitimate boobs since she was twelve.

I steal a glance at her sitting in the lounge chair on the side of the pool, reading her Kindle. She looks like Mom in her bikini. She has hips and everything.

I still wear my purple one-piece. I refuse to wear a bikini. It would only draw attention to my wimpy boy body, not that it matters. Other than the few snide comments the bratty girls in my class have made, it doesn't affect me that I have no curves whatsoever.

I get a running start off of the diving board, and thinking big and heavy thoughts for maximum splash effect, I jump as high as I can before grabbing my legs and crashing my balled-up body into the water with what I'm sure is an epic splash.

When I surface, Jax calls out, "Seven, max. Maybe even a six and a half."

"No way!" I protest. "That was at least a nine!" I tread water as I wipe the drops from my eyes. "What do you think, Kee Kee?" I direct my question to my nine-year-old sister.

She is adjusting her face mask and snorkel. She has been practicing her snorkeling abilities nonstop lately.

Her eyes appear bigger, showcased through the thick plastic of the hot-pink face mask she's wearing. She spits the snorkel out of her mouth. "I don't know, Lily. I wasn't really watching." She shrugs her shoulders.

"That doesn't matter, Keeley! You should always side with me. I'm your sister!"

She shrugs again before placing her face in the water to resume her snorkeling.

Jax chuckles. "Ah, poor little Lily. Can't get your sister to cheat for you? As I said, six and a half."

"Hey, mister, you said seven first! You are not taking it back. Besides, I give yours a five!"

He slaps his hand through the water, sending a wave into my face. "You're a sore loser, Lil."

"No, I'm not because I didn't lose. You got a five," I say indignantly. I swim to the front of the pool where I can stand.

Jax follows. He grabs my hands in his, entwining his fingers through mine. "Name That Tune?"

I grin. "Okay. You go first."

Hands intertwined, we take a deep breath and let our bodies sink into the water. With our heads submerged, Jax begins to belt out a song under the water. I listen really closely because it is very difficult to hear the song through the water. It reminds me of what that teacher from Charlie Brown would sound like if she were singing.

We run out of breath and come up for air.

"Any guesses?" he asks.

"Hmm. It sounded like Whitney Houston's 'I Will Always Love You.'"

"Huh?" Utter confusion is etched across his face. "I have no idea what song you're talking about."

"I know you have heard that song before!"

"No, Lily, I haven't," he answers seriously.

"It is a classic. Haven't you ever watched *The Bodyguard*?"

"Body what?"

"*The Bodyguard*. It's an old movie with Whitney Houston and that other actor guy." I love to watch all my mom's old movies.

"Lily, seriously. Guess a song that I would actually know."

I let out a sigh. "Fine, but it sounded exactly like that song."

"Um, no, it didn't. Now, give me a real guess." He smirks.

"That was a real guess, but fine. Let me think. 'Get the Party Started' by Pink."

He laughs. "No. It sounded nothing like that."

"Fine, I give up. What song were you singing?" I remove my hands from his and cross my arms as I pout.

"Work It by Missy Elliot."

"What?" I ask in confusion.

"I heard it on Landon's iPod, and it's about sex, I think."

I cover my mouth in a gasp before hitting him on the chest. "Ew! Why would I know about that song? That's gross! Does your mom know that Landon listens to that type of music?"

"He's seventeen. I'm sure my mom doesn't care. Anyway, the song is funny. Lighten up."

"Gross. No, I'm never going to listen to a song about that. That is disgusting, and you shouldn't be listening to it either. Plus, you have to pick a song that I'd know, or this game is stupid." I resume my crossed-arms, pouty position.

He chuckles. "Okay, fine. Your turn. The same goes for you—pick a song that I'd know."

"Okay. Ready?" Releasing my arms from my display of irritation, I grab a hold of his hands, and we go under the water once more.

After we've gone through six songs and six unsuccessful guesses, my mom brings out a tray of food and beverages and places it on the patio table under the shade of the umbrella.

"Kiddos, lemonade and chicken salad pitas are ready. You must be hungry."

"Thanks, Mom," I say as I climb out of the pool.

"Thanks, Miranda," he addresses my mom as he follows behind me.

"Jax, your mom texted me a while back. Landon will be over to pick you up in an hour. Your dad's benefit is tonight, and you have to go home to get ready."

He groans. "Ugh. Seriously? Did she say if I could bring Lil?"

"I don't think so, honey. I think your dad just wants you and Landon there today."

"This sucks." He plops down in a lawn chair and takes a big bite of the pita sandwich.

Mr. Porter is the CEO of a big advertising firm in Kalamazoo that's about forty minutes away from here. The firm seems to always have some dinner or event that requires the Porter family to dress up. Jax hates it, but he hates it less when I'm allowed to tag along. When I go, we manage to make it fun.

We live in the country, outside of the small town of Athens—and I'm talking, a one-blinking-red-light-in-the-center-of-town small. We have one gas station, a bar, a family-owned ice cream place, and that's about all.

Jax's dad is probably one of the most successful people in our town, and although they are good people, his parents carry themselves with an air of superiority, especially his dad. My dad is a lawyer, working in the same city as Mr. Porter, but I'd say our family is more easygoing.

I grab a pita and a glass of lemonade, and I collapse onto the lounge chair next to Jax. "It won't be that bad." I nudge him with my shoulder.

He gives me an unenthusiastic grunt and finishes his pita in four bites. "Well, I have an hour. What do you want to do? Play Mario?"

"No. I don't want to be inside. Ride bikes?" I ask.

"Yeah, that's cool."

My mom approaches me with a metal aerosol can in hand. "Lily, let me spray you again with sunscreen."

I stand without argument and put my arms out, preparing for the SPF onslaught. Even though I just lathered up over an hour ago, I know better than to question my mom when it comes to my skin protection. I am engulfed in an SPF cloud smelling of coconut and chemicals.

"Okay, let me get your face with the lotion."

"Mom, I can wipe lotion on my face," I say. I turn toward her and watch her lather up her hands with the greasy cream.

"I know, honey. I just want to make sure you're good and protected. The sun is hot today."

I have a light splattering of freckles across the brim of my nose, which my dad insists is the cutest part about me. If it weren't for my mom's commitment to skincare, I would probably be covered in them. I'm definitely the most fair-skinned person in my family. My mom and Keeley have blonde hair and blue eyes as well, but both their skin and hair are slightly darker than mine.

"All right, Jax. Let me get you now."

"I'm fine. Really, Miranda," he protests.

"Nope. Your skin needs protection, too. Come here, you."

I giggle at his expression as my mom rubs sunscreen onto his face. He is definitely the opposite of me with his raven hair and olive skin.

His emerald eyes look mildly annoyed as he turns away from my mom. "Ready?"

"Ready, Freddy!"

"Don't forget your helmets!" my mom yells as we make our way toward the garage.

I wave my arm in acknowledgment of her directive.

We pedal along the country road that weaves between expansive cornfields. The cornstalks are taller than me now, which is an indication that summer will soon come to an end and we will welcome our seventh grade year.

"What do you want to do for your birthday this year?" he calls out as we glide speedily down a hill.

"I don't know. What do you think?"

Both our families make a big deal of birthdays, throwing extravagant parties.

"Well, thirteen is, like, an important one, isn't it? I'm sure your mom is going to go all out."

My birthday is at the end of August, right before school starts up. "Not sure if I want a huge party this year. Maybe I should just do something with you and my family."

"What about all our friends from school?"

"Meh," I let out an uninterested sound.

Sure, I have friends at school, but Jax is my best friend, and he's the only one who really matters.

"Come on. You don't want to invite our whole class and have a giant bash? We could have a bonfire outside and put on music for dancing. Maybe we could play Spin the Bottle or something. You're going to be thirteen. Don't thirteen-year-olds do stuff like that?"

"Jax! What has gotten into you today? First, songs about dirty stuff, and now, kissing? I'm not letting our whole class put their germy mouths on mine. Ew. No, thank you. Dinner and a movie, it is!"

He throws his head back and laughs. "You're a prude sometimes, Miss Lily Madison. I feel bad for the first guy who tries to date you."

"You're being so weird right now. I think we both have a while to worry about that."

"I've been thinking about asking Katie Phelps out."

Katie is one of the most popular girls in our class. I'm not sure how much that is saying, considering we go to such a small school and our class consists of sixty kids. I think of her as a friend, but she can be bossy sometimes.

"Really? How does that even work? You are too young to date." I feel tightness in my chest that I can't quite explain.

"Yeah. Well, obviously, I wouldn't literally take her out, but we would talk on the phone and see each other at school. We could have our parents drop us off at the movies or something, too. You and I do that all the time."

"I know, but that is different. We are friends. Will your parents really let you hang out with a girl you like?"

"I don't know. I guess I'll see."

"Well, when would we hang out?"

I don't want to share Jax. He's too good for Katie anyway.

"We would hang out like normal. That wouldn't change." He sounds sure.

"Yeah, it'd better not," I say with authority.

"You're silly. Come on. Let's head back."

I nod, knowing that Landon is going to be at my house shortly to get Jax.

We pedal back to my house in relative silence. I'm lost in my thoughts, wondering why he wants to date. It seems kinda odd to me. If I'm honest with myself, I'm nervous. Jax has been my partner in crime since we could crawl. I don't want to share him, not yet.

I change my mind on things a lot, but Jax is the one thing I'm sure of. He's my best friend, and I'm not letting him go.

11

one

five years later

I scan the crowded stands for my friend Kristyn as I walk toward the packed seats. Everyone from our town came out for tonight's football game against our rival school. I stop a moment in front of the concession stand near the chain-link fence surrounding the football field and watch the band's preshow. The cheerleaders are in sync with the music as they dance on the track that circles the field. They are wearing their skirts today due to the unseasonably warm autumn air. I love Friday night football games on our home field, especially when the weather isn't awful.

"Lily!"

I hear my name and turn to see Kristyn waving at me from the third row. I wave back and make my way toward her.

I shuffle my way in front of the seated people, inching closer to Kristyn in the center of the row.

"Hey." I smile when I reach her. "Sorry I'm late." I don't offer up an excuse because I don't have one. Sometimes, I'm not always the most punctual person. Even though I was supposed to meet Kristyn in the parking lot twenty minutes ago, I'm just proud of myself that I made it here well before kickoff.

"No worries." She smiles warmly at me.

Kristyn is my closest friend at school besides Jax. She is great and would do anything for me. I adore her.

I look out onto the field in search of him. I know it sounds silly, but I feel his stare on me. I catch his gaze as he stands there, all padded up while holding the football to his chest. I wave, grinning enthusiastically, before giving him a thumbs-up. He shakes his head, and his eyes shine with humor. Though I can't hear him, I know he chuckles before turning away from me, throwing the football to another player.

Jax has been the varsity starting quarterback since last year. It is unusual for a sophomore to start on varsity, especially as the quarterback, but when it comes to Jax, I'm not surprised. He is naturally talented at most things. He gets great grades with minimal effort and has excelled at every sport he's attempted.

"How is Jax feeling about the game?" Kristyn asks.

"Good. I think he is confident that we'll win tonight."

I focus on his arm muscles as they flex with every throw. He truly is a hot specimen, and I can totally understand why every girl here—and from the surrounding schools, for that matter—is all gaga over him.

"Well, the other team is undefeated so far this season," Kristyn notes.

"Yeah, so are we. I'm not worried."

My leg is forcefully pushed to the side, and I pull it back and look up to see Maeve, Jax's current girlfriend, walking in front of me.

"Oh, I'm sorry, *Lily*," Maeve says with a voice that shows anything but. She puts emphasis on my name, and it sounds vile coming from her mouth.

I grin reluctantly, acknowledging her pseudo-apology, and wrap my arms around my shins, holding my legs out of harm's way, while she and her posse continue their way across the row to the seats at the end.

Kristyn leans over and whispers in my ear, "Have you told Jax about her yet?"

I shake my head, indicating that I haven't.

"Why not? He would never be with her if he knew she was such a bitch to you."

I turn toward Kristyn. "He will figure it out on his own. He always does," I say in a low voice.

"No, you should really tell him, Lily."

"There will always be bitches in this world, Kristyn. They don't bother me too much. I just ignore them." I shrug.

"Promise me, if she ever crosses the line, you will tell him." Her voice is heavy with concern.

"I promise." But as I say it, I know that it will never come to that.

Jax will discover Maeve's true character before I have to say anything. I didn't know Maeve much before she and Jax started dating about a month ago. She is a senior, and we didn't have too much contact with each other prior to this year. I'm not surprised that she is rude to me. Many of his girlfriends in the past have been as well. They always start out cool, but I think jealousy eventually kicks in when they realize how close he and I actually are, and then the claws come out. Jealousy really isn't attractive on anyone.

It seems that Jax has had a girlfriend of some sort pretty much since seventh grade, but I will say that it hasn't affected our relationship too much. Our friendship is solid, and he puts me first. It's not like I've asked him to choose between his girlfriend and me because I haven't, and I would never ask him to. He values our friendship and always makes time for us. As soon as he notices a girl's jealousness or rudeness toward me, he ends the relationship without a second thought.

The game is exhilarating the entire way through. The two teams go back and forth, but we come out a touchdown ahead. I love watching Jax in his element, and I'm so proud of him. The guys are going wild on the field, raising their fists in triumph.

I'm happy we won, especially because having to hang out with the guys tonight after a loss would have been a complete downer. There is a big bonfire in a secluded field on a classmate's property. Those of us from small town Michigan might not be known for much, but we have sweet-ass bonfires.

I watch as the players exit the field and head toward the doors leading to the locker room. Jax breaks away from the line of rowdy football players and jogs toward me. I stand and leave the bleachers, followed by Kristyn. I weave my way through the celebration to meet him halfway.

He pulls me into a sweaty hug, squeezing me with a fierce intensity.

"Great game!" I congratulate him.

"Thanks! Wait for me, and you can ride with me to the field." He pulls away and locks me in his intense stare.

"It's okay. I'm going to catch a ride with Kristyn. I will meet you there."

He skeptically looks at me. "Are you sure?"

I smile. "Yes, I'm sure. I will see you there, okay?"

He pauses for a moment. "Okay."

"Good game. Seriously, I'm so proud of you, Jax."

"Thanks, Little. See you soon." He uses his personal nickname for me.

It stems from when he was a toddler. He thought my mom was calling me Little when she was saying Lil, and it has stuck. I used to hate it when I was younger, but I love it now.

I hear the shrill tone of Maeve's voice calling out Jax's name behind me, and I give Kristyn a subtle look. We leave Jax and make our way toward the parking lot.

I bounce off the seat in the cab of Kristyn's pickup truck as we careen down the bumpy path to the field. As we get closer, I see the huge fire already well ablaze. Logs and bales of hay are positioned around the fire, forming a circle around the flames. Another larger ring of hay bales is around the first one, creating two seating areas facing the bonfire. Poles are positioned in equal distances from each other between the two circles. Little white Christmas lights are strung from one pole to the next, surrounding the seating areas in a blanket of soft white light. Beyond the twinkling lights are the outskirts of the field surrounded by dark woods. Music is pounding with deep bass coming from the speakers positioned in the back of someone's rusty Ford F-150.

After we park in the line of cars at the edge of the woods, we head toward the fire.

"It's going to be a crazy one with that win tonight," Kristyn says.

"Yeah, I figure it will be." I scan over the crowd of my schoolmates already congregating with red Solo cups in their hands. "Do you want to find the keg? I can drive you home if you want to drink."

I'm not much of a beer fan. I know they say it is an acquired taste, but I don't think I will ever acquire it. It tastes bitter and dreadful to me.

"No, I'm good. I don't feel like drinking tonight," she responds.

"Yeah, me neither, especially something that tastes like pee." I scrunch up my nose.

She giggles. "Exactly."

I hear my name and turn to find Alden heading in our direction.

Alden is a great guy. We have several classes together. His grandfather owns this land that we are on. He has been increasingly friendly with me lately, and I get the impression that he likes me. I'm not a very good judge of that sort of thing though. I haven't ever had a boyfriend, but I admit that I haven't put any effort into getting one. My life is pretty full with my family activities, studying, my friends, and Jax. Unlike Jax, I actually have to study hard for my good grades. It's only the fall of my junior year, so I don't feel like I'm missing out on the high school relationship deal yet. I have time.

Alden closes the gap between us and hugs me. He releases me before pulling Kristyn into one. Letting go of Kristyn, he turns to me, "So glad you could make it. Can I get you something to drink?"

"No, we're good. Thanks though." I smile up at him, and I take note of how close we are standing.

I bet I could feel his breath against my face if I leaned in a fraction more. I am terrified to do so. It probably smells like beer or something else unappealing. It's better to imagine it in a positive light.

I'm spoiled with Jax. He is the only guy my age who gets this close to me, and he always smells wonderful. I know it sounds cliché, but he really is walking perfection. Any guy I date is going to have big shoes to fill. Jax and I aren't like that, but I know I will inadvertently compare everyone to him. He is what I know.

"Come on. A group of us are over there." Alden nods toward the seating area.

"Sure," I agree.

He places his hand against the small of my back and leads me to the warmth of the crackling flames. We are making our way around the fire and in the direction of the bales he indicated when I hear Jax.

"Lil!"

I stop walking and pivot on one foot in the direction from where we just came. I'm met by Jax's open arms as he pulls me into a hug.

"Have you been here long?"

"No, we actually just got here," I reply.

"Oh, good. Hey, I have to go talk to Paul. You coming?"

"Um, sure. Just let me..." I look behind me to speak to Alden, but he is no longer there.

My eyes skim the faces congregated around the fire, all cast in a warm golden hue, and I spot him on the opposite side of us, speaking with some friends. He raises his head to meet my stare and smiles shyly, giving me an upward nod, before returning to his conversation.

"Okay, never mind. Let's go."

Kristyn and I hang out with Jax and most of the football team for the majority of the night.

Maeve showed up shortly after Jax, and she has been draped all over him ever since. She really does annoy me to no end. It's not jealousy I feel but simple irritation with her obnoxious behavior.

I contemplate expanding my social circle, and I go to talk to others, but I don't venture too far away from Jax. I never do. Maybe it is the fact that he has been close to me from the moment he was born, but I feel unsettled when I'm too far away from him.

As the night wears on, the gathering thins, and the random groups of people sporadically positioned around the fire come together to become one single crowd.

"Hey."

I hear Alden's voice at the same time I feel his hand on my arm. I turn to him. His eyelids appear heavy as if he is concentrating on keeping them open.

I chuckle as he sways. "How's the beer?" I ask, motioning to the red cup full of sloshing liquid in his hand.

"Good! Can I get you some?"

I shake my head. "No, I'm still good. Thanks."

Letting go of my arm, he lifts his free hand and takes a strand of my hair in his fingers. He studies it before he tucks it behind my ear. Despite his obvious inebriated state, the gesture is sweet, and I'm mesmerized as I watch him take in my face.

"You're so pretty, Lily."

"Alden."

Jax's voice comes from behind me, and I jump, startled. The trance that drunken sweet Alden had me under is shattered.

"Oh, hey, man," Alden addresses Jax. "See ya, Lil." He smiles weakly before he turns to someone beside me and starts up a conversation.

I take a few steps away from Alden before addressing Jax, "What was that all about?"

"What?" he asks innocently.

"Um…that"—I motion to Alden—"thing between you and him. You ran him off."

Jax nods. "He was hitting on you."

My eyebrows rise. "So?"

He shrugs. "He's not good enough for you."

I sigh. "That's what you say about every guy. Alden's really nice."

"He's drunk," Jax says matter-of-factly.

"Yeah, and so are most of the people here. Who cares?"

"I do."

"You have to stop scaring away every guy who wants to talk to me. You're worse than my dad."

Jax feigns innocence. "I only do that to the ones who aren't worth your time."

I scrunch my lips into a pout and look up to Jax in annoyance before answering, "Apparently, that is every boy in our high school."

"Basically, yeah," he agrees. "Don't be mad." He pulls me into a hug and kisses the top of my head.

"I'm not. It would be nice to expand my friendship circle, is all. You can't always be around, Jax."

"For you, Lily, I can. I'm always here for you. You know that." He kisses me again on top of my head before he is yanked away.

"Jax! I miss you," Maeve whines. She has become increasingly drunk as the night has progressed, as evident by her speech morphing into one long slurred mess and the decibel of her voice passing the point of obnoxiously loud.

Vomit explodes from Maeve's mouth onto the grass in front of his feet.

"Whoa!" Jax yells, jumping back. "Damn!" He makes his way behind Maeve to steady her as she expels everything from her stomach.

Becca, Maeve's best friend, steps beside Jax. "Seriously?" I hear the annoyance in her voice. "I will take her home."

Becca glares at the now dry-heaving mess. Maeve is bent over with her arms propped on her knees as she coughs toward the ground.

"Are you sure?" Jax asks, appearing concerned.

I know that he is trying to camouflage his relief.

Becca wraps her arms around Maeve's waist. "Yeah, I got her. It's fine." She leads Maeve toward the line of vehicles parked up against the tree line.

I turn to Kristyn. She is smirking in the direction of the retreating girls. She briefly shakes her head and then steps closer to me.

"I think I'm actually going to get going, too. Do you want me to take you home?" she asks.

Before I can answer, Jax says from behind me, "I got her. Thanks, Kristyn."

We say our good-byes, and I turn toward Jax.

"So, is it going to be refrigerator exploration or Denny's?" he asks, leaning in close to my face.

When we are together on weekend nights, we usually hang out and have a late-night meal. We either hunt through the refrigerator at one of our homes to see what yummy leftovers await, or we drive thirty minutes to the next town where a Denny's is open twenty-four hours.

"I think it is a Denny's kind of night."

He flashes me his all-American boy smile. "I agree. Let's get out of here."

Grabbing my cell from my back pocket, I shoot my mom a text, letting her know I'm going to eat with Jax and will be home late. As long as I'm with Jax and keep her posted on our plans, I don't have a curfew. She adores him and completely trusts him.

I love our late-night dinner dates. Jax and I spend a lot of time together, but the older we get, the less uninterrupted quality time we have. We can spend hours talking and laughing at Denny's, and we have many times. We never run out of things to say. He is my favorite person in this world to be with.

Now, the only question is, what am I going to order tonight? I'm always so indecisive. I could go with sweet and get French toast or savory and get a burrito. Or I could do something different altogether.

"So, what are you in the mood for tonight?" Jax asks in an amused tone.

I chuckle. I swear, he can read my mind sometimes.

I shake my head. "I'm torn. I don't know."

"Okay, give me your options, and we'll go over the pros and cons of each."

Giggling, I begin to tell him my meal choices, and so begins our twenty-minute conversation on what I should order. As I said, we can talk about anything.

two

Tilting my head to the side, I peer into the full-length mirror adorning the bathroom wall and take in my appearance. My black dress is long and tight, accentuating every curve of my body. The front dips just enough to display my very average cleavage in an attractive manner. I rotate to the side to catch a glimpse of the back of my dress, and my pale skin reflects back at me. The dark silky fabric falls from my shoulders, leaving almost the entirety of my back exposed, and ends in a swooping fashion at the base of my spine, seemingly millimeters from the crack of my rear.

I can see my cheeks getting pink as I wrap my head around the fact that I'm going out in this dress. The dress is sexy, simple as that, yet that term *sexy* in itself is not one that I would use to describe myself. Normally, I might use pretty, athletic, and maybe a bit plain. But sexy? No.

I went dress shopping with Kristyn, and she about squealed herself into a frenzy when I tried on this dress. She all but insisted I get it. I decided to be bold and go for it, but now, I'm having second thoughts.

A small chuckle escapes from my glossy lips as I remember my parents' reactions to this dress. I tried it on for them when I got home from shopping. As I twirled, showing off my prom dress, they both sat stoically on the living room sofa. My dad's mouth was held shut in a tight line, and his big blue eyes bulged from their sockets. My mom had on her classic nice face, the one she gives someone from town when she doesn't agree with what the person is saying but doesn't want to be rude. Her unmoving expression, although containing a smile, wasn't one of authentic approval. Yet they didn't say anything negative about it, and I still don't know why. From a parent's perspective, this dress is a little intense.

As I breathe deeply, working to bring my cheeks back to their normal color, I can now admit to myself that this dress isn't me. But at the same time, why not? It's gorgeous, and I feel beautiful in it.

"Doesn't she look so pretty?" Keeley beams as she faces her iPhone my way.

I can see Amy on the screen, her mouth wide in a smile.

"Yes, she does." Her voice comes over the phone's speaker. "I'm so sorry I couldn't make it home for your first prom, Lil."

"It's fine, Amy, really." I take the phone from Keeley and blow a kiss toward the screen.

I wish my big sister could have been here as well, but I understand. She had to take incompletes in her classes at the University of Michigan this past semester due to a vicious bout with mono. So, she has had to stay up at school for a few weeks longer to finish all her coursework. If she can't be here, FaceTime is the next best thing.

"Are you excited to go with *Jax*?" She enunciates all the letters in Jax's name, like it contains four As instead of the one it has.

I look to the screen, taking note of her raised eyebrow. "Why do you say it like that?"

"Oh, no reason," she answers in a singsong voice. "I bet he will look hot, all dressed up in his tux."

Of course he will. "Um, yeah, obviously," I answer, shaking my head.

Jax is always gorgeous. I've seen him in a tux several times before, and he definitely hasn't disappointed in that attire either. This is Jax's third prom. Older girls asked him to their proms during his freshman and sophomore year. This is my first one, and I'm so happy that Jax is currently without a girlfriend. There is no one I would rather experience prom with than my best friend.

My mom walks into the bathroom where I currently have primping materials strewed about the granite countertop. "Lily, honey, Kristyn and her parents just pulled in." My mom stops next to me and runs her hand down the length of my arm before gently squeezing my wrist. "Oh, honey, you are so beautiful."

I lean in for a hug. "Thanks, Mom."

"Hi, Mom!" Amy yells from behind my mother's back where the phone still rests in my hand.

We all chuckle, and after I release the embrace, I hand the phone back to Keeley.

Sucking my tummy in, I bend at the waist to buckle my heels. The material clinging to my body is making it a more strenuous task than normal. Once my shoes are on, I grab my clutch from the counter and take one last look in the mirror before following my mom and sister out of my room.

I skip down the carpeted stairs to the kitchen—as best as one can skip in three-inch heels. I stop at the mirror at the bottom of the steps and apply another thin layer of pink lip gloss for good measure. I head out the back sliding glass door to the deck where a group of friends and their parents have started to congregate.

Shielding my eyes from the warm May sun, I scan the small crowd. Everyone is here but Jax and his parents.

"Lily!" Kristyn calls.

She approaches me in a poufy princess-esque dress made of coral satin material with gold embellishments on the skirt. She looks stunning with her long brown hair curled into ringlets and pinned together in an elegant side ponytail resting over her shoulder. She is wearing more eye makeup than I've ever seen her wear. The gold metallic hues decorating her lids make her big brown eyes seem even larger. She really does look like a princess.

"Kristyn, you truly look amazing." I examine her from head to feet once more.

She blushes. "Thanks. You, too."

Ben, Kristyn's boyfriend, walks up and wraps his arm around her middle. "I told her the same thing." He stares down at her with a look of appreciation. "Gorgeous."

She playfully hits him on the chest. "Stop it." Turning to me, she says, "So, what did we decide on for dinner? Red Robin?"

"Yeah, I think so." I nod my head. "They do have the best food ever." I'm a huge fan of their fries dipped in ranch.

"I agree," she answers.

Kristyn and I are taking some group selfies with the other girls when Susie's enthusiastic voice cuts through the yard, and I turn to see Jax's mom speaking to my own.

A huge smile graces my face when I see Jax standing across the lawn, his eyes fixed on me. A sigh escapes my mouth as my eyes devour him. My friend is so beautiful. It's true. I totally think it is acceptable to call a guy beautiful, especially if that guy is Jax Porter, because, holy heck, he is.

I begin walking across the grass toward him, my steps a giddy bounce. We meet in the middle, and he wraps his strong arms around me, pulling me close. He smells like Jax, and there are no words to describe that smell, other than intoxicating.

His hold on me lingers. Loosening his grasp slightly, he scans my body from my heels to my face. His tongue darts out to lick his lips. "You look beautiful, Lil." His deep voice penetrates my skin, causing goose bumps to appear.

"You, too. Well, handsome, I mean. You look very handsome." Okay, so you can't call a guy beautiful to his face.

"Thanks, Little." Jax's full lips form a grin as he looks down at me.

Something in his expression is different, almost hesitant.

"Smile!" My mom beams, touching her iPhone screen.

We turn toward the rapid-fire clicking of the phone with my mom's bright expression peeking out from behind her pink case. Jax's arms retreat from behind my back and squeeze gently at my arms before he releases me.

After a plethora of pictures, we all hop into the limo to take us to dinner. Everyone chats excitedly at the restaurant as we wait for our food, except for Jax. He is quiet, and it's an odd change from his normal exuberance.

My knee brushes his, and I squeeze his forearm. "You okay?"

His gaze meets mine, and I see a multitude of emotions in his stare.

I wonder if something happened before he came to my house earlier. Sometimes, Jax gets in quiet moods, and they are usually a result of an argument with his dad. Mr. Porter is a good man, but he is tough on his boys. He wants Landon and Jax to be the very best at everything, and he doesn't ever seem quite happy with their many accomplishments. It's never enough for him, and it is so infuriating.

As I hold on to Jax's arm, I get the sense that his mood isn't a result of a confrontation with his father. Something is off, but I'm not sure what it is.

He lowers his head and kisses my forehead. "I'm good."

"Promise?"

"I promise," he replies.

The waitress sets my burger down in front of me. I scan the delectable contents of my plate, noticing that she forgot my ranch. I can't eat Red Robin fries without their heavenly ranch. I open my mouth to ask her for some, but before I get the first word out, Jax has placed his plastic cup of ranch on my plate.

Closing my mouth, I turn my face in his direction, and I'm greeted with a wink. "Thank you."

"Anytime."

Throughout dinner, Jax's temperament morphs back into something resembling his usual demeanor. I catch him directing a few thoughtful glances my way through his bites of burger. But other than that, he seems more like himself. He talks and jokes with the rest of the group sitting around our table.

Walking into the reception hall of the hotel is a fun experience. I've been to many fancy dinners with Jax and his family through their connections in the business world, but prom is different. It could be the overabundance of balloon usage. Giant balloon arches cocoon the dance floor in the center of the room. Large bundles of balloons sit in every corner along with some smaller balloon arches scattered about, which I'm assuming are backdrops for photos. The prom theme this year is *The Wizard of Oz*, and I smile as I walk on the glittery yellow brick paper road leading to the dance floor. Off to the side is a large sparkly red shoe, and I see some girls sitting in it for a photo op.

I grab Jax's hand. "Oh! Let's get our picture in the shoe! Kristyn, can you take it for us?"

"Of course," she answers.

We make our way to the shoe and wait for our turn to hop in it. When the girls in front of us finish all their selfies, Jax and I climb in. He sits behind me and wraps his arms around my middle. I lean back into him as I smile big, holding his hands resting on my stomach.

I pivot around so that I can see his face. "Thanks for bringing me to prom, Jax."

A small grin spreads across his face. "I wouldn't want it any other way, Lil."

We stare into each other's eyes for a moment before Kristyn's voice breaks through my happy haze. "Can you take ours now?"

I clear my throat. "Um…yeah, sure."

The pounding rhythm of the music pours through the speakers, and I'm all smiles as I dance with Kristyn and some other girlfriends under the giant balloon arches. I look toward our table to find Jax's gaze on me. He lowers his stare, swirling a bit of red punch in the plastic tumbler. I watch as he continues to glare at the remaining punch at the bottom of his glass, deep in concentration. Something is definitely off with him tonight.

Is he upset that he's not here with a girlfriend?

He broke up with his last girlfriend about a month ago, which gave him plenty of time to find another girl to date. But he didn't.

No, that couldn't be it anyway. He was sincere earlier when he said he was glad to be here with me.

So, what is it? He is acting strange, and that's worrisome.

I tell my friends that I will be back, and then I make my way over to him.

"Let's dance!" I reach down, take his hand in mine, and pull. "Come on. You love dancing. Why are you being a stick in the mud?"

Jax chuckles and takes my hand, following me onto the dance floor. The troubled expression on his face melts away as we move to the music.

I squeal softly in excitement as the thumping loud beat changes to the soft melody of my new favorite slow song that has been getting a lot of airtime on satellite radio.

"It's my song, Jax." I wrap my arms around his neck.

"I know, Lil. I'm with you every day, and you freak out each time it is played." He circles his arms around my waist, pulling me close to him.

"I do not freak out."

"Uh, yes…yes, you do."

I chuckle. "Fine, maybe a little. But can you blame me?"

Jax's warm hands rest against my skin exposed from the low swoop of my dress, causing a heated shiver to run up my spine. I am cognizant of everything about him as I lean my head against his chest. I can hear his heartbeat through the smooth fabric of his dress shirt, and that simple sound causes butterflies to flutter in my belly.

Apparently, Jax isn't the only one who is acting odd tonight. I'm aware of my issues this evening, and they are all centered around my body's reaction to this hottie who I'm currently pressed against. I'm not blind to his good looks and charm. I spend more time with him than anyone, so if anyone knows how wonderful he is, it is me. Yet I've never been so *aware* of...him. I'm always conscious of the attractive qualities in Jax, but I'm usually able to push it out of my head.

But tonight?

Tonight, I can barely breathe correctly with his arms around me, and it is maddening.

Why am I reacting like this?

I want to end this crazy act of betrayal that my body is committing, but I can't. The attraction is so strong that it is out of my control. But I have to rein it in. It isn't an option. My seventeen-year-old hormones might be going out on a suicide mission, but I refuse to follow. Nothing is worth making things awkward with Jax. Wearing my crazy attraction on my sleeve would definitely cause weirdness between us, and I'm not about to do that.

I hear the first three notes Elvis's "Can't Help Falling in Love," and I squeal again as Jax pulls me in closer. My mom is a huge Elvis fan, and Jax and I have danced to this song more than a hundred times in our lives. It is one of my favorite songs. I can't help but love it and the timeless beauty portrayed with every note and lyric. I wrap my arms tighter around Jax's neck. Our bodies are flush against each other, moving instinctually to the music that holds a special place in our lives.

A warm smile spreads across my face. "I can't believe they are playing this song."

"I requested it, and I made it extremely clear to the DJ that my Little had to dance to this song tonight."

My heart fills with even more love for my sweet friend. "Thank you." I lean my head against his chest. I close my eyes and hum along to the song.

We are in our own little world on this dance floor, and I'm so happy that I feel like I could float away on a cloud.

Jax and I are still wrapped up in each other, dancing to another song, when Ben comes up behind us.

"Hey, guys, let's get out of here."

"So, what should we do?" Kristyn asks as we stand outside the banquet hall.

Having gotten enough dancing in, everyone in our group agreed that we should leave fashionably early. We have the limo until one a.m., so we have three hours to kill before we call it a night.

"We could have him drive us to South Haven?" I suggest.

The white sandy beach of Lake Michigan is Jax's and my favorite place to go in the summer.

The group murmurs their approval, and we all climb into the limo. Blasting music, we dance around in our seats and chat adamantly until the limo pulls into a parking area alongside the beach.

We all pile out of the limo.

"Wait. Let's leave our shoes here," I suggest as I bend to unclip the buckles on my heels. I love the way the soft sand feels between my toes.

"Okay," Jax agrees. He removes his dress shoes and socks, and then he rolls up the cuffs of his pants.

The air has a bit of a bite. The sun's absence along with the cool air from the water blowing across the beach sends a shiver down my spine. Jax gives me his jacket, and I hike up the bottom of my dress, holding it in one hand as we walk through the cool sand. The other couples have dispersed, no longer visible to me in the faint glow of the moon reflecting off the rippling water.

"So, this is what prom is like?" I ask, looping my free arm through Jax's.

"No, this prom is much cooler than the other ones I have gone to."

"No way. You are just saying that." I nudge his side.

"No, I'm not. I'm serious. Of course it is better. I'm with you. You make everything more fun."

"Well, had I gone to prom before...I'm sure this one would be better, too. Is everything okay? Are you feeling all right? You seem quieter tonight."

"Everything's fine."

"You promise?" I ask softly.

I know him better than anyone, and I know he's not being truthful, but I won't push him if he doesn't want to talk about it.

"Yep. I'm good, Lil." He squeezes my hand that is looped around his bicep.

"Okay." I remove my arm from his and pull my dress up further, so it rests above my knees. "Race through the water?"

Chuckling, he says, "What do you want to wager?"

"Just bragging rights." I smile wide.

I call out in rapid succession, "One. Two. Three." Splashing through the water, I take off, running, giggling, and shrieking from the cold bite of the water.

"Cheater!" he calls out.

I hear his splashes behind me.

I sprint through where the sandy beach meets the shallow water. It is painfully cold, and my feet begin to go numb. "Cold, cold, cold," I chant.

Jax's arms snatch me up from behind, pulling me to his chest, and he lifts me out of the water as if he were carrying me across the threshold of a doorway. His chattering teeth still as he whispers huskily in my ear, "That doesn't count, you little cheat."

I laugh through my shivering. "Yes, it does. My challenge, my rules."

"Fine. Even with your obvious shadiness, I caught up to you and very well could have passed you, so I win." He carries me away from the water before setting me down in the cool sand.

"Okay, I'll give you that one. You did catch up pretty quickly."

We stand in the dry sand on the beach. My body trembles as my feet regain feeling from the icy water. He tugs me toward him, wrapping his arms firmly around me while rubbing my back.

I lean my head against his chest. "Brrr. It's going to be a long time until we can actually swim in there, huh?"

The water in Lake Michigan isn't bearable for swimming until July.

"Yeah."

He holds me close against him and gently kisses me on the temple.

It is quiet for a moment until Jax blurts out, "Can I kiss you?"

I whip my head back and study his face. My voice is shaky as I say, "What?"

This is all so weird. I'm not sure what is happening or why, but I know I like it.

My focus goes to Jax's lips as he speaks, fumbling over his words, "Never mind. I don't know why I even asked. I was just thinking that—"

Instinct takes over, and my hands move of their own accord, pulling on Jax's neck until his face is close enough for my lips to cover his. Our lips meet, and that connection sends a rush of emotions through me. It is a new sensation, so powerful and exhilarating, and I want more.

The kiss is slow and tentative at first. I cautiously brush my lips against his, feeling the fullness of his moving in rhythm against mine. As his needy breath mingles with mine, it fills me with an intoxicating hunger. I groan into his eager mouth, and his fingers thread into the curls of my styled hair. He pulls me closer as he gifts me with the entrance of his tongue, and I want to explode because the feeling is almost too much. He firmly grasps my face between his hands, and my tongue greedily entangles with his. I lick and taste all the recesses of his mouth as the blood pounds feverishly through my veins. His lips pull on mine, and I continue to kiss, lick, suck, and taste all that is Jax.

My Jax.

I am kissing Jax, and it is more than I dared to imagine. It shouldn't be a surprise that it is beyond perfect because that is what he is to me.

Perfect.

Our knees give way, and we kneel in the sand. I whimper into his mouth as my tongue continues its flawless dance with his. The next thing I know, I'm lying on my back in the sand, and he is leaning above me. His one arm is resting on his elbow in the sand, and his other hand is exploring my face, neck, hair. My hands echo his in their exploration of his face.

His hand is burning me with its touch. It's not the burn of pain but one of desire. Desire is an understatement. I have never wanted anything more in this life than I want Jax right now.

The chill of earlier is gone. The bitter air does not even bear recognition in my thoughts. I feel nothing but pure satisfaction as my mouth continues to be consumed by Jax's.

In the distance, I hear a car horn, three beeps in quick succession. It takes me a moment to realize that the sound is most likely coming from the limo as I'm sure our time here is coming to a close.

He pulls his lips away from mine, and I think I hear an audible protest escape from both our mouths. He leans his forehead against mine as we struggle to calm our breaths.

"Um, Jax?" My voice sounds raw and needy through labored breaths.

"Yeah?"

"That was…"

"Yeah."

"I think that we are supposed to be going back to the limo now," I whisper.

He sighs. "Yeah."

He stands and offers me his hand. He pulls me up, and we proceed to wipe the sand off our clothes. He threads his fingers through mine, and we make our way back to the limo in silence, lost in our own thoughts.

Inside the limo, the music plays through the speakers, but the atmosphere is different than it was on the ride to the beach. Everyone is quiet. Each couple keeps to themselves on the forty-five–minute drive back to our town. I hear the evidence of kissing happening around us, but I stay curled up against Jax's side, his arm hugging me around my shoulders.

This isn't the time or place to discuss what just happened, and for that, I'm grateful. Jax and I obviously have to talk about it, but with that conversation, I know that change is going to come. I have either made my life infinitely better or infinitely worse, and either way the coin lands, I'm scared to death.

three

What do I even say to that kiss?

That kiss…was amazing. For starters, it was freaking mind-blowing. I've never been kissed like that. Okay, I've never been kissed, period, unless you count the slobbery pecks from eager thirteen-year-olds when we used to play Spin the Bottle. But I don't. Those kisses aren't even in the same universe as Jax's kiss.

What does that kiss even mean? Does he see me as more than a friend? Was it mere curiosity or fleeting hormones? Does he want to repeat it?

As I sit here, snuggled against Jax's chest, I realize that I want him to want to do it again because goodness knows I do. Maybe I shouldn't want it. But that kiss elicited emotions in me that I never knew existed. His lips created an almost painful burning desire to feel him again.

The drive back from the beach seems to take forever, but we eventually arrive at my house where everyone has left their cars. Jax and I say our good-byes to our friends and stand in my driveway as we watch the limo pull away.

I take a deep breath. "So…"

"Yeah," Jax replies. A few more uncomfortable moments of silence go by. "Do you want to go to Denny's?"

I think for a moment. "No, I'm kind of tired. Want to talk inside?"

"Yeah, sure."

We walk around the back of the house, taking care not to step on my mom's flowers. I slide open the glass door facing the backyard, and we enter the quiet dark basement. I flip on a side lamp and watch as Jax takes off his tux jacket and tosses it on the arm of the leather sofa. He repeats the action with his tie. His white dress shirt is already untucked and hangs loosely over his black pants.

"I'll be right back," I say.

Jax nods and makes his way to the mini bar, grabbing a bottle of water out of the fridge.

When I return in my yoga pants and T-shirt, he is sitting on the sofa with his feet out in front of him. In one hand, he holds the bottle of water, and in the other, he has the remote. He is idly flipping through the TV channels with a dazed expression. He looks so grown-up and sexy. His dark hair is tousled but perfect at the same time. His shirt is wrinkled from where it was tucked in. I've always known that Jax is exceptionally gorgeous, but my pulse has never raced this much when looking at him. It's like that kiss has kicked my attraction to him into hyperdrive. It is hard to even look at him now and not want his lips on mine.

When he sees me, he smiles and mutes the TV. I plop down next to him, crossing my legs under me.

"So, I guess we should talk about that kiss," he says.

"Yeah, I guess so." The sound of my blood rushing through my veins is pounding in my ears, and I realize that I'm nervous. I have no idea what Jax is going to say, and I'm terrified to find out. Part of me wants him to confess his undying love for me, and the other part wants to go back to the way we were yesterday, simply Jax and Lily without the awkward air of intimacy between us.

"Look, Lil, I don't know what to say. I'm not sure what came over me. You were so beautiful tonight. Don't get me wrong. You're always beautiful. It's just that something about you tonight really affected me, and I needed to kiss you. I physically needed to feel your lips on mine. I know that sounds crazy. Am I making any sense?" His words come out in a rush.

"I think so. What does that kiss mean for us?" I ask in a hushed voice.

Jax faces me, taking my hands in his. "I'm not sure. It doesn't have to mean anything if we don't want it to."

My heart sinks at his words, and I know now that, deep down, I wanted it to mean something.

"First and foremost, we have to think of our friendship. It makes sense that we would be attracted to each other. I have loved you my whole life. You are gorgeous, and obviously, you are a girl." He pauses, gifting me with an adorably sexy smirk. "So, it would be weird if I didn't find you attractive, right? It doesn't mean we have to act on anything though. What are you feeling?"

"You are right." About what part, I don't know.

"I'm thinking that we should just say that, as two friends who find each other attractive—"

I cut him off there. "Hey, I don't remember me telling you that I find you attractive," I tease, poking him in the side. My comment has the desired effect I wanted.

43

He laughs, and I watch his body relax.

"No, you are right. You didn't. So, you aren't attracted to me at all?" His voice is hesitant, and I fear I might have bruised his ego.

"Maybe a little, but let's not assume." I grin.

He smirks, and his green eyes shine down on me. He is so darn sexy that I can barely settle my newfound hormones.

"Yeah, I knew it. Okay, back to my thought. As two friends who find each other attractive—maybe one of us more so than the other"—he closes his lips, and his mouth turns into a sly smile as he quirks one eyebrow in my direction—"I think it is normal that we would also crave the physical connection, especially tonight with the whole prom gig—you know, with the dressing up and dancing and stuff. But just because we find each other attractive doesn't mean we have to change anything about our relationship. You are the most important person in my life, and I value our friendship above everything else. I would never do anything to jeopardize what we have. I know the crap and drama that relationships bring, and I would never want that with you. So, I'm thinking that we should just say that we had an amazing...like, totally hot kiss, but now, we need to go back to normal. Don't you think?"

Do I think so? I'm not so sure.

My head tells me that he is right and completely spot-on in his assessment. A relationship would change everything. *Wouldn't it?* It seems it would have to, and it would never be worth it to lose any part of what makes us, us.

We have been the perfect pair since before I can remember. People rarely speak about one of us without mentioning the other. We have always gone hand in hand.

I don't think it is simply from the fact that we were raised together either. I have grown up with my sisters my whole life, and although I love them completely, we don't have what Jax and I have. What we have is the absolute rightness of two souls born into this world to complement the other flawlessly. Everything that Jax is and everything that he does is always exactly what I need. He is my center when I need it. He can make me laugh like no one else. He makes me feel important, beautiful, and cherished every day. *Best friends* isn't even a title that begins to sum up the importance of our relationship. I don't know what title would. The closest I can think of is *soul mates*, if that label can work in a relationship without the physical actions.

So, if everything that Jax is saying makes perfect sense, then why do I have a desperate ache in my chest? Why is my heart being squeezed with a vise of panic at the thought of never feeling Jax's lips on mine again? Rationally, I know that a relationship would mess everything up. I do. *Yet is it horrible for me to want to take the risk?* If we are this attached in friendship, imagine what we could be like as an intimate couple. I have no doubt that we would have the connection that people write books about.

But let's face it...high school sweethearts never last. They don't.

Am I willing to pay a price to see what it would be like?

No, I guess I'm not. If the price would be losing Jax, then no physical connection, regardless of how earth-shattering it might be, could ever be worth it.

"Lil?" Jax's husky whisper breaks through my thoughts.

I clear my throat, willing the lump of emotions resting there to retreat. "No, you are right. It would mess everything up, and that wouldn't be worth it." I force my voice to remain calm when, internally, I'm feeling anything but. I want to scream at the unfairness of it all. I want to cry for the loss of something I never had, something so monumental that the idea of losing it is breaking my heart.

"Okay, good. Then, it is settled. So, do you want to watch a movie?"

"Yeah, that sounds good."

I watch as Jax flips through the movie channels, and we settle on one involving gladiator-type men with extremely hot bodies fighting in some past fictional world.

Jax pulls me to his side. I snuggle into the crook of his arm, resting my head on his chest. He wraps his arm around me, hugging me tight. I inhale his scent, the familiar smell of his body wash and cologne. Like everything else, it is overwhelmingly perfect. The scent wraps me in a blanket of need. I close my eyes to block it all out. I focus on the blackness beneath my lids, the sound of my breath, and the feel of my beating heart. I concentrate on the rhythmic calmness of the blood whooshing through my veins and the void of nothingness where my heart is still unaware of the feeling it gets when Jax's lips touch mine. In this void, I am naive and oblivious, and it is right where I need to be.

The soft glow of the morning sun finds me asleep on the couch. The scent of Jax is gone. I lie on my side with a blanket tucked around me. I take my hand and touch my lips. Closing my eyes, I remember the kiss on the beach.

Ugh. Suck it up, Lily. Get over it already.

I hear the soft plop of feet descending the carpeted steps to the basement.

"There you are." Keeley's excited voice echoes through the quiet room. "So, how was it?" She drops into the recliner next to me.

I sit up, wrapping the blanket around me. "It was really fun." I give her the details of dinner, dancing, and the limo ride to the beach.

I leave out the kiss, not wanting to share that moment with anyone. If it is the only kiss I'm going to get from Jax, I'll be keeping the memory whole, so I can always have it. I'm sure I'm being overly dramatic, but I don't see anyone topping it. I might need to pull from that memory for a long time to come.

I grab my heavy calculus book before shutting my locker. I sense him approaching before I turn around. The recent flutters that come when he is near are now dancing around in my belly. I take a deep breath and turn to meet his piercing green stare.

"Hey," I greet him with forced nonchalance.

I start strolling down the hall toward the Mr. Brown's classroom where Jax and I sit daily to endure the horror that is calculus. Okay, it is only horrendous for me because it makes no sense whatsoever. I sit in class every day, fuming while wondering why on earth I have to learn this gibberish. You can't tell me one situation in which I would ever need to know this crap.

Jax walks beside me. "So, are we still on for tonight?"

"You bet. You know, I think the only one worth seeing that we haven't already seen is the one about the guy coming back from war and searching for his past love." To be honest, it sounds way too romantic for me.

Things have been typical this week between Jax and me. Our weekly routine hasn't changed. We have most of our classes together, so we see each other a lot during the day. We eat lunch together and study at one of our houses at night.

We are going on our weekly Friday date night tonight, and it all seems so normal. Yet, for me, it's not. I have had to force all my interactions this week. It's not because I don't enjoy being around Jax, but now, I enjoy being around him in a different way, and I have to get past it.

"Yeah. It actually looks good and is getting great reviews. Do you want to do dinner somewhere before?" The deep timbre of his voice causes a goose-bump epidemic to break out across my arms.

"You know what? Let's do a movie-theater dinner. We haven't done that in a while." My voice is excited as I think about the popcorn with extra butter, nachos, and peanut M&Ms we'll have for dinner. It's just what I need to get out of my funk—a sugar-and-carb meal laced with chemicals and preservatives.

Jax laughs. "Okay, but remember, the last time we did that, you felt like crap afterward."

The memory of my bloated stomach and the sick full feeling that accompanied it come back to me. Okay, so maybe the idea of that meal is more appealing than the meal itself. Jax is correct. The last thing I need to feel on top of the unease already permeating every pore is ill.

"You are totally right. Subway?"

He chuckles, shaking his head. "Sounds good."

"Would you rather live on a deserted island with a serial killer or live naked in a dump for the rest of your life?" I ask from across the table at Subway.

Jax's lips release the straw of his soda, and they turn up into a smile. "Okay, but if I were in a dump, don't you think I could find some discarded clothes? Why would I have to go naked?"

I playfully slap his hand. "Just answer."

"I would live on the island. I'd kill the murderer before he could get me and live the rest of my life lounging on the beach, sipping coconut milk." His lips form a wide grin before closing into a smirk. "Okay, would you rather lick a stranger's toes or wear a stranger's underwear on your head after he ran a marathon?"

"Would I have to wear the underwear around my face, or could I just wear them on my hair?"

"I don't know. I guess around your face."

"I would lick the stranger's toes and then go throw up and brush my teeth." Yep, sounds like the better choice. "Okay, would you rather go to school naked every day or sleep with the lunch lady?"

"The portly old one who is balding?" Jax smiles. "Of course I would come to school naked every day. Heck, I'd be doing the school a service."

He mischievously quirks his eyebrow, and I laugh.

"And by the way, why am I always naked in these scenarios?"

I feel my cheeks flush. "Shut up, and go."

"Let's see. Would you rather eat a teaspoon of poop or take an hour-long bath in a tub filled with poop?"

"Ew! That is so gross. I don't think I could stand to be surrounded by poop for an hour, so I guess I would have to take my chances with eating it."

"That's really sick, Lily. I can't believe you would eat poop." Jax is peering at me with his best attempt at a face filled with disgust.

"Oh, hush. Would you rather sleep with the love of your life one time and then never see her again? Or would you rather be able to see her every day for the rest of your life through glass and never be able to touch her?"

"Why won't I see her again? Is she dead? What kind of glass are you talking about? And why is there glass between us?"

"Jax, you can't always get clarification, you know. That's not the way this works."

"Yeah, but I don't understand your question. I need answers, so I can make an informed decision."

"Fine. She doesn't die. She just moves away to…Antarctica."

"Why Antarctica? Don't you think she could find somewhere better to move to?"

I sigh. "Maybe she studies penguins and really likes Antarctica. Quiet. Anyway, the glass thing…I guess she is in jail, so you only get to see her through that glass and talk to her on those phones."

"Why is she in jail? What did she do?"

"Jax!" I whine.

"Am I in love with a murderer or a bank robber? I mean, that would change my thoughts and my possible answer."

"I don't know. Fine. Maybe you are the one in jail for running around the school naked, indecent exposure and all."

"There you go, getting me naked again, Lil. Is there something that you are trying to tell me?"

I ball up a napkin and throw it at him.

"Just kidding. But do you really think I would get life for showing off this body? I mean, really?"

"No one said the scenarios had to make sense." I shake my head with a wide grin on my face. "Okay, fine, you robbed a bank, naked, and when you were coming out of the bank, you jaywalked across the street, kicked an old lady in her shin, and then threw a rock through a storefront window before stealing a car, running a red light, and then leading the cops on a fifteen-mile high-speed chase. So, now, you are serving life for robbery, indecent exposure, jaywalking, assault, vandalism, stealing, traffic violations, speeding, and resisting arrest. Basically, you're a complete idiot. Now, answer the question."

Jax's deep chuckle resonates through Subway. "Okay, fine. I'd sleep with her once and then lose her because I think it would be pure torture to have to see her every day but never be able to really have her. That way, at least I would have had her once."

I nod at his answer.

"Okay, would you rather have to watch your parents doing it every day for the rest of your life, or would you rather join in with them once and never have to see them do it again?"

I almost choke on the bite of turkey wrap I'm chewing. I hold my hand over my mouth and cough violently as I try to dislodge the piece of lettuce stuck in my windpipe. My eyes water as I take a drink of my pop. "Jax Porter, that's disgusting, and I'm not answering that. Just gross."

His grin goes wide. "Well, Lil, when you have been playing Would You Rather with someone for years and know everything about her, you have to get creative with your questions. You have to answer it. It's the rules."

"There are no rules."

"Yes, there are, and rule number one is that you must answer," he says simply.

"Whatever. There are no rules, but fine, I would watch them. I would never join in. That is sickening. I guess, in this imaginary scenario, if I'm forced to watch them every day, then I would eventually become immune to the grossness of it, and it would become inconsequential, like watching my mom make coffee or something."

Jax chuckles. "Yeah, I'm sure it would be just like making coffee."

I wrap up the remainder of my wrap, having lost my appetite. "You ready? We'd better get going anyway. Plus, I think you have ruined this game for me for a while."

"How long is a while? Like a day?"

"Definitely at least a week." I grin as I stand to throw my trash away.

The movie is good. I think. I'm struggling to pay attention. My focus is on Jax's knee as it rests against mine and his arm beside mine on the armrest. When I can't take the feeling anymore, I move my arm to my lap. I cross my leg, so it is no longer touching his, and my bottom leg bounces nervously. Then, the warmth of his breath assaults me against my ear as he leans in to tell me something about the movie that I'm not watching.

I lean my head against the back of my seat and close my eyes. My mind plays memory after memory of the innocent times I have had with my best friend. The movie entitled *The Friendship of Jax and Lily* shows in my head, reminding me of the importance of our friendship.

I see it all so clearly, every amazing moment.

Jax and I playing Capture the Flag with my sisters when we were eight.

Playing hide and seek in the cornfields.

Dressing Jax up in my dresses as we played my favorite game at the time, Twins, when we were six.

Picnics under our favorite oak tree in the field behind my house.

Deciding to make our moms cookies for Mother's Day when we were ten but having it turn into a giggling food fight. The look on my mom's face as she walked into the kitchen that was covered from top to bottom in flour while Jax and I stood there, like guilty powdered ghosts.

Lying on the trampoline on a hot summer's night, looking at the stars and asking each other Would You Rather questions until we couldn't keep our eyes open.

I have so many memories of growing up with Jax. He is embedded in every recollection, and each one brings a smile to my face.

I jump when he speaks against my ear once more, "Is the movie boring you that much?"

It takes me a moment to realize that he is referring to me sitting here with my eyes closed. I open my eyes and give him a shy smile before turning back to the screen in a mocked effort to pay attention.

The night air is warm, and it speaks to the summer that is just around the corner, the summer before my senior year. I step up into Jax's new Durango, an early eighteenth birthday present. I snap my seat belt in, and the vehicle begins moving away from the theatre.

Jax drives in silence for a few minutes before turning into an empty department store parking lot, and he shuts off the car.

I look around at the dark pavement outside. "What are we doing?"

"Let's talk."

"Okay…" I drawl out my response.

"So, I've been thinking a lot." Jax pauses.

"About?" I ask

"About the kiss."

I sigh. *You're preaching to the choir, buddy.* "What about it?"

"That I really want to do it again and again and again."

Holy. Wow.

"What do you have to say about that?" Jax's voice is soft, hesitant.

"I'd say that I've been thinking the same thing, like, all week," I admit.

"Me, too. I seriously can't stop thinking about it. Lil, I don't know what to do. I know we talked about it already and decided what we thought was best. But why can't I get it out of my head? Maybe we should try the whole relationship thing."

"Really?" I can't help the excitement I hear in my voice. "What about messing things up and all that?"

"I know. I've thought about that. A lot. This is what I think. I think that you and I together would be unlike anything I've experienced. Yes, most of my relationships have been annoying and filled with drama, but they weren't with you. I realize that being with you would never be like that. You never annoy me, and our friendship now never has drama. So, why would it be any different? I can't compare what I've had with others to what I could have with you. You are my Lily. There is no comparison."

"I don't want to do anything that would risk our friendship. I could never lose you." My voice cracks at the thought of a life without Jax.

"You wouldn't. Here's the thing. Our relationship would be built on an almost eighteen-year friendship. If our romantic relationship doesn't work out, then we'll end that part, but we'll still have our friendship. We'll always have each other in that way, no matter what. We have too much love and respect for each other to ever lose our friendship completely. I honestly never see that happening. Do you?"

I think about his words, and it all makes sense. Even if we didn't make it as a couple, we could simply go back to being friends. I know there is nothing that Jax would ever do that could change that. He is right. We would never throw away a lifelong friendship because a romance didn't work out. *And what if it did work out? It could.* Our current platonic relationship is already so wonderful.

I get giddy just imagining what else we could be. "No, I think we'll always be friends."

"Exactly. Always. Nothing will change that. We just have to make a promise to each other that, if a relationship doesn't work out, we'll go back to being friends. I can promise you that. Can you?"

"Yes. Definitely." My insides burst with happiness from this conversation.

Jax pulls in an audible breath. "Lily, would you rather try a romantic relationship with your best friend with the knowledge that it might not work and your heart could get broken? Or would you rather play it safe, guard your heart, and remain solely friends, always wondering what could have been?"

I unbuckle my seat belt and climb over the middle console, placing my legs on either side of Jax so that I'm straddling him. I hold his face between my hands, his piercing eyes shining brightly. I pull his face toward mine as I lean in. Giving into necessity, I kiss him softly, moving my lips against his. I feel the yielding firmness of his full lips and the way in which they move perfectly in time with mine. I push my tongue into his mouth, and a groan rumbles from the back of his throat. That sound sends pure hot liquid desire shooting through my body.

My need for Jax borders on painful as we take the kiss deeper. His arms wrap tightly around me, his hands kneading the skin on my back, as his tongue explores my mouth. I tangle my fingers in his silky short hair and hold him to me. I cannot physically get enough. My lips throb from use, pulsing with pleasure. I kiss him like this is my first and last kiss. I never want it to end.

In my whole life, I have never been happier, and I feel that this is exactly where I am meant to be. There isn't another soul that I would want to experience this with. I hope to experience all of my firsts with Jax. There is no one who could love me and guard my heart the way Jax would.

Our tongues dance, our lips explore, and our hands feel until the vehicle is filled with the dense fog of lust-fueled air. Our skin shimmers with sweat in the warmth of our surroundings.

I finally pull away, my mouth protesting from the loss of contact. Our chests heave as we attempt to regulate our breathing. I open my eyes and get lost in Jax's expression. His eyes are filled with love, desire, and happiness, and they mirror my own feelings.

In a husky whisper, he asks, "You never answered my question. Friends or more?"

"More. Definitely more."

four

Despite my worries, transitioning our status from *just friends* to *dating* really wasn't a huge deal. Most people didn't give us a second glance when they found out. It definitely didn't come as a surprise to anyone.

The Sunday after our movie date, our two families had dinner over at Jax's house. During the meal, Jax and I announced that we had something to say, and we proceeded to tell everyone that we were now officially together.

Everyone smiled.

Jax's mom said, "That's nice, honey. Do you mind passing the vegetables?"

Landon and Amy, who were both home from college, started whispering among themselves at the end of the table, and I caught Landon with a gloating expression.

He said, "Pay up, Amy, baby. I won fair and square."

To which she replied, "Shut up, Landon."

I turned to Jax, and he had a bemused expression on his face, which I was sure mirrored my own. We both shrugged and immediately started laughing.

It was the same way at school. Most people reacted with an attitude of nonchalance. Others said comments about it being a long time coming, and we heard several, "Finally," responses. Okay, so maybe this monumental decision in our lives wasn't so monumental after all.

Regardless, I got the guy…the perfect guy.

More than that, I have a relationship that started from such a pure place and evolved into something so meaningful. I know that a relationship like ours is rare. I can't fathom that many people get to experience something so amazing. The love that we share is beautiful. It's the kind of love that fills my lungs, allowing me to truly breathe in fully for the first time in my life. It is all encompassing, bringing so much clarity and joy. It has filled me up in places that I didn't even know were vacant.

It is the last day of our junior year.

We're walking in the hallway from our last class, Jax's fingers entwined through mine. I can sense his stare on me. My skin warms, a tingling sensation dancing over it, as his eyes take me in.

"What?" I ask as we reach his Durango in the student parking lot. Raising my head to meet his gaze, I'm met with his half-cocked smile.

"Nothing, Little. All's good."

"Why are you looking at me like that?" I ask, feeling the heat creep onto my cheeks.

His eyes dart from my eyes to my lips and back again. He scrapes his teeth along his bottom lip and says, "I can't help it."

He raises his arm and tucks a loose strand of my hair that fell from my ponytail behind my ear. He studies his movements and my hair with an almost reverent expression.

"You," he whispers as his body leans toward me, backing me against the side of his SUV, "are my walking dream."

His voice, all husky and hoarse, does something crazy to my insides. He places his hands on either side of my head, bracing himself against the passenger window while pinning me against his vehicle with his intensity. His hot mouth is mere inches from my ear.

"You, with your hair pulled back, taunt me with your creamy skin all day. I just want to taste every part of you." He leans back marginally, running the tip of his finger down from my earlobe to my neck and over my collarbone, searing me with his touch. "And those tight little shorts make your butt look amazing, and your long legs..." He lets out a breath. "You look like a fucking runway model."

His finger works its way back up, sliding around to cup the nape of my neck. "And your little freckles are back." His stare studies the light spattering of freckles across my nose that fade in the winter months. "Your big blue eyes do something to me, Lil. You have the power to make me insane. I will never be able to get over how beautiful you are."

I take in the sincerity of his words and the love shining from every pore of his gorgeous face. He has rendered me speechless, and I'm just looking at him, my eyes wide. He lowers his head to mine, joining our lips. He feathers light kisses over my lips, warm and gentle. He is always so tender with me, treating me like a porcelain doll. Sometimes though, I wish he wouldn't. I'm constantly turned on around Jax, and it is slightly maddening. He has had many girlfriends, and he has lots of experience in the physical department. Yet he has been holding out with me and simultaneously driving me crazy.

I don't have to ask him to figure out why he is so cautious. I know how much I mean to him, and he is trying to be respectful of my lack of experience by taking it slow. It is a cruel twist of fate that I finally get to call the hot-ass player of our school mine, and he's taken this opportunity to turn into a saint.

He pulls away, and my body chills, missing his heat despite the fact that it's a seventy-five–degree day.

Moving on, he asks, "So, what should we do today to celebrate our last day?"

"What do you want to do?" I ask. "We don't have to do anything special. You can come over and go swimming, and we can just hang out or whatever."

It doesn't matter where Jax and I are or what we are doing. It is always special when we are together.

"Sounds good. Do you want to go get some ice cream?"

I hop with excitement. "Yes!"

If I can't kiss Jax into oblivion to relieve some of my pent-up energy, the next best thing is mint chocolate chip.

Jax looks at me, and his mouth quirks in amusement before going wide, his pupils dilating once more. "God, Lily."

Leaning in, his lips whisper lightly across mine. Unable to contain it, I let out an audible sigh. He deepens our kiss, his perfect lips moving against my own. His tongue enters my mouth, and I can't stop the groan that resonates from deep within my throat. Our tongues collide in this dance, and then I pull away.

"Ice cream?" I say in a broken whisper, my voice laden with desire.

I want him but not here in the school parking lot.

Jax clears his throat. "Yeah, right. Ice cream." He grabs my ass, tugging me toward him, before placing a quick peck on my forehead. Then, he walks around the front of the vehicle to the driver's door.

We order our ice cream cones, and Jax drives us to my house.

Hand in hand, we walk past my house and through the field and trees until we reach our favorite old oak tree. The trunk is wide in circumference, and about six feet up, a myriad of thick branches extend out, creating a peaceful canopy. It is the perfect climbing tree, and when we were younger, we spent a lot of time climbing it, having imaginative adventures. Since we got older, we still come out to the tree often, but we usually sit at its base and talk.

With our legs extended, we lean against the tree and use the trunk as a backrest. Jax plops the bottom part of the cone with the warmed ice cream into his mouth. I lean my head against his shoulder as I finish my cone.

I swallow the last remnants of the sweet wafer. "Delish!"

We chat idly for a few moments, and then Jax's voice changes, becoming deeper and even sexier somehow. "I can't stand not having my hands and lips all over you. I need you more than I've needed anything in my whole life. I can't believe I have gone almost eighteen years without being with you like this."

ELLIE WADE

I clear my throat. "I want you, too, like, a lot. I'm not going to break, Jax." The words feel strange leaving my mouth.

I'm so inexperienced when it comes to dating, but with Jax, I feel safe. Even if I say or do something idiotic, I know that it won't change the way he thinks of me. We have a trust that I'd bet is more secure than most people in the world share with another person. Period. I've spent my entire life falling in love with him. Now that we are together, I know deep in my heart that nothing in this world could tear us apart.

With my words, he leans down and places a line of soft kisses on my exposed shoulder. When he reaches my neck, he licks the skin at the base of my ear. "You taste like the perfect combination of heaven, sweet and salty all rolled up into one."

His voice amplifies my want for him, and a small whimper escapes my lips. He groans, a guttural and needy sound, before throwing his leg around my waist so that he is straddling me. He takes my face in his hands before our lips crash in a fiery collision of lust. Our tongues collide in heated desire as we both try to take the kiss as deep as humanly possible. He pulls my bottom lip between his teeth and begins to grind against me. I moan as he moves the hardness beneath his shorts over my core.

He rotates off of me and begins to unbutton my shorts. My eyes go wide as I watch his hand pulling my zipper down.

"We won't go farther than this, Lil. I just need to feel you. Is this okay?"

I nod my head, taking my bottom lip between my teeth, not having the words to tell him that he is misreading my reaction. I'm far from concerned. I'm full of anticipation.

He pushes his hand beneath my shorts, placing his fingers at my entrance. "Oh, Lily." His exclamation is almost a prayer. "Baby, spread your legs for me."

I drop my knees to the sides, allowing him better access. He inserts one finger, and I cry out, overwhelmed with new sensations. He catches my cry in his mouth, and begins a desperate rhythm with his tongue. He takes it slow, waiting for me to adjust, before inserting a second finger. My whimpers vibrate in his mouth.

"So good, Lily. You feel so good. God, I love you. You are so fucking perfect," he chants his adoration for me against my neck in between kisses.

My body starts to writhe beneath his lips. Using his thumb, he starts to apply circular pressure to my most sensitive spot as his two fingers continue their assault.

"Jax!" I cry out, grabbing a hold of his arm.

I'm experiencing something unlike anything I ever imagined. I dreamed about what it would be like the first time that Jax touched me, but my dreams had nothing on this experience. I didn't know to dream these feelings. I didn't know they existed. My body is chasing something, a release. I'm almost afraid to get to the finish because the journey is so good. My heart is beating rapidly. All in the same breath, I want to yell at Jax to quit and beg him to never stop touching me. The sensations are intense, almost too much, but so amazing at the same time.

"It's okay, Lil. It's okay," he reassures me. "Concentrate on the feeling. That's it. Deep breaths." He peppers my face with soft kisses.

My eyes are scrunched together, and my breathing is erratic and heavy.

"Jax." My voice comes out ragged and uncertain.

"It's okay, baby. Just let go. Don't fight it. You are so perfect. Let go, Lily."

I emit a deep moan as the release spreads through me in a wave of warm pleasure. My body starts shaking as the ecstasy fills me up from my scalp covered in goose bumps to my toes curling down, digging into my sandals.

When I cease to shake, he removes his fingers, pulling them out of my pants. He buttons my shorts and zips them up while I sit against the tree. My chest rises and falls forcefully, my arms hanging limp at my sides. A light sheen of sweat coats my skin, and I can feel the heat in my cheeks as I exhale, my lips slightly parted.

"You have never been more beautiful," he says, tucking the persistent loose strand of hair back behind my ear.

"Oh my God, Jax. That was…that was…I don't know," I choke out.

He chuckles. "Good, I hope?"

"Fuck, better than good. Amazing. Unreal." My eyes are closed, and my head is leaning back against the bark of the tree.

He laughs loudly. I'm sure it's because hearing the F word fall from my lips is rare, but if anything deserves the F word, it is that experience.

"That would be called an orgasm, Little Love. Have you never had one?"

My eyes pop open and go wide as I look at him. "Of course I haven't. When would I have had one? You know I've never been with anyone."

"Yeah, I know, but…haven't you ever touched yourself?"

"No! Of course not!"

He shakes his head and grins. "Lily, it is okay to touch yourself."

I can't wrap my brain around his words. *No way.* "No, Jax. That's just…I don't know. But I feel weird about it. I can't do it."

"Lily"—he takes my hands in his—"it is totally normal to touch yourself. Most people do. Hell, I do it a lot."

I giggle. "That's different. You are a guy. That's normal for guys."

"It's normal for girls, too. Listen, you should be an expert on your own body. You need to know what feels good. You need to know how to read your body, so you can ask for what you want."

I shake my head. "I didn't ask you for anything, but you did just fine, more than fine."

He smirks, and he has every right to. "Well, I'm just good like that but not everyone is."

I hit him on the chest. "Well, I'm not with everyone, am I? I'm with you. You apparently know what you are doing, so I'm in good hands. No need to go there."

"I know what I'm doing, huh?" His smile is wide.

"Uh, yeah…apparently." I don't want to imagine how he learned to be so skillful.

"So, you liked it?" he asks.

I look at him and roll my eyes. "Yeah, obviously."

He huffs out a laugh. "Okay, well, promise me that you will touch yourself at least once. I want you to understand your body. And let's face it…thinking about you doing that is a total turn-on."

I giggle again as he pulls me to his chest and wraps his arms around me.

"I will think about it."

"Good, and after you do it, I want a play-by-play."

"Jax—" My voice comes out whiny, but it is stopped abruptly as his lips find mine once more.

I have no complaints. I will try anything this man wants because kissing Jax Porter is something I will never tire of doing.

The summer speeds by in a happy, lust-filled haze.

My days have been spent with Jax, and while that isn't any different than previous summers, the ways in which we fill our days are. We've been spending the hot, humid hours before our senior year literally wrapped up in each other.

Most days, a considerable amount of time consists of me enveloped in his arms in the pool. We've also spent equal amounts of time under our oak tree with me leaning against him, my back to his front with our hands entwined, as we talk for hours. During the nights, we're usually snuggled up against one another in my basement as we mindlessly watch movies. We have done the summer dates that we always have—water-skiing, movies, putt-putt, and go-karts. We even went to Cedar Point, the best place in the world for roller coasters. We have also spent a few weeks at his family's vacation home on Lake Michigan. The only thing better than relaxing on the white sand and listening to the waves rolling onto the beach is doing it with Jax by my side.

Jax's lips and hands have gotten quite the workout this summer. He has explored every inch of my body many times every day. We haven't taken it all the way, but man, do I want to. I should win some award for the level of my willpower. I'm almost positive that most women wouldn't have been able to hold out for this long if they had someone as irresistible as Jax at their side. But it takes two, and I'm letting Jax call the shots. He has chosen the pace, and although I want more, I have enough. I have more than I could have ever imagined.

five

"So, you don't have any guesses?" Keeley asks, lying across my bed. Propped up on her elbows, she's flipping through the latest issue of *Us Weekly* magazine.

"No. He said to bring a bathing suit, but other than that, he didn't give me any clues." I hold up my two bikinis, deciding whether to go with the teal with purple polka dots or the white ruffled one, before shaking my head and throwing them both into my bag. I've packed enough clothes for a week even though I'm only going to be gone for two nights. But seeing as I have no idea where I'm going, I want to be prepared.

Jax has a surprise planned for my eighteenth birthday. I can't wait to find out what it is, but honestly, regardless of what we are doing, I'm going to love it. I'm looking forward to some quality time with him. Football practices started a month ago, and I miss not seeing him every second of the day.

I find myself not able to think straight when he's not around. I crave him—mind, body, and soul. Always. Yes, I'm slightly pathetic, but I have no shame.

"I heard Mom saying something to Dad about meeting up with some friends," Keeley says, not taking her eyes from the glossy pages below her.

"Really? What friends?" My interest is piqued.

"Not sure. Didn't hear that part. Hey, did you know that Jennifer is pregnant?" Keeley is slightly obsessed with celebrity gossip and refers to them on a first name basis.

"They always say that. I doubt it. According to the tabloids, she's been pregnant a hundred times."

"I think she really is this time."

"Well, I guess we'll see. So, did you happen to hear any other details?" I'm dying to find out some information about this weekend. I haven't been able to persuade Jax into giving me any clues even though I used all of my fail-proof techniques.

"Nope. Just that."

"Hmm…well, that's not really much to go on. I wonder what friends?" I say more to myself than my sister. "What are you doing this weekend?" I ask her.

"Not much. Just shopping with Mom," she answers absentmindedly as her eyes scan an article.

In a week, Keeley is going to be starting her freshman year of high school, and I'm going to be a senior.

"Are you getting excited to go to high school?"

"Yeah, sure. Shouldn't be too much different than last year, right?"

My sister is so easygoing. Out of all the females in the house, she is the one who is least led by emotions. I guess if my dad has been blessed with three girls—four, including my mother—at least the last one hasn't added much to the girl drama of the house.

"You're probably right," I answer her as I zip my bag. "Well, I guess that's it. I'm going to go sit out on the deck with Mom until Jax comes."

"Okay, I'll join ya," she answers as she hops off my bed.

Sitting in a deck chair, I hear the gravel of our driveway crunch under car tires, followed by a door shutting. A few seconds later, Jax appears after walking around the house to meet me in the back.

I will never tire of the way my body reacts to Jax. At the mere sight of him, my skin warms, humming with desire. My heart rate accelerates, and a broad grin automatically appears on my face.

He is wearing a pair of khaki cargo shorts and a fitted navy T-shirt that clings to his toned arms and chest. His olive skin is several shades darker from exposure to the summer sun, allowing his already captivating eyes to shine that much brighter.

When his green eyes connect with mine, I stand immediately, and an instinctual desire to be closer to him propels me forward.

"Hey, Lil." Jax's face beams with excitement.

I wave enthusiastically as I walk toward him. I can tell he has something fun up his sleeve for this weekend. I don't know what it is, but somehow, he convinced my parents to let him take me away for my birthday.

"Hey," Keeley greets him.

"Hi, Jax, honey," my mom says.

Jax speaks to my mom and sister for a moment before turning to me. "Ready?" He asks.

"Yes!" I say a little too eagerly.

I give my mom a hug.

"Be safe, Lily. Please keep your phone on at all times and check in with me."

"I will, Mom. I promise. But I'm going to be an adult tomorrow, so you really don't need to worry," I say with a smirk.

My mom lets out a forced laugh. "Watch it, baby girl. I can change my mind about this little excursion." Her lips pursed together, she looks at me with mock warning.

"I'm kidding! You know I'm kidding. I will call you."

She pulls me in for another hug. Softly, she says, "Just remember that age does not make you an adult. You are an adult when you make mature adult decisions."

I pull back with a serious expression. "I know, Mom. You're right. I'm wrong. You're an adult. I'm a child. You're smart. I'm dumb. You're beautiful. I'm ugly."

She bends at the waist, laughing hard. I hear Keeley and Jax laughing from behind me, and I start in, too.

My mom stands, wiping the tears from her eyes. "You are too much, Lily Anne. What am I going to do with you?"

"Love me," I answer back with a wide grin.

"Oh, I do." She kisses my forehead. "Have fun. Happy birthday, baby."

When I saw the route we were taking as we were halfway to Lake Michigan, I suspected that we were going to Jax's family's lake house.

We are now winding our way over the narrow drive to their vacation house with towering pines on either side. This is one of our favorite places on earth. Their house is nestled atop a hill of tall evergreen trees. A long wooden staircase weaves its way from the back deck to the sand below. At the bottom of the hill, mounds of sand are covered with sea grass. A sandy path through the sea grass leads to a private beach.

The end of August is the best time to go to Lake Michigan. The water is finally warm, and it is so much fun swimming in the waves. I can't wait.

I turn to Jax, and a smile spreads across his face.

"Happy?" he asks.

"Very. Thank you. This is perfect."

"I knew you would approve."

"So, who's all coming?" I question as he parks his SUV.

"Just you and me, Little Love."

"What? How? Really? My sister said that friends were coming."

"I might have lied some." His eyebrows rise as his lips form into a smirk.

"Do explain." I giggle.

"Well, I knew I wanted to take you away this weekend. I wanted to celebrate your birthday with just the two of us. I told your parents that one of my friend's parents was having a big end-of-summer weekend party at their lake house, and I asked if I could take you. I laid it on thick, reminding them that we would be leaving for college this time next year. I explained that, after this summer, we wouldn't have time to go away with friends like this."

"But they know all our friends and their parents. They are going to find out."

"They don't know my friends from football camp or their parents." Jax's face lights up with a mischievous grin.

"You're bad." I laugh. "What about your family? What if they decide to show up this weekend?"

"They won't. Landon is already up at college, and my parents have a benefit. Don't worry. We have the next two days all to ourselves. No one is going to bother us, and no one is going to find out." He threads his fingers through mine and pulls our hands to his mouth. He kisses each one of my fingers, never taking his emerald eyes off of mine.

My heart immediately starts racing. Jax has an intense effect over my body. He is able to set me on fire with a simple touch.

"I...I can't believe my parents didn't do more investigating, like calling these so-called parents or anything."

Pulling his lips from my hand, he leans over the gearshift, bringing his mouth to mine. He kisses me softly before releasing my lips. "They trust me." His voice is a husky whisper.

"Bad mistake," I whisper back.

Jax trails kisses from my mouth to my neck. "Very bad."

His hot breath hits my skin, causing me to shiver.

An unpleasant cooling sensation takes over when he removes his mouth all too soon. "Come on. Let's go inside."

I nod.

The interior of the house isn't anything new to me. The five-bedroom home is beautifully decorated in what I would call rustic beach chic. The colors are muted, consisting of different shades of cream with aqua and tan accents. The dark mahogany floors contrast with the pale walls, but at the same time, it pulls the look together.

As I remove my flip-flops at the door and feel the cool smooth wood beneath my feet, an odd sense of excitement comes over me. The energy in this space is different, invigorating.

I've been alone with Jax many times but never *alone*.

With our bags, Jax disappears into one of the bedrooms. It's not the bedroom with the set of twin beds. It is the one with a singular king-sized bed. The thought of that brings me to a state of nervous excitement.

On the wall past the kitchen is a large shadow box with a white frame and gray cracks flowing through the wood, antique in appearance. I stop before it. Inside the bottom of the frame sits small glass vials of the perfect white sand that graces this part of the lake. Next to the sand lies a group of shells, ones I remember collecting. Above this simple but sweet homage to the majestic lake below us is a collage of photos from the summer before I turned ten.

There are various shots of me, Jax, and Landon doing numerous beach activities—building sand castles, riding the waves on our boogie boards, lying together under a large brightly colored beach umbrella.

Raising my finger, I touch the glass over a photo of Jax and me. We are wearing our swimsuits, standing on the beach. We are both as skinny as can be, the shot taken long before Jax acquired the muscular physique he has now. Even then though, he stood a head above me. Jax's skin is a golden brown. My skin is pale, like always, but the sprinkling of freckles over my nose is just visible, a clue to my summer spent in the sun. I'm holding a blue pail in one hand, and my inside hand is entwined with Jax's. We aren't looking at the camera. Instead, our faces are turned in, looking at one another. I'm laughing, my mouth open wide. I know he must have said something funny. I wish I could remember what it was. Jax is wearing his signature smirk. I can't count the amount of times I've seen that expression in my life. I will never tire of it.

This photo brings out a thousand emotions in me, the strongest being gratitude. It is beautiful and sweet and brings me right back to that time. It's amazing how much love shines through this photo. Even at nine years old, it is radiating off of us.

Everything with Jax was always effortless. It was never a discussion. It was pure. It was special. It was perfect. We were the perfect pair.

We still are.

This photo was taken years before we became romantically involved—that evolution happened only three months ago—yet even in my nine-year-old body, he was all I saw. He is all I have ever seen. He was made for me, and I for him. The warmth that thought brings me is indescribable.

"That was a fun summer." His deep voice breaks me out of my nostalgic reverie.

I immediately feel his strong presence behind me. "Yeah, it was."

His firm arms turn me around, and he pulls me into him. I rest my cheek against his chest and circle my arms around his back, hugging tight.

He kisses the top of my head, letting his lips linger, as he speaks, "What should we do for dinner, my Little Love?"

There are numerous restaurants in the quaint town down the road, including some of our favorite places to eat, but I don't want that tonight. I don't want to share Jax with anyone this weekend. I want all of his beautiful energy to myself.

"Let's order in."

"My sentiments exactly," he agrees.

The sunset is breathtaking over the lake. An array of oranges and purples sprawl across the horizon as the bright sun starts to descend, appearing to sink into the rippling water. I sit cross-legged on a plush comforter out on the deck. Jax mirrors my position, sitting across from me. A steamy pizza lies between us in all its sausage and mushroom glory. It's our favorite, and it really is the best pizza in the world.

Jax grabs a slice. Leaning down, he brings it to his mouth. A line of melted cheese trails from his piece to the rest of the pizza below. Through a mouthful of goodness, he declares, "The best."

I take a bite of the slice in my hand. "Totally," I agree.

"Have you put any more thought into college?" Jax asks.

I swallow before answering, "I'm not sure what I want to do yet."

"I thought you wanted to go into photography?" he asks.

"I do, but I don't know. It's kind of a flimsy degree, don't you think? Not many people can make a living being a photographer. You have to be really good."

"You are really good. And who cares? Do what makes you happy," he urges me.

"I know. I have to think more on it." I sigh. "What about you? Any definite decisions?"

"Just waiting on offers. If U of M's is decent, I'm there. My dad talked to his friend in the recruiting office, and he reassured Dad that it would be good. I'm assuming they'll come talk to us soon, probably mid-season."

"I'm sure they will. They'd be stupid not to want you."

"You know, Lil, U of M's a great school. Come with me." His voice is pleading.

We've talked about this already, and I simply don't know what I want to do. This is the first time that a choice involving Jax isn't blatantly obvious to me. There is something unnerving about the whole thing, so I can't commit yet. I have to think it through.

"I know. I need time to figure out my best option."

"Your best option is with me."

His stare is intense, and I want to avoid this debate right now. We've been over all the aspects of choosing a college so many times, and none of those conversations have made my decision easier. In fact, it is quite the opposite.

I don't want to put a damper on our weekend.

I put the remainder of my crust down in the pizza box and crawl around toward Jax. When I'm within reach, my lips find their target, right below his ear. He groans, and the sound sends electricity down to my toes.

His voice breaks as he says, "Lily Madison, are you changing the subject?"

"Mmhmm," I answer against his skin.

The cooling night air swishes around me as he lifts me and lays me down on the blanket in one smooth movement. His body is above mine, heating my already sensitized skin. His mouth is on my lips, devouring me with a powerful hunger. We are all tongues, hands, and moans as we frantically explore each other's body.

Jax breaks the kiss. "God, Lily, I want you."

"I want you, too," I breathe out.

"Are you sure?"

A smile forms on my lips. "I'm sure."

I have wanted to be with Jax since our first kiss on the night of our junior prom. He has insisted on waiting until it was right. I can't understand that because Jax and I are nothing but right.

"But I want our first time to be perfect, romantic...not initiated by a hormone-crazed kiss while sitting outside next to a pizza box. I made plans..." He breaks off between kisses. "Candles and stuff."

"Jax"—my hands go to his face, and I hold his cheeks, locking our gaze, allowing him to feel my words—"our entire life together has been perfect. We have had eighteen years of foreplay. I don't need candles or flowers. I need you. Take me to bed and make me yours in the only way that I'm not."

His eyes go wide. "Holy fuck, Lily."

Before I register the movement, he is off of me and pulling me up to meet him. He lifts me, and I wrap my arms around his neck and my legs around his waist. I feel his desire for me straining against his shorts.

Once in the bedroom, we lose our clothes in a flurry of lust-filled movements, each article dropping to the ground.

He lays me down on the bed. Leaning in, he gives me a sweet kiss that wraps my stomach into anxious knots.

Pulling his head back, his green eyes latch on to mine. "I love you so much, Lily."

My emotions spin out of control, and my skin is practically vibrating in anticipation. "I love you, too." My voice quivers.

His gentle kisses burn down my neck, over my collarbone, over my breast, and across my belly. All the while, he sighs my name over and over between kisses. *Lily* is a chant, a plea, a declaration coming from his lips, and it causes me to ache with a need so intense that my fingers grasp the sheets for stability.

He uses his hands and his lips to dedicate extra attention to all the places on my body craving his touch. I'm ready, writhing beneath him. He is above me now, pressing his forearms into the mattress on each side of my head, boxing me in with his arms.

I feel him at my entrance, and my heart rate spikes, my breaths coming in ragged bursts.

"You ready?" he asks in between kisses.

I nod, biting my lip.

He takes my mouth in a soul-devouring kiss. His tongue wraps with mine, kissing hard, licking greedily. He pushes into me, past the barrier, and I feel a stinging sharp pain. I cry out into his mouth, my eyes closing tight.

Pulling his mouth off of mine, he kisses me all over my face, voicing his love, while waiting for my body to get used to this new intrusion. "You okay?" he asks.

I nod, releasing the breath I was holding.

"You sure?"

"Yeah," I offer.

He begins to move slowly. The burning sensation disappears, and I'm left with the overwhelming feeling of awe. No longer painful, I take in these new sensations, the way my body is coming together with Jax's. I begin rocking back and forth, meeting him thrust for thrust.

It is everything I hoped it would be and nothing like I thought because it is so much more. Connecting with Jax this way floods my heart with so much love that it's difficult to process.

He is gentle and carnal all at once, and my first time is utter perfection, save the initial pain. Then again, everything with Jax is amazing. He takes me to new highs I didn't know existed, and he fills me with more love than I knew possible. I become his in every sense of the word.

We lie on the crisp linen sheets, exposed and naked. Our legs entwine together as I snuggle into the crook of Jax's arm, my face against his chest still damp with sweat. His fingertips lightly dance across my back as we calm our breaths.

Exhausted and exhilarated all at once, I sigh into his skin. The connection that we shared was everything I'd known it would be, and I pray that I'm not too sore to do it again tomorrow—hopefully multiple times.

"So?" Jax asks.

"Amazing." And it's true.

"That it was, my Little Love."

"I love you."

"I love you more."

"Forever," I state.

"And always," he answers.

I know, with every fiber of my being, that these words are true, and I'm so very thankful because a life without Jax's love wouldn't be a life at all.

six

three years later

Leaning my head against the cool window, I let out a sigh. My breath creates a circle of fog on the passenger window of my dad's SUV, concealing the passing blur of trees. Since we passed Lansing, trees and cornfields have been my view for the last thirty minutes. I'm estimating we have a little more than forty minutes of all things rural before we make it to Mount Pleasant.

I don't know why the scenery is bothering me. The same landscape surrounds my parents' house. Even though this view looks familiar, it's not. These aren't my fields, and they're not my trees. None of this greenery holds any of my memories. None of it has been the backdrop of my life.

My heart aches for our tree—the old grand oak that stands tall and strong in the middle of our field of grass. Jax and I have spent countless moments in our lives under our tree. It has always been our special place. When we were young, we played under it, using our imaginations to create thrilling adventures that would keep us occupied for hours. It was where we built our fort and conducted our secret missions. In our teen years, we lounged under its shade, doing homework or gossiping about the latest high school drama. After the end of our junior year of high school, when Jax and I decided to allow our lifelong friendship to evolve into a romance, it was where we discovered one another through this new perspective, both with our words and our bodies. And over the past two years, while Jax has been away at college, it is where I sprawled on a blanket and talked to him for as long as I could on the phone. Although he wasn't physically with me, just being in our spot and hearing his voice coming through my cell phone made me feel closer to him.

A barely audible whine reaches my ears as my finger pulls along the fogged window, making a heart shape in the traces of my breath. I watch while the outline of the heart disappears as the window slowly returns back to its former temperature. When my eyes focus again at the landscape beyond the highway, a tall oak stands amid a field of green cornstalks.

Whatever.

I turn away from the window, and closing my eyes, I rest my head against the back of my seat. Instead of becoming more excited the closer we get to our destination, I feel increasingly down as the distance from my home to my new college diminishes. The sense of sadness coursing through me is irritating.

I'm annoying myself.

In reality, I'm an upbeat, cheerful, positive, and non-annoying person. I don't do drama or pity parties…yet here I am, sitting under my cloud of melancholy, when I should be doing a happy dance, spinning around and celebrating in a shower of glitter in my metaphorical party.

After high school, I wasn't sure what I wanted to do with my life. Jax encouraged me to go to the same college as him, but that prospect didn't feel right at the time. The tuition is high there, and I just thought I should stay home and attend our local community college, taking the basics, until I figured out what I wanted to do. I didn't want to put myself or my parents into debt, especially over courses I could take at a fraction of the cost while living at home.

When I finally settled on a degree in photography, I started researching programs. The best one I found in Michigan was at Central Michigan University in Mount Pleasant. I know nothing about that city. I didn't even visit the campus before I committed to going.

Jax was supportive of my decision, but I knew it was an act. I've known him my whole life. I know when he's being less than truthful. Jax has only been an hour-and-a-half drive away for the past two years. Now, he will be a little over two and a half hours away. So, we'll be farther apart. I'm sure he wasn't a fan of the longer distance, and with the fact that I'm not bringing my car up this first semester while I get acclimated to college life, I might not see him as much these first few months, but I think that is the best decision. Even though the thought of seeing him less this semester is sobering, I know that part of me wanted this space.

Jax is my past, my present, and my future. He is all I have known and all I want to know. He has been my companion since before we could walk, and he will be at my side when we can no longer walk while our wrinkled fingers entwine across the arms of our wheelchairs. He has always been my protector, and although my love and appreciation for him is endless, I need to know that I can do this on my own.

I know that marriage will come shortly after college, and then Jax will be caring for me forever. This knowledge fills my body with warmth and tingly happiness because there is nothing that I want more. I love Jax Porter with everything that I am. But I'm compelled to prove to myself that I can be independent. I need to know that I can be strong and independent.

"Lily, honey." My mom's comforting voice breaks into my thoughts.

Already knowing what she is going to say by the intonation of her voice, I tell her, "I know, Mom."

We've had this conversation in a variety of forms more than once over the past month.

Apparently, my mom feels one more time is in order. "Honey, I'm so proud of you. You are doing the right thing, following your dreams."

"I know." And I do know. This is my choice.

Jax had all but begged me to transfer to the University of Michigan, but I didn't. I did what I thought was right for me and the course that I want to take in my life.

Then, why do I have this aching, unsettled feeling?

It is the same type of anxiety I have when I'm watching a scary movie. In the movie, when the music starts playing, the tune tells me that something crazy is about to happen. The scene drags on, and my heart pounds in my chest as I wait for it to happen. It always does, whatever version of terror it is, and each time I scream, jumping halfway out of my seat.

That is how I feel right now, and it is terrifying me. My body is in a state of stress, waiting for the disturbing, horrible event to occur. But why? I don't understand it, yet I can't stop it. To be perfectly honest, it is making me question my sanity a little.

People go off to college every year. Couples have long-distance relationships all the time. My fear—of what, I haven't figured out yet—is irrational.

"Then, why the long face? You and Jax have been apart for the majority of the past two years. This is no different. He has been following his dreams, and now, you are following yours. You can both do what is right for each of you and still end up together in the end. This isn't going to change anything between you two. You should be happy, baby. This is going to be great."

I let my mom's words sink in, but they seem wrong. It's not the same. Something is different. I just don't know what it is.

She is right in the fact that Jax has been away for most of the past two years. He started his freshman year of college at the University of Michigan in Ann Arbor where he is a starter on the football team and attending the prestigious business school. His intense course load and rigorous practice schedule haven't left much time for us. I've been able to go stay with him at least two weekends a month, and while not ideal, it's been enough. Plus, add in the fact that we text and talk on the phone multiple times a day, it's been fine.

With football, Jax was barely home for a month this summer. He surprised me by coming home last weekend to spend time with me before I left. Yet, even though I've seen him recently, it just doesn't feel right, going off to college without saying good-bye to him in person.

That has to be it.

Ah, let it go already, Lily.

"You're right, Mom. I just miss him, but it will be great. I know I will feel better when I get there."

87

With one arm resting on the door and the other loosely holding onto the bottom of the steering wheel, my dad peers at me through the rearview mirror. I see his bright blue eyes, identical to my own, reflected there.

"You will, Lil. Just wait. This is an exciting time for you. You are going to meet new people and make friendships that will last a lifetime. This is your time, baby girl. Enjoy it."

"Definitely," my mom adds. "You have the rest of your life to focus on Jax. Focus on yourself for now."

"Yeah," I answer. I know they're right, and once again, this was my choice.

Jax has a larger than life personality and is great at everything he attempts. Everyone in our town and the surrounding areas know who he is. He was the star quarterback of our high school football team and had several college scouts trying to recruit him. One can't help but take notice of him when in his presence. He is tall, built, and gorgeous. His olive skin and dark hair make his deep green eyes stand out, captivating every audience. He is stunning.

Being Jax's best friend and then girlfriend has been my main defining quality in life. People whom I have encountered in the past didn't always know me personally, but they knew me through Jax. I have always been identifiable as his girl in one way or another.

I'm Jax's Lily.

I love that.

I do.

But I think, as much as it hurts my heart, that just for once, for a small amount of time, I need to be Lily.

Just Lily.

I'm nervous and sad, and I miss Jax already, but this change is important to become the best version of myself.

Don't get me wrong. It's not like I'm a hermit with no personal connections other than Jax at home. I have a life. I have friends and hobbies. I do things with my parents and my two sisters. I'm happy. But all of that, the life that I'm living, has Jax entwined through it. He has grown up with all those people as well. My friends are his friends. My family is his family. My experiences are his.

I want my own thing just once. I haven't admitted this out loud to anyone. It is hard enough to be honest with myself. Besides my parents, I don't think others would understand. I'm afraid people would think less of my love for Jax, but this in no way has anything to do with my love for him. It has everything to do with my confidence and proving to myself that I am strong.

Yeah, so…this funk has to go. I will give myself the rest of this car ride, but then there will be no more feeling sorry for myself. I'm going off to college for the first time.

This is necessary. This is important. This is going to be great. I give myself an internal pep talk, and then my phone dings.

A smile spreads across my face, and my mood immediately lifts when I see Jax's name across the screen.

Jax: Hey, Little Love.

Me: Hey, mister.

Jax: I miss you.

Me: I miss you, too. What are you doing?

89

Jax: Morning practice. Coach is giving us a ten-minute break. Wanted to see how your morning was going.

> *Me: It's fine. Not there yet. How's practice?*

Jax: Brutal. You excited?

> *Me: Getting there.*

Jax: You'll love it.

> *Me: I hope so...but I'll miss you.*

Jax: Obviously. ;-) I'll miss you, too. Nothing's really changing though. We'll be apart, same as last year.

> *Me: Yeah, true.*

Jax: Gotta run. Talk to you later. Have a great day.

> *Me: Okay. I love you.*

Jax: Love you more.

Jax: Always.

I press the top button on my phone, clicking it once. I watch as the screen goes black, and then I hold the phone to my chest. *It's going to be okay. Why wouldn't it be?*

I still have Jax.

I will always have Jax.

I'm going to enjoy this time. Jax has been my other half for almost twenty-one years, and he will be mine for the rest of our time here on this earth. This is my chance to be on my own for the first time in my life, and I'm going to make the most of it.

seven

Driving onto Central's campus is like being transported to a different land, a place where all my worries and anxiety are immediately replaced by ecstatic joy.

The downer who was Lily Madison this past month and especially on the car ride this morning is gone.

Just like that.

Poof.

This place must have some sort of magical powers, but I'm not complaining. The exhilaration that I feel right now is what I always hoped I would feel. Even an hour ago, I couldn't imagine ever feeling like this.

I thought the guilt of not choosing to attend the college where Jax is would remain, like a cloud of regret raining sprinkles of depression on me during my entire time here.

But it left.

Gone.

Or maybe it's still here, but the overwhelming weight of the eager anticipation rushing through my veins is blocking it from surfacing. That's okay, too.

I'm here. I'm actually doing this.

I stare in excitement at the rectangular brick building towering before me. At first glance, it doesn't appear to be anything special. In fact, I would venture to say it would definitely be classified as boring. Yet the tingles of pure elation dancing on my skin are a dead giveaway that I know a huge secret that random passersby might not know about this structure. This dorm will house eager young students from all over Michigan and perhaps many from other states. Nothing is more thrilling than immersing oneself into a group of eager, hopeful, and enthusiastic new adults recently liberated from the clutches of their parents' grips.

The possibilities of fun and discovery to be had are endless.

I find myself wanting to jump up and down on the balls of my feet and squeal like a five-year-old on Christmas morning. I'm so terrified that I'm giddy—if that makes any sense. I've been protected my whole life. I know I'm fortunate to belong to such a loving family and, of course, to Jax, who is the biggest blessing of them all. Yet in a few hours strangers will surround me, and that thought both thrills and terrifies me. I will be able to figure out what I am made of. I can finally see what it is like to be me—not the Lily of Jax and Lily and not Lily Madison, middle daughter of respected Mr. and Mrs. Madison.

Just Lily.

I'm going to miss Jax like crazy, and when I allow myself to think about it, my heart hurts. It more than hurts. It aches with a fierce intensity. Yet I don't regret my decision, even now. I need to have this time. Someday, I know that I'll be Mrs. Porter, and Jax and I will be living the American dream. I will forever be linked to him, just as I always have been, and that is great. I couldn't ask for anything more.

For now though, while I can, I need to experience life on my own. Even if only for a short time, I have to know what it is like to be just me.

All around me is the chaos of college move-in day. An assortment of vehicles are parked in random angles, completely ignoring the painted white lines indicating appropriate parking spots. People are obviously jostling to be the closest to the entry doors, white lines be damned.

I want to experience the walk through the hallways and the first view of my dorm alone, so with promises to return in a moment, I leave my parents struggling with the awkward round wooden frame of my favorite chair. I opt to carry a few duffel bags with convenient over-the-shoulder straps into the brick building standing before me.

Inside the metal entry door, I immediately notice the unpleasant air, a musty scent with a dose of chemicals. I'd imagine it's what an abandoned building that has been exposed to water and mildew damage would smell like after it was cleaned with the expired harsh chemical cleaners in the school's janitorial closet. It is nothing I can't handle, and it will be fine once my dorm window is open, allowing the warm summer breeze to carry the funk away.

I take deep breaths—wait, no...shallow breaths as I continue to walk toward my room, watching the numbers on the doors get closer to 216. When I reach the room, I see a square blue paper with *Lily Madison and Jessica Rose:*

Suite 1 written on it in black Sharpie. Underneath our names, it reads *Tabitha Hunter and Molly Smith: Suite 2.*

I take a quick glance down the hall to make sure no one is watching before I bring my hands in front of my face and do a quick succession of claps. I couldn't resist. All smiles, I open the door.

Standing before me is a girl in khaki shorts and a black V-neck T-shirt. She's arranging books on a shelf. She has black leather bands around both wrists and a chunky silver chain attached to her belt loop, disappearing into her pocket. She turns to me and smiles. Her deep brown eyes are kind, and they complement her dark brunette hair that is styled in random small chunks. The shortness of her hair makes the large black gauges in her ears stand out, drawing my attention.

"Um, hi," I stutter, suddenly hit with a case of the nerves. "Hi. I'm Lily."

The girl approaches me, her hand extended. "I'm Jess. So, you're my new suite mate."

I shake her hand. "Yeah."

At first glance, I would describe Jess's appearance as skater meets tomboy. The warmth radiating from her eyes makes me feel immediately at ease. If first impressions are correct, I think I'm really going to like rooming with Jess.

She lets go of my hand and helps me remove the duffels from my shoulder before setting them onto the ground. "Awesome. Well, we'll be sharing the dorm with Molly and Tabitha. They aren't here yet. I think they are coming tomorrow. The three of us have been together since freshman year. My roommate the past two years was a girl named Carrie, but she fell in love with drinking last year and bombed all her classes. So, that left a spot for you."

She chuckles, and when I realize my mouth is open, I close it.

"Oh," is all I can say.

"Is this your first year of college?"

"Yes—I mean, no. I went to community college for the past two years. But this is my first time going to a university and living away from home."

"Ah, I see. Well, no worries. We are all pretty easy to get along with. Molly is a sweetheart, a little on the shy side but very nice. Tabitha can be a bitch—not gonna lie—but you will get used to her. She means well, most of the time, but she can be hard to take. She is blunt and spoiled. But believe me, we could have it worse. And I'm pretty cool, I think. Let me know if you decide otherwise." She gives me a wink.

I let out a nervous laugh. "Okay, will do."

I hear rustling behind me and turn to find my parents jostling with the wooden chair frame.

Addressing Jess, I say, "I hope you don't mind that I brought my big chair. It is crazy comfortable, and I promise to share. It will take up a little room in here though." I gesture to the joint living space separating the two bedrooms.

"Cool. Whatever," she replies.

My parents set the frame down in the corner. My mom fans her face, which is slightly wet from sweat.

"Thanks for grabbing my chair. Hey, Mom and Dad, I want you to meet my roommate Jess." I nod in her direction.

She gives them a wave and a tame grin. "Yes, we are going to be sharing this room." Jess points to the room to the left of the door. "Two other girls are sharing that room on the other side of the bathroom." She points to the door across the main living space.

"Oh, great. Nice to meet you, Jess. I'm Miranda Madison." My mom extends her hand.

"Pleasure to meet you, Mrs. Madison," Jess says as she takes my mom's hand.

"Oh, sweetie, Miranda's fine," my mom reassures her.

"Hey, I'm Anthony. Nice to meet you, Jess." My dad shakes her hand.

The four of us bring up the rest of my stuff from downstairs, and then we go out to dinner at a local Chinese restaurant that Jess raved about.

We do Chinese in typical Madison style, ordering a number of entrees and sides and putting them in the center of the table on the wooden spinning platter. We all get empty plates and dish up little bits of each entree from the center smorgasbord of Chinese deliciousness.

"This is awesome. I love it," Jess says in reference to our food setup.

"Yeah, Anthony and I started doing this when we were dating," my mom says. "I could never decide what I wanted, so on one of our dates, he ordered all the meals I was choosing between, and we shared them. We've been doing it ever since."

"I love it, too. I can be indecisive, like my mom, so this works for me." I chuckle before taking a bite of a crispy egg roll.

Over rice, noodles, vegetables, and various sauce-covered meats, Jess more than impresses my parents, not that it is difficult because they are very loving people. She is one of the most fascinating people that I have ever met. She is so bold, saying exactly what comes to her mind, yet at the same time, she's humble and likeable. She likes music, sports, and the arts. She is double-majoring in music and design.

I stare at her as she struggles to eat with chopsticks. She sends a water chestnut flying across the restaurant, initiating a round of laughter from my parents. I find myself marveling at how lucky I am to have such a cool roommate.

My parents and I continue to talk about our family. Jess doesn't give too many details about hers, except that she is an only child. I tell Jess all about my two sisters. I explain that Amy lives in Ann Arbor where she graduated last year from the U of M's nursing program, and she now loves working at Mott Children's Hospital. I tell her about Keeley, who is at home, school-clothes shopping with her best friend as they get ready to start their senior year of high school. Then, I briefly mention Jax and explain how he goes to school in Ann Arbor.

"Wait," Jess stops me. "You mean Jax Porter? Like U of M's hot-ass quarterback?" She addresses to my parents. "Sorry for swearing." Then, she turns back to me. "Really?"

"How do you know Jax?"

"Lily, anyone who follows college football knows Jax."

"Oh, yeah." I forget that Jax is known to more than just those from our community now, especially since last year when he took over as the starting quarterback.

"Wow. That's crazy. How cool. I'm a serious football fan."

I look to my parents, and their focus is on me. They look like they want to say something, but they don't.

I address Jess, "Yeah, I kinda came here to do my own thing for a bit, you know? But, I'm sure at some point we can make it to a game."

Her face beams with excitement. "That would be awesome."

After many hugs from my parents, I'm alone with Jess in our room, finding a home for all my stuff. Katy Perry is blasting, which was my choice in music. Jess wanted to go old school with Pearl Jam, but Rock-Paper-Scissors made the final call.

When the space is livable and my body is beyond exhausted, I plop down on the futon, and Jess sits at the other end.

"So, Lily, what is your story?" Jess asks.

She learned the gist of my life over dinner. She got a rundown of my sisters and knows about Jax. However, she knows him only by name, so she doesn't truly know him. I start rambling, and I fill her in on the amazingness that is Jax, the real Jax. I tell her how I've known him my whole life, how we've always been inseparable, even before things got romantic between us. I mention how he is remarkable at everything he does and that he is the hottest guy I know. I fill her in about junior prom and the events leading up to how we ended up together.

Jax and I have a beautiful love story. Retelling it reminds me of how much I love him, and that thought makes me miss him even more. I look down to my phone, and I still don't have any messages from him. Since I got here, I've called him several times throughout the day and sent various texts, but I haven't heard back from him yet. I know he's busy, but I ache to hear his voice.

"Wow, you make him sound like the hottest, most amazing guy on the planet." Jess chuckles, shaking her head.

"Oh, he is," I reply. "You just wait and see. You'll like him."

"I'm sure I will. If he has you so enamored with him, he must be pretty decent."

"He is more than decent."

Jess throws her head back in laughter. "Yes, Lil, so you have said, numerous times."

We decide to call it a night. My body aches with exhaustion. I lie in bed, clutching my phone to my chest, halfway between reality and the dream world. My entire body and mind are drained from move-in day. My phone vibrates, and I squeal, becoming completely alert, as I slide the screen to answer.

"Little."

His voice does me in, and I immediately start crying—why, I'm not sure.

"Lily, what's wrong? Why are you crying?" Jax's tone becomes concerned.

I hiccup. "I-I don't know."

"Are you okay?"

I sniffle. "Yes, I'm fine, great actually. I'm just...tired, and I miss you like crazy. I had a fantastic day. I've been waiting to talk to you all day, and I don't know why I'm crying. I'm exhausted but happy." And I'm rambling.

Jax's deep laugh resonates through the receiver. "Oh, Lil, I love you so much. I miss you, too, baby. I'm sorry I wasn't around all day. It has been busy here, you know?"

"Yeah, I do. I'm just so happy to hear your voice."

"Me, too. I've missed you, too. So, tell me all about your first day. What do you think of Central? How's your roommate? How did your parents take leaving you? Tell me everything."

I start talking, telling Jax everything from the way the dorm looks to how it smells to the feeling I got when I stepped foot into my new home for the next eight months. I tell him about Jess and about how much fun we had over dinner. I don't give him time to respond to my incessant chatter as I don't take a break in my story until I end with me lying in bed, holding my phone while waiting for him to call.

"Wow," is all he says.

"I know, right? What a crazy day."

"I'm glad, Lil. Jess sounds cool. I look forward to meeting her. You two should come up with a plan to keep all the horny fuckers away from you."

"Oh, stop. Like that would happen anyway."

"You don't know guys like I do. It will happen, and it worries me."

I dismiss his concern. "I will be fine. I love you. Tell me about your day. Tell me everything."

Jax's day consisted of two practices, a nap, and several meals with his three roommates, who are all on the football team as well. The four of them are actually getting ready to head out to a frat party, but Jax wanted to call before he left.

"Please be careful. Don't drink too much and kiss some random chick."

He chuckles. "Are you kidding? You know that would never happen. You're it for me. You know that."

"I do, but I still worry. Promise me you'll be careful."

"Of course I will." He pauses for a moment. "Hey, Little Love?"

"Yeah?" I answer.

"Happy birthday, baby."

I look over to the clock on my nightstand, and the red digital display reads *12:00*. It is my twenty-first birthday.

"Thanks."

"I wanted to be the first to tell you."

"I know. You're the first." I smile in the darkness.

"Your first everything." His voice is deep and sexy.

My body immediately becomes aroused. "Mmhmm," I answer.

"Do you remember your eighteenth birthday?"

I chuckle. "You know I do."

"So do I. In fact, I'm thinking about it right now." The low timbre of his voice tells me he is just as turned on as I am.

"Maybe that's not a good idea, considering you're about to go out."

"True. God, I wish you were here. I miss you."

"Me, too. Call me tomorrow?"

"Of course."

"Have a good night. Be safe."

"I will. I love you, Lily."

"I love you, too," I answer.

"Love you more," he says.

I hear the click and know he's gone.

I hold the phone to my chest as my eyelids close with acute heaviness. A hint of nervousness fills my body as I think about my first night sleeping away from home, far from Jax and everything I know. But the exhaustion kicks in, and before I can really contemplate my feelings, I'm fast asleep.

eight

The sun streams in through the cheap vinyl blinds covering my dorm window. I stretch my arms above my head, unable to suppress the smile on my face since my dreams of Jax are still fresh in my thoughts.

I reach over and grab my cell off the end table next to my bed, knowing he would have texted this morning before his practice.

> *Jax: Happy birthday, my beautiful girl. I will be thinking about you all day. I love you.*

I text back the emoji that is blowing a kiss and then sit up.

I hear voices on the other side of the bedroom door. Looking toward Jess's bed, I see that she isn't there. After pulling my hair into a messy bun, I head to the living room.

"Oh, look. The flower child herself has emerged from her beauty sleep," a voice that can only be described as snarky says.

"Lily, this is Tabitha. Tabitha, Lily," Jess says as a quick introduction.

"Hi." My voice is hesitant. It's then I notice the very distinct smell of…lilies.

Looking around, I see five vases, each one full of at least a dozen lilies. Ignoring my roommates for a moment, I walk over to each vase and grab the cards, stopping to inhale the scent of the flowers. I'm sure I appear slightly crazed as I bounce around the living room space.

Offering an explanation, I state, "It's my birthday. They're from my boyfriend."

I open the cards and read each one.

HAPPY BIRTHDAY, LITTLE LOVE.

I LOVE YOU.

I LOVE YOU MORE.

I LOVE YOU ALWAYS.

The last one makes me laugh.

DON'T DRINK TOO MUCH TONIGHT AND KISS SOME RANDOM DUDE.

"Happy birthday," Jess says warmly.

"Thanks. It's my twenty-first."

Jess nods her head in approval. "Nice."

Tabitha speaks, "So, listen, don't touch my stuff, don't eat my food, and don't flirt with my boyfriends, and we should be fine. Okay?"

It catches me off guard. Through all my warm and fuzzy feelings, I almost forgot she was here.

Is this girl for real? I lean toward yes, taking in her expectant icy stare.

"Okay," I try to say normally, but I can't help to drawl out each letter of my response.

"As I said, she can be a bitch, but she's harmless. She'll grow on you," Jess says.

"Yeah, okay." I take in Tabitha's appearance.

She really is gorgeous. She is tall—well, taller than me. She's maybe five feet seven inches or so. Her lean long legs are showcased perfectly under her very short shorts. She's wearing a tight T-shirt that stretches over her ample chest. Her shoulder-length black hair falls perfectly, every piece shiny and in place. She has full lips and a slightly pointy small nose, but what stands out the most are her big captivating eyes. They are so dark that they are almost black.

"Okay, great," Tabitha says, her mood lighter, almost friendly.

I wonder if she has some sort of personality disorder.

"So, your twenty-first? We are definitely going out tonight. Right, Jess?" Tabitha asks.

"Of course," Jess answers. "You in, Lily?"

"Sure. Sounds fun." I've gone to college parties with Jax but never with a group of girls.

"Looking hot, girl," Jess says as she buckles her black leather belt. She is wearing jeans, a black T-shirt, and black Chucks.

I'm sensing Jess has a very simple wardrobe. So far, I haven't seen her in anything other than black.

"Thanks. You look great, too. Am I overdressed?" I look at my ensemble in the mirror. I'm wearing a short black tube dress with a chunky gold belt and strappy gold heels. My blonde hair is down and curled. *Maybe it is a little much? But it is a special day.*

"Hell no. You look great. Don't mind me. I'm just not one to dress like that. But no worries. You will fit right in with Tab and Molly."

Molly, our fourth roommate, showed up this afternoon. She is nice, sweet, and quiet, just like Jess explained. She looks like the typical girl next door with wavy long brown hair and brown eyes. Her oval face makes her look innocent, and she probably is.

"Ready to do your first night out as an independent college chick?" Jess asks.

"Yeah, definitely," I answer.

Jess was correct. My outfit is fine next to what my other roommates are wearing. Tabitha has on less fabric than I do.

I text Jax, letting him know we are going out. I haven't heard from him since he called me after his practice this morning. It makes me anxious when he doesn't text back. *But that's why I'm here, right? To discover myself without being connected to Jax.*

I let out a sigh.

This is what I wanted. This is what I needed. It's only day two. The anxiety will lessen as the days go on. I know Jax is busy, and he can't always be attached to his phone. I just miss him. It feels weird to go out on my birthday without him.

"Why the long face, Flower Child?" Tabitha asks, already developing a nickname for me.

I guess she thinks she is clever, given that I'm named after a flower and our dorm is full of them, but it's actually not that creative. Just saying.

"I'm good. Are we ready?"

They take me to The Pub. The atmosphere is great. Half the bar is like a sports bar, and the other half is a dance club.

The night speeds by rapidly, aided by a combination of drinks and dancing. My feet ache, but I'm having so much fun. At the moment, I'm not missing Jax.

"Let's get another shot in honor of the birthday girl!" yells Tabitha.

I know I should say no. My legs feel like Jell-O as it is, and my fingertips are tingling, two signs that I've had enough. *But who cares? It's my birthday.*

"Yes!" I state enthusiastically.

The four of us line up at the bar, each grabbing a lemon drop and holding the glass out.

"To a new year, new friendships, and a new roommate!" Jess cheers.

"To roommates!" Tabitha, Molly, and I shout before the four of us down our shots.

"Let's dance!" Molly yells.

Her personality has come out tonight. She's definitely not shy and quiet when she drinks.

I stand on the dance floor, eyes closed and hands raised, as I sway my body to the beat. I'm completely drunk, and I like it.

Happy twenty-first birthday to me.

Big hands grab my hips, and I sense a body behind me. I smile and lean back into the warmth, the movement of my hips mirroring the ones behind me. The hands move up my hips, stopping at my waist, and they rub the fabric covering my stomach as they wrap around me.

Wait. What am I doing?

I snap out of my drunken haze into crystal-clear clarity as I realize that I'm dancing with some strange guy. I forcefully lunge my body out of his grasp and turn to face him.

"Hey, where are you going, pretty girl?" His voice is deep, but it does nothing for me.

"Um, I'm sorry. I can't dance with you. I have a boyfriend," I stammer out.

"It's just a dance, sweetheart, not a big deal." He sounds cocky.

I don't like it.

"It is to me." I scan the through the dancing bodies in search of my roommates.

He grabs my arm, and I look down to where he holds me and then look back up to his face.

"A pretty girl like you shouldn't have to dance all alone."

He isn't bad-looking. In fact, I would venture to call him attractive. He has short sandy-blond hair and a handsome face. I can't get a good view of his eye color in the dark mood lighting, but I would guess that they are brown or hazel.

"It's just a dance," he says as he rubs his hand up my arm.

I pull my arm from his grasp, edging to the side, but before I respond, I hear Tabitha say, "If it isn't Trenton Troy."

"Ah, Tabs. How are you? I'm sensing, as bitter as ever?" He directs his attention toward my roommate.

"Wouldn't you like to know?" Tabitha says in her snarky voice.

She really is amazing at pulling off that tone. I would sound like an idiot if I tried it.

"No, I'll pass, like always," he says.

I think I see a hurt expression grace Tabitha's face, but it is gone before I can really study it.

"Well, I see that you've met my new roommate, Lily," she says coldly.

"No, actually, we haven't gotten to introductions yet. Lily, is it? I'm Trenton."

His heated stare is on me, and it makes me feel uncomfortable.

"She doesn't care what your name is. She has a boyfriend, so leave her alone."

I'm starting to really like Tabitha and her bitchy side, especially when it is aimed toward this guy.

"So I've heard." His voice is cool with an air of arrogance.

Tabitha takes my hand. "Let's go, Lily." She pulls me behind her, and we distance ourselves from Trenton.

I foolishly look back and find his eyes on me. Our gazes lock, and he smiles.

Whipping my head back around, I say to Tabitha, "That was weird."

"Yeah, he's an ass. Stay away from that one."

We find Molly and Jess playing pool on the other side of the bar. This side is a welcome change. There is slightly more light, and the music isn't as loud. It's already my favorite side because it's away from him.

"What's the story with you and Trenton? It seems like there is some history," I ask Tabitha.

"Hell no. I hate him. He wishes." She huffs. "I'm going to go get us another round. Be right back."

I watch her slender form as she walks away.

"So, you met Trenton Troy, huh?" Jess asks.

"Yeah, on the dance floor."

"He's a douche. He thinks he's hot stuff, but he's a total dick."

"Tabitha doesn't seem to like him either."

Jess chuckles. "Now."

"What does that mean?"

"She chased his sorry ass all last year. He wouldn't give her the time of day. He's a player, and I think that's what made Tabitha so mad—you know, that he sleeps around but not with her. Her ego's hurt. She's not used to rejection."

"Oh. Interesting."

"Yeah, I guess. Do you play?" Jess asks, gesturing toward the table.

"Not well."

She smiles. "Us neither."

We drink more, play pool, and laugh. I haven't laughed so hard in a long time, and it feels great. My anxiety disappears, and my obsession with hearing back from Jax is forgotten.

We dance through last call. We finally call it a night when the lights come on and the music stops, a very obvious sign that the bar is closing.

When we get back to our dorm room, I literally fall into my bed. Too tired or drunk to get undressed, I decide to sleep in my dress. Glancing at my cell phone, I see the texts that Jax sent. Struggling to keep my eyelids open, I opt to wait to read them and respond tomorrow. I'd say the day was a success with awesome roommates and a great birthday celebration.

I'm a lucky girl. I take that to heart as my breathing evens out, and I fall asleep to the smell of lilies filling my room and my love for Jax filling my heart.

My first month of college flies by in a blur of repetition.

I have been getting along great with my roommates and loving my classes.

Jax and I text periodically throughout the day, but usually, we only get to chat at night. Now that classes have started, he is busier than ever. Between his two-a-day practices, meetings, and business school courses, Jax has little to no free time.

When I spoke to Jax the last couple of nights, I could sense an edge to his voice, and it made me sad for him. I know he is stressed, and I don't know how to help him. Personally, I think that the degree he chose to pursue paired with the time commitment to the football team was a little too ambitious, but that's Jax. I'm not sure if he had much of a choice in the matter though. His father demands nothing but the best from his boys and has always pushed Landon and Jax to their limits. His father's high expectations mixed with Jax's insistence on personal perfection has created a powder keg of stress that I'm praying, for Jax's sake, doesn't explode.

Jess's voice breaks my concentration. "You wanna go grab some lunch?"

I look up from the textbook I'm reading to see her standing in our bedroom doorway. I was so engrossed in studying that I didn't hear her come in.

I could use a study break. "Sounds good." Putting the heavy book down beside me, I reach up to the ceiling and stretch before hopping off my bed.

"We're going to meet Tab and Molly there," Jess states as we step into the bright dorm hallway.

"Sounds good."

I decide on the salad bar. I've never been concerned about my weight, nor have I ever had to watch what I eat. I'm blessed with a high metabolism. Plus, all the heavy starchy foods served in the cafeteria make me tired, and I could use all the energy I can get. So, I've really been trying to cut down on any useless calorie intake.

I grab a milk and make my way to our usual table. Tabitha is talking adamantly when I set my tray down next to Jess. I would bet money that it is about her most recent conquest. I wouldn't go as far as calling her a slut because that would be cruel…but let's just say that Tabitha has many male friends with benefits.

My roommates greet me as I slide onto the bench seat. While Tabitha continues her rambling, my phone dings from my pocket. Pulling it out, I see a text from Jax.

Jax: Heading to my next class. Whatcha up to?

Me: Eating in the cafeteria.

Jax: What's on the menu?

Me: Salad.

Jax: Boring.

Me: I know. Miss you.

Jax: Me, too.

Jax: If you could only eat one thing for the rest of your life, would you rather choose salad or pizza?

Me: Easy. Pizza.

Jax: Is that a very healthy choice?

I laugh, hearing Jax's voice in my head asking that question. I can see his face, knowing that he would be raising one of his eyebrows with an adorable smirk.

> *Me: No but don't care. It's the yummier choice.*

Jax: You would get fat and unhealthy.

> *Me: So? I'd be happy, and you'd still love me.*

Jax: That I would.

> *Me: Would you rather smell like fish or skunk spray for the rest of your life?*

Jax: Fresh fish or rotten fish?

> *Me: No questions. I don't know. Fish! ;-)*

Jax: Then, fish because fish doesn't always smell bad, but skunk spray does.

> *Me: Good call.*

Jax: You'd still love me regardless, fishiness and all.

> *Me: True, but I might invest in a nose plug.*

Jax: Hey, gotta go. In class now.

> *Me: Love you.*

Jax: Love you more.

I smile as I click my phone off and put it in my back pocket.

"How's the boyfriend?" Tabitha asks.

"Good."

"So, when are we going to meet this enigma?"

I look across the table toward Tabitha. "I don't know. Why do you call him that?" I ask, curious.

"I just want to meet this guy who is so great that he has had you wrapped around his finger for twenty-one years, is all."

"Yeah, he is pretty great." There is no point in downplaying the awesomeness that is Jax.

"So we've heard. When is he coming to visit?"

"Not sure. He's really busy with football. I don't think he would be able to make it here until next semester."

Molly speaks, "That's too bad. I bet you miss him."

"Like crazy. I wish I had my car here."

"You can borrow mine anytime," Jess offers.

"Really?" The thought of driving to see Jax sounds too good to be true.

"We should totally make a weekend trip to Ann Arbor! I bet the parties there are so much better. Does he have any roommates?" Tabitha asks.

I smile, her enthusiasm contagious. "Yeah, three."

"We should go, and you should surprise him!" Molly exclaims.

Tabitha agrees, "Yes. Surprises are the best."

"So, when should we go?" Jess asks.

"I'm not sure, but if we want to see him, it should definitely be during a weekend when he has a home game."

"Do you think we can get tickets?" Jess reaches for her phone.

"I'm sure. I don't see why not. Jax should know someone who isn't using theirs."

Jess starts typing into her phone. "I'm just pulling up the schedule. If we are going to a game, it has to be a good one. Let's see. This weekend, they play Indiana, and the first weekend in October is against Northwestern. Oh! The State game is in Ann Arbor this year. We have to go then, yeah? It's the last weekend in October." She looks up with a hopeful expression.

"The State game would be fun," Molly chimes in.

Michigan State verses U of M would be a great game to attend. Besides Ohio State, I'd say State is U of M's biggest rival. The fact that it is over a month away is a downer, but I know how much Jess would love going to that game, being the big football fan that she is. She would be the one providing the transportation after all, so it would only be fair.

"Sounds great," I agree. "You think I should keep it a surprise though? What if he has plans?"

Tabitha screws on the cap to her empty water bottle and then tosses it on her tray. "Definitely keep it a surprise. It is more fun that way. Plus, what would he be doing that he couldn't incorporate you into?"

"I guess you're right. He'll probably be going out on Saturday after the game. We can go along. It will be fun." The knowledge that I'm going to see Jax in a month sends happy jitters through me, and my excitement starts to grow. I enthusiastically clap my hands together a few times. "Yay! Thanks so much, Jess, for the ride, and you girls, for coming."

"No thanks needed. It's going to be a blast for all of us," Jess states.

Tabitha enlightens us with all the stories she has heard about U of M's parties. I let her talk, but I've been to many parties with Jax, and they weren't like what she is describing. I hope she won't be disappointed when we get there. However, something tells me that if she finds a cute guy to hang out with, then it won't matter how epic the parties are.

The girls decide to go out to Wayside, a local club that we've already been to a handful of times during my month here. I take a rain check this time with the excuse that I have to study. My excuse is a half-truth at least. I could use some uninterrupted study time, but actually, I just want to call and talk to Jax.

The girls have been talking about our trip to Ann Arbor all day, and it has been making me miss Jax like crazy. Knowing that I'm going to see him in a month, which is sooner than I thought I would, is thrilling.

I text him.

Me: Call me when you can.

Me: Miss you.

Me: Love you.

He doesn't respond, so I call him for good measure and leave a voice mail.

I stare at my phone, willing it to ring.

Nothing.

Maybe I should have gone out with the girls?

Now that I'm on a mission to talk to Jax but can't, I'm unable to focus on anything else, especially reading.

I let thirty minutes go by, and I decide that it's a respectable wait period, so I text him again. I'm so eager to talk to him, but I don't want to jump on the crazy train of girlfriends either.

Still nothing, and I wait.

Lying back on my bed, I decide to pass the time by scrolling through my pictures on Facebook. I have thousands on my account, the majority of Jax and me. I slide my finger across the screen, changing the photo, and each one brings back a different memory, each one special. I smile despite my need to talk with Jax. I can't help but to be happy when I think about all the great times we've had.

After several minutes of scrolling, I get to the photos of junior prom and grin wide, thinking back to the night that started it all.

nine

I can't stop the chuckle that erupts at the sight of Tabitha's very large brand-name suitcase leaning against the wall, next to the door.

"It's only one weekend, Tabs, like two nights. How could you possibly need that much stuff?" I ask through a large grin, shaking my head.

"Hey, Flower Child, we don't know what the weekend will bring, so I'm taking options." Tabitha tucks a loose strand of her hair behind her ear as she admires her reflection in the mirror on the wall.

"I'm pretty sure that whatever the weekend brings, one or two outfits would suffice," Jess states matter-of-factly as she grabs her compact duffel off of the futon.

"Nope, not for me," Tabitha states unapologetically. "Hey, Molls, you ready?" she calls back to her bedroom.

"Coming," Molly yells.

We make our way out the door.

The ride to Ann Arbor seems to take forever. I'm so giddy with excitement. I haven't seen Jax since August, and I'm almost jumping out of my skin in anticipation.

Jax's busy schedule paired with my own has left us limited time to talk or text. This is the longest that we have gone without seeing each other, but in addition to that, it is the furthest I have ever felt from him, in all aspects. To say these past two months have been difficult would be the understatement of the year.

My entire being—mind, body, and soul—desperately need this weekend. I crave my connection with Jax.

I'm so grateful for Jess and her offer to drive me here. But I have learned a valuable lesson. A car at college, for me anyway, is a necessity. I know that Jax doesn't have the time in his schedule to drive to Mount Pleasant to see me. So, after I go home in a month for Thanksgiving, I will be bringing my car back. I will not go this long without visiting Jax again.

We navigate the one-way streets through downtown Ann Arbor until we are approaching campus and our destination. We are lucky to find a spot to park on the street just around the corner from Jax's apartment.

Opting to leave our bags in the car until after we announce our arrival, we start toward the apartment building on foot. The cold brisk autumn wind is in full effect, causing me to wrap my arms around myself.

"Are you, like, so excited right now, Lil?" Tabitha asks.

"You don't even know. I can't wait. I just hope he is there."

Based on my previous texts with Jax today, I know that his practice is over by now. He didn't mention having any plans, so he should be in the apartment.

I don't think he had plans to go out tonight. Jax usually doesn't go out the night before a game.

My shaky hand grabs the cool metal railing leading to the apartment entrance as we walk up the steps to the door. Before we have to ring Jax's apartment buzzer, the front door swings open, and a guy exits. He holds the door for us, and we scurry into the building.

I knock eagerly on Jax's apartment door. In a matter of seconds—albeit very long seconds—Jax is swinging the front door open. His expression is one of pure surprise and happiness as he stares at me, eyes bulging and mouth slightly agape.

He stands there, gorgeous as ever. He is wearing a pair of track pants and a faded T-shirt that clings to all the right places. His hair has that sexy tousled style going on and appears slightly damp. I can smell his body wash, and it immediately warms my body, taking away all traces of the chill from outside.

I'm pretty sure I hear Tabitha say, "Damn," in that sultry way that she's perfected, but I ignore her.

I throw myself into Jax's arms, lifting my body off the floor, and I wrap my legs around his middle.

He catches me and holds me close. It feels so right, being in his arms. We fit perfectly together, like a second skin. All my anxieties fade, and I'm left with nothing but a feeling of peace.

"Little Love, what are you doing here? I'm so happy to see you. I couldn't be happier, but what are you doing here?" he asks in astonishment.

"I wanted to surprise you," I mumble into his neck. I squeeze him tight and remember what it is like to have my arms around him.

I release my legs from around his waist and lower myself to the ground.

He runs his hands through my hair. "Well, you definitely did. How long will you be here?"

"Until Sunday. Is that okay?"

"Of course. Yes. Of course."

His hands pull my head forward as he leans toward mine until are lips are together. It is a short soft kiss, but it sends a current of pleasure through my body, and I curl my toes into the soles of my pink Chucks.

Recalling our audience, I pull away. "Oh, yeah. My roommates." My voice is almost a whisper as I'm in my Jax-induced haze.

I proceed to introduce Jax to the girls, not missing how Tabitha's hand lingers in their handshake before Jess playfully pushes her aside to shake his hand.

"We've heard so much about you. I hope you don't mind us crashing here this weekend," Jess says to Jax.

"No, not at all. I've heard a lot about all of you as well. Glad to meet you," he says to Jess before turning his attention back to me. "I still can't believe you were able to keep this from me. You're horrible at keeping secrets."

I laugh. "I know. Believe me, it was hard."

We head into the apartment, and Jax quickly introduces my friends to his three roommates—Jerome, Josh, and Ben. This is their third year rooming together, and they are great friends. The foursome has picked up the name Ben and the Three Js around campus. The name makes me laugh because they are all adorable and could be a boy band of some sort—a buff, muscly one that doesn't sing but a group nonetheless.

Ben is actually our friend from home. We've gone to school with Ben since we were five. Ben and Jax have always been friends, but going to the same college and playing on the same team—not to mention rooming together—has made them even better friends.

"Ladies, now, you've met Ben and the Three Js," I say in a dramatic fashion with my best Vanna White hand gesturing toward the room packed with testosterone sexiness.

I told the girls all about Jax and his roommates prior to our arrival. I became pretty close with the guys over the past couple of years when I would come to stay with Jax two weekends a month.

Jess immediately starts talking football with Jerome, the current starting wide receiver on the team. Tabitha works her flirting magic on Ben and Josh while Molly watches, content to hang back.

Jax entwines his fingers in mine and starts leading me down the hall toward his bedroom. Once inside the room that he shares with Ben, Jax closes the door and locks it.

After he pushes me against the closed door, his mouth is instantly on mine. Our tongues plunge into each other's mouths, starved of this taste, this feeling. The rhythm of Jax's tongue and the warmth of his mouth elicits a moan from deep within me. The sound coming from my mouth amplifies the kiss, and Jax's mouth works harder, faster, rougher.

A desperate desire to connect that can't be sated with a kiss erupts within me. Our breaths are heavy as our lips pull, our tongues explore, and our teeth bite. It's everything, this kiss, but it's not enough.

I can feel the pool of warmth between my legs, and my hips start rocking against Jax of their own accord. His hard length mimics the rhythm against my hip.

"Lily." His voice is strained, and my name sounds like a plea. "Lily," he says again into my neck between kisses.

His hot breath against my skin initiates a new round of shivers to course through me.

"I need you, Lil."

"I'm here," I whisper.

"I need to be inside you."

"Take me."

He licks from my collarbone, up to my neck, and then over to my ear where he whispers, "I will, but I need something else first."

He pushes me to the side, so I'm against the bedroom wall, and then he drops to his knees. He unbuckles my jeans and pulls them down my legs, removing them along with my panties and shoes before tossing them to the floor. I stand in front of him, bare from the waist down.

On his knees, he looks up at me, and our eyes remain connected as two fingers enter me. His expression shows love, desire, and pure lust. He starts moving his fingers in and out, and when he pushes against the front of my inner wall, I whimper.

"You're so wet, so perfect."

Simultaneously, he breaks our gaze and removes his fingers. Taking his two hands, he opens me and plunges his tongue in as deep as it will go. I want to cry out from the sweet torture, but I hold it in, my breaths becoming ragged. He moans into my wet flesh as he continues to make love to me with his mouth, sliding his tongue up and down my slit.

"Fuck, Lil. So good. So sweet. So everything." His voice is low, deep, and broken as he chants his adoration into my skin.

His tongue concentrates on my most sensitive spot, and it takes mere seconds before my body starts to convulse in absolute ecstasy. His hand reaches up and covers my mouth as his tongue continues its assault. I bite down on his hand, blocking my screams, as the sensations continue to pulse through me.

I come hard, releasing the weeks of pent-up need. Eyes closed and knees bent, I slouch down against the wall, unable to hold myself up straight, as my body recovers from the onslaught of sensation.

One of Jax's arms wraps around my waist, pulling me up to a standing position. I feel his skin against my own. Opening my hazed eyes, I see he is now naked. He takes his free hand and pulls my shirt and bra off over my head, and we stand against each other. I revel in the feeling that our skin-on-skin contact brings. He grabs one of my legs and wraps it around his middle, opening myself to him. Then, he grips both of my wrists and firmly holds them above my head.

"You still on birth control?"

"Of course."

"We'll go slow later. Right now, I just need you—hard."

I nod once before he slams into me. The way in which my leg wraps around him allows him to get in deep. He relentlessly pounds into me, and it burns in the most exquisite way. It's painful pleasure.

In between thrusts, Jax's strained voice chants fragmented words of desire, "I. Need. You. Fuck, Lil. Yes. So. Good."

Our breathing is heavy. The sound of our skin slapping together echoes throughout the room. My eyes remain closed, and I take it all in. The feeling of his body entering mine with so much power mirrors his desire for me.

The noises, the smells—it is all too good, too much.

My orgasm hits fast and hard, and I bite down on Jax's shoulder as my body quakes forcefully. Jax thrusts in even deeper, and I feel his body start to shake against me.

His grunts sound almost pained as he keeps them quiet behind his closed lips.

Spent, our sweaty bodies glide against one another as Jax holds us up against the wall. It is quiet in the room, except for our breaths.

After a few moments go by, Jax lifts me and walks me to his bed. Lying side by side, he holds me with a fierce intensity, like he's afraid to let go. His face is nuzzled into the crook of my neck, and his strong arms wrap around me.

I lightly trail my fingers up and down his back. "Jax," I say tentatively, "are you okay?"

He seems different, so intense...almost sad or perhaps mad. It is hard for me to pinpoint his emotions, but his demeanor is off. Maybe he is just getting all his feelings in check after not seeing me for so long.

"I'm fine. I just have a lot going on. I've been so stressed lately."

"Can I help you? What can I do?" I kiss him on the head.

"You're already doing it." He pulls me even closer. "I love you. You know that, right? That I love you so much?"

"Of course I do. And I love you."

"You know that, no matter what, I will love you always."

"Jax, what is it? What's wrong?"

He is worrying me.

"Nothing. I just want to make sure you know that."

The room is silent again, and I take everything in— his words, his demeanor, his intensity. I know something is wrong. I just don't know what it is. I will give Jax time, and hopefully, he will open up to me this weekend and let me help him.

We lie still for a while, holding each other tight, lost in our own thoughts.

Tabitha's distant laugh catches my attention, breaking through my Jax fog.

"My roommates," I say. "We should go back out there."

"No." Jax's answer is quiet, but definite.

"Jax, I brought them here. I just can't leave them to fend for themselves."

"They'll be fine. Ben will set them up with sleeping arrangements."

I feel guilty that not only is Ben going to be sleeping out on the couch, which has been his and Jax's agreement from the beginning for when I visit, but now, Ben also has to find somewhere for three additional girls to crash.

"Jax," I coax, "come on. I can't just ignore them. We should go out there for a bit."

"No, Lily. No."

I'm taken aback by Jax's firm tone.

He softens a bit. "Listen, I just need it to be me and you tonight. Okay? I need this. I need you. No one else. Please?"

"Okay. Of course."

I tilt my head down so that my lips can find Jax's. I softly kiss him, trying to communicate my love for him, my unwavering support for him. He is everything to me, and I want to be everything to him. Whatever is hurting him, I want to take it away.

I pull my lips from his. "Do you think you can get us tickets to the game tomorrow?"

"Yeah, hold on." Jax rolls off the bed and retrieves his jeans from the floor. Reaching into his pocket, he pulls out his phone. His face goes hard as he stares at the screen.

"What is it?" I ask, concerned.

"Just a message from my dad. He has been such an asshole lately."

"What does it say?"

"Nothing worth talking about. It's fine. Lily." His thumbs move over his phone screen, typing.

"Who are you texting?"

"Ben. Asking him to set the girls up and score you tickets."

A couple of seconds after Jax's thumbs stop moving, a ting comes from his phone.

"There. All set," Jax states before tossing his phone on his desk and climbing back into bed with me.

"What did he say?"

"He's taking care of your friends and the tickets. No worries." He kisses me on the forehead. "Now, back to more important matters."

Jax's signature coolness is back in his voice, and I can't help but giggle.

"What matters are those?" I ask, already knowing his response.

"You and me," he states between kisses. "I'm going to make love to you, slowly this time, until we both pass out from exhaustion."

Jax kisses me, pulling my lip between his, and it is heaven. I know I should be worried with his intense behavior and random mood swings since I got here, but right now, with his lips on mine, I can't. All I can think or feel is Jax. It might be selfish, not talking things through with him and helping him with whatever is bothering him, but when my amazing boyfriend wants to make love with me, I do it.

And I plan to until, like Jax said, I can't keep my eyes open any longer.

ten

I wake up to Jax's lips on my forehead. I partially open my eyes and see his fuzzy outline through my sleepy haze.

"Hey." I yawn and stretch my arms out above my head.

Coming into focus now, I see Jax sitting on the side of the bed, studying me with an expression I can't place.

"Morning." Jax's tone is very businesslike. "So, I have to run. We have some stuff to do with the team before the game. Our friend Stella is going to stop by sometime this morning and drop off your tickets. I'll find you at some point afterward, once the team has finished going over the game, okay? I'm not sure how long it will take, but I'll text you when we're done, and we'll meet up. A spare set of keys is hanging on the hook by the door. Just lock up when you leave, all right?"

"Okay. Good luck. Love you."

"Me, too." He bends down and kisses my forehead again. "Always." He gets up and heads toward the door. Before he closes it, he says, "See ya later."

"Bye," I say as the door shuts.

I wait until all the male voices from the hallway are gone, and I get out of bed and put on my outfit from yesterday. I walk across the hall to the bathroom.

I grab my toothbrush, squirt a big blob of toothpaste on it, and start brushing. My reflection stares back at me, and I can't help but smile. I'm a hot mess. My mascara is smudged, black streaks trailing toward my cheeks. My hair is a heaping rat's nest. But my pale skin has some color to it, my cheeks glowing a light pink. I look like I just spent the night getting thoroughly screwed, and I guess I did—in the best way.

I find the girls by the kitchen the counter, waiting for the coffee pot to finish brewing.

"Morning," I say cheerfully.

"Well, look who it is—our roommate who ditched us to have a sex marathon," Tabitha says in a serious voice.

The grin on her face lets me know that she's just teasing.

"Sorry I ditched you. We didn't feel like coming back out. I hope it wasn't uncomfortable for you out here with the guys."

"Girl, no need to apologize," Jess says. "It was fine. The guys are great. And don't let Tabs give you a hard time. She wasn't without a warm body to sleep with last night either."

I turn to Tabitha, my eyebrows rising in interest. "Who was it?"

"Josh," she says matter-of-factly, shrugging her shoulders. She grabs the pot of coffee and pours the steaming liquid into her mug.

I laugh. "You never cease to amaze me. So, how was it?"

"It was fine. We didn't do it. Jerome was in his bed in the room. I didn't care, but I think Josh did. We just made it to second base," she says in a bored tone. "Tonight will be a different story. I'll let Josh do me in the bathroom, if he wants. He's fucking hot."

"Classy," mutters Jess into her coffee cup.

"Jealous," snaps Tabitha.

"Hardly," says Jess.

"Well, Josh is really cute, and he's such a great guy," I offer.

Tabitha turns to face me, her straight hair swishing as she does. "He's not really cute. He's fucking hot. And speaking of hot, damn, Jax is gorgeous, Lil—like *People* magazine's Sexiest Man Alive hot."

I smile. "Yeah, he's pretty gorgeous."

We retrieve our bags from the car. We all shower and get ready.

The intercom buzzes, and I go over and ask, "Who is it?"

"Stella," the voice says through the speaker.

I buzz her up.

Stella introduces herself. Apparently, she has a lot of classes with Jax since they have the same major, and they study together. She is a gorgeous girl. As far as looks go, I would say she is the female equivalent of Jax. She is taller than me, has wavy long dark hair, and hazel eyes. Her whole appearance is pleasant, and she radiates kindness.

For a brief moment, an emotion that I'm not used to feeling when it comes to Jax rushes through me— jealousy. But as soon as it appears, it goes away.

I listen to Stella yammer on, and I get a really good vibe from her. Either she is a great actress, or she is quite possibly the sweetest girl in America.

"So, I hear you are into photography? Jax has shown me some of your photos. You are really good," she continues talking.

I find it a little strange that Jax has shown his study buddy pictures that I've taken. I shake my head, trying to rid it of these thoughts. I'm being silly. *Why wouldn't Jax show off my pictures?* He loves me and is proud of me.

I'm in my own thoughts when I realize that it is silent in the living room, and all eyes are on me. I'm not sure what I'm supposed to be saying or what question I was asked. But I think it's safe to say, "Well, thank you so much for bringing over the tickets. We really appreciate it. We're all so excited to go to a game."

"Oh, no problem. I'm only a couple of rows away from your seats. Maybe we can get together after the game. One of my friends is having a postgame keg party. It will take the guys a while to meet us."

The girls all voice their agreement, and we exchange numbers with Stella in case we lose her in the postgame exodus of the crowd.

"Sweet. I'll text Jax and let him know where we'll be," Stella says.

"Yeah, sure. Okay," I answer.

It's a little cold as we walk around the tailgating area prior to the game, but thankfully, it has warmed up a bit from yesterday. The sun is shining, and the leaves are bursting with vivid autumn colors. The four of us are decked out in our maize-and-blue attire and block M temporary tattoos on our cheeks.

Of course, Tabitha friends some drunk college guys with an awesome tailgating setup. We play cornhole, drink some, and eat some grilled goodness. It is a great time, and the girls are loving it. I can't help the smile adorning my face because I truly am having a fantastic day, but a part of me can't wait until all of this—the tailgating, the game, and the partying—is over, so I can see Jax. I have such limited time with him. When my thoughts go to when I have to leave tomorrow, I miss him again.

The game is awesome. Jax is in his element, and nothing is sexier than Jax on the football field. I know he works hard to be as good as he is, but he makes it look effortless. He's a talented team leader and has really helped the football program here get back on track. I'm so proud of him.

The game is close and intense. Sitting in the student section at a Michigan football game is an experience in itself. There is something thrilling about standing in a large group of loud, enthusiastic die-hard fans who love my boyfriend. It is surreal really.

When the game is over, the team rushes the field in celebration, and Jax looks toward the student section. I don't know if he can see me among the sea of maize and blue, but I feel his stare nonetheless. I know it is for me alone.

We meet Stella in front of the stadium and start walking toward downtown. Her friend's house is on one of the side streets a few blocks away. The party is already going when we arrive. Groups of people are congregating all over the front yard and porch. Loud music is booming the house, and I can hear laughter and muffled voices from the people inside.

My roommates and I, along with Stella and some of her friends, make our way into the house. Tabitha and Molly immediately break away, heading in the same direction as the keg. Stella introduces Jess and me to a few people, but I can't really hear most of the people's names with the music blaring.

We hang out for several of Molly's and Tabitha's keg stands, numerous conversations, loads of fantastic people-watching, and countless ear-piercing songs before Jax comes. I can feel him, and I know he is behind me before he wraps his arms around my waist. I lean back into his chest as his arms tighten around me.

"There you are," he says into my ear.

Immediate goose bumps take up residence on my skin.

I turn, still wrapped in his embrace, until I'm facing him, and I put my hands around his neck. "Great game. You were amazing, Jax."

He smiles, and it is both shy and prideful. "Thanks. I'm glad you could be there." He bends down, and his lips find mine.

Our surroundings become muted white noise as all of my focus is concentrated on the pair of silky soft lips currently caressing mine. I could kiss Jax for an eternity.

Jax pulls away from the kiss, and the expression on his face is what must be the opposite of my own. I feel content warm love radiating from my pores, yet Jax looks stressed, almost pained.

"Let's get out of here," he says.

I don't question his reasons. I simply nod.

We find my friends among a big group of people in the next room, including Jax's roommates and Stella. I tell the girls that I'm going to head back with Jax, and they are fine with staying to hang out here. I watch Jax say something to Ben and Josh, and they both nod while looking toward me.

Jax turns back to me and grabs my hand before winding me through the now larger crowd of people occupying the house.

On the way to the door, I hear, "Good game," "Awesome job," "Fucking epic, dude," and some other congratulatory comments directed at Jax.

He also receives several slaps on the back and some fist bumps.

Once we are on the sidewalk, away from the party, I say, "Quite the celebrity you are." Leaning in toward our entwined hands, I playfully bump Jax with my shoulder.

"No, I'm not," he says seriously. "I'm just a football player."

I disagree, "No, you are way more than just a football player, Jax Porter."

He is silent.

"Babe, what's going on with you? You don't seem like yourself. You are worrying me," I say as we stop at a corner and wait for the crosswalk sign to change.

"I'm fine. I'm just tired and stressed. There's a lot going on right now, so much pressure."

The white Walk sign flashes, and we head across the street.

"What exactly is stressing you out? Your classes? Football?" I ask.

"Yeah, all of it. My dad, everything—it's too much."

"How can we make it better? Can you give something up? Maybe take less classes?" I think aloud.

"I don't know…" Jax's voice trails off.

We walk some more in silence before we head into Pizza Bob's, a local restaurant with the best chipati sandwich in the universe. Both of us feeling hungry, we get a take-out order.

Back at the apartment, we sit cross-legged on the living room floor, facing each other, with our chipati sandwiches laid out before us on the square sub paper.

"Do you know what day I always think back to?" I ask.

"What day?"

"I'll give you a hint." I smirk. "Subway."

Some of Jax's charm returns as he smirks. "Oh, I know exactly what day you are thinking of."

"What?" I chuckle, bumping his knee with my own.

"Our first friend date after the infamous prom kiss."

"Yep," I answer. "The night that we took the leap into the *more* category."

"I'll tell you what else I recall about that day. Remember how all your Would You Rather questions focused around me being naked?" He breaks into a mocking smile while quirking up his eyebrow.

"That is not true!" I whine.

"Oh, Little Love, it is totally true. I wish I could recall your exact questions, but I do remember them all revolving around my nakedness."

"Whatever. If they did, I'm sure it was because you made them that way."

"Nope, it was all you. You wanted me."

"Well, obviously." I chuckle, shaking my head. "Can you believe that was, like, three and a half years ago?"

"Yeah, pretty crazy."

"Looking back, I don't know what took us so long to get together. You were hooking up left and right with anything with boobs but not your best friend," I tease.

"Hey," Jax says in mock offense. "First of all, not anyone with boobs. I had standards. And secondly…" He pauses. "You know why." His voice is serious.

"Maybe, but tell me again."

"Because you were different than the others. You were special. You were important, and most of all, you were needed."

I stare into his emerald eyes, imploring him to continue.

"I needed you, and because of that, I couldn't fuck it up and lose you. Us, like this"—he motions in between us—"was an unknown. I wasn't going to chance a known that was as amazing as our friendship on an unknown and risk losing it all."

"What was it exactly that changed our minds? Do you remember?" I wonder aloud.

Jax laughs, shaking his head. "Hormones. After our kiss at prom, there was no way that we could have just been only friends. Chemistry is something we have always had going for us."

"We have a lot more than that going for us."

He nods, and his gaze becomes unfocused as he stares at something behind me. "Yeah."

"So…" I say in a cheerful voice. "Would you rather—"

He puts his hand on my knee. "Little, can we just lie down for a bit? I'm exhausted."

"Sure. Of course."

We bawl up our trash and throw it out in the kitchen. Then, we go to Jax's room, and he locks the door behind us.

I lie on my back, and Jax climbs in next to me. He lies on his side, so that one of his legs and an arm are draped over me. He rests his head on my chest and closes his eyes. I draw my fingers through his hair, just thinking. His breathing slows, and I know that he is asleep. I continue touching his hair. He didn't put any product in it since his shower after the game, and it is so soft. The motion of dragging my fingers through it calms me, but inside, I am anything but.

I feel like crying, and I'm not sure why or for what reason. Something is very wrong. I've seen bits and pieces of my Jax this weekend but not very much. I need to figure out what is causing this funk that he is in, so I can pull him out of it.

My heart hurts for my sweet boy. He's the boy who captured my heart before I knew what love was, the boy who showed me what love was through his words and his actions, the boy who loved me so fiercely that not returning his love wasn't an option for me. Loving Jax has never been a choice, but it's always been a privilege. When he hurts, I do, too.

I'm just hoping that I can fix whatever is causing him pain.

As I lie here, listening to his even and steady breaths, I pray that his troubles aren't too much for us to conquer together. Jax has to know that, in this lifetime, he will never be alone. Everything that he faces, he will face it with me. I will support and love him always. I have to believe, with our unwavering love, we can overcome it all. We will conquer the world, our perfect little world.

eleven

I awaken to warm hands caressing my stomach under my shirt. I open my eyes to find Jax peering at me, a thoughtful expression gracing his face. He appears wide-awake, and I get the impression that he might have been watching me for some time.

"Jax." My voice is quiet, my vocal cords still waking up from the very comfortable and needed nap. "What time is it?"

The apartment is still quiet, indicating that our drunk friends haven't returned from their night of partying.

"It's eleven."

Eleven at night is still early for a Saturday, so it is no wonder that no one is back yet.

The pained look in Jax's eyes has returned, but before I can really look at him and analyze his expression too much, his lips find mine.

All lingering drowsiness vanishes immediately as my body responds to its favorite thing in the world—Jax, and more specifically, his lips on me. The kiss is gentle and sweet for a moment, and the quick space in time is filled with several of my heartbeats before the kiss accelerates. The softness is gone, and the hunger ensues. His mouth, lips, and tongue devour my own.

Our hands are everywhere, tugging and pulling, frantically removing items of clothing. Moans fill the air around us. Desperate hungry sounds speak of the longing of two souls bursting to connect in the manner in which they were designed to.

This right here with Jax and me, our bodies and our souls acting on pure instinct and desire, is what I was made for. To be part of him and him me. To become one in the most beautiful way imaginable. There's only one thing in this world more beautiful than Jax, and that is our connection, the way we are together. There is nothing more right, more pure, more destined than us together.

The first time we make love, it is hard and rough. Jax's thrusts are forceful, sending my body jolting back toward the headboard each time. It is powerful, raw need coming out, and I love it. We both come hard, our bodies shattering simultaneously, our voices yelling out into the lust-charged air around us.

Jax falls on top of me, his sweaty chest rising and falling as he works to catch his breath. He buries his face into my neck and breathes in and out against my skin. I gently run my fingertips across his back, feeling his slick muscles beneath my skin.

No words are spoken as we come down from our highs. My body hums with fulfillment. My heart beats with the fullness of my love for Jax.

He places light kisses on my neck, my entire being immediately recharged and ready for him again. This time is different though. He moves his lips over my body—sucking, kissing, and licking every inch of my skin. He spends a lot of time on my breasts, working the sensitive skin into his mouth so flawlessly—pulling, kissing, and lightly biting—until my back is arching off the bed, begging for more.

Despite my plea, he doesn't take me again right away. His lips continue their descent all the way down my legs to my toes. It's as if he's memorizing every indent and curve of my body. He works my body with both his mouth and hands, kneading my muscles in a unique sensual massage. It brings so much calming satisfaction that I simply close my eyes and take it all in—every sensation, every kiss, every touch.

Jax works his way back up my legs, and his mouth stops at my entrance. The lavish attention he has shown to the rest of my body is now focused to this spot, the bundle of nerves that brings me the most blissful sensation. His tongue flicks slowly, savoring the experience. I feel his moan resonate into my flesh as his tongue continues its skilled movements.

My orgasm comes quickly, so intense that it borders on painfully aching ecstasy. Using his hands, he keeps my legs spread, as his tongue continues to work over me through the exquisite shudders coursing through me.

I yell out, "Oh my God, Jax. Yes. Yes. Yes."

Completely spent, I feel Jax working his kisses up my leg, over my stomach, and around my breast. He moves my knees open with his own, and he enters me again, torturously slow this time. I open my eyes as Jax starts a gentle rhythm, the passion between us still there. But unlike the first time, which was dominated by raw desire, this is now fueled by pure adoration, a deep love, and a controlled longing.

My gaze connects with his deep green eyes shining down on me, taking my breath away. His eyes are wet, full of unshed tears, and it breaks me.

"Jax." The ache in my voice reflects the agony I see in his eyes.

"I love you." His words come out short, broken.

"Oh, babe, I love you." I reach my other hand up so that I'm cradling his beautiful face.

"Always," he whispers.

His face lowers, and his tongue enters my mouth. He continues to move in and out of me as his tongue mimics the motion in my mouth.

We're lying side by side now, both coming down from our release. Our sex life is never lacking. Sometimes, Jax likes it rough, and other times, he likes it slow and sweet. I love it every way. But the way that he just made love to me is new. It was heartbreakingly delicate. His eyes and movements sent melancholy through my heart. The sated contentment the experience left on my body compared to the confusing sorrow it left in my heart are at odds, leaving me to wonder how I should be feeling right now.

An unknown fear washes over me. "Jax? Please talk to me."

His breaths are still labored, but our bodies have had time to recover.

He exhales. "Little Love…" My long-standing pet name sounds like an apology. "We need to talk."

Those three words send terror through my veins. The tone of Jax's voice isn't one I'm used to hearing, and deep down inside, I know that whatever he is about to say is going to ruin me. I only hope that I will be able to recover.

"What is it?" I ask, almost frantic. In reality, for some reason, I no longer want to know.

Jax is silent for a beat. "Lil, I don't even know how to say this. Fuck!" he yells, dragging his hands through his hair.

His outburst startles me, and I instinctually move back, wrapping the sheet around me, and lean against the headboard. He jumps off the bed, retrieving his boxers from the floor, and he puts them on. He paces back and forth in front of the bed, his elbows bent as his fingers entwine behind his neck.

I sit silently and wait, my heart beating out of my chest.

He removes his hands from behind his neck before dragging them down his face as he lets out an audible huff of hair. His hands fall to his sides, and he looks at me with a haunted expression. "I just have to say it. I just have to say it all at once. I'm sorry."

I nod, but I'm not quite sure why.

"This is the hardest thing I have ever done, and I don't even know why I'm doing it." His words come out quickly, almost rehearsed.

It makes me wonder how many times he has had this conversation in his head.

He starts pacing the room again. "I love you, Lily. You know I do. I love you so much. You are fucking perfect. Do you know how perfect you are for me?"

I don't answer, knowing his question is rhetorical.

He continues, "You are everything to me. I want you to know that I love you. I've always loved you, and I always will. Always."

My eyes widen even more as he stops pacing and comes to sit on the side of the bed. I instinctually scoot toward the far side of the bed, away from him. I'm not so much afraid of him but of his words. I can't predict what is going to come out next, but I just know that it's not going to be okay. *I'm not going to be okay.*

Although he is now sitting on the bed, he doesn't look at me. It's as if he can't. He looks out the dark window past his bed, his eyes unfocused. "This isn't something that I take lightly. I know it is a big deal, but the thing is that, right now, I just don't see any other way. I'm sorry, Lil, but we have to end things for a while."

"What?" I blurt out.

"We need to do our own thing for a while…apart."

His words are dripping with remorse, but the regret I hear doesn't damper the hurt and confusion exploding through me.

"I don't understand. What are you talking about?" I cry.

"Listen, Lily, I've been thinking about this for a long time. There is just so much going on. I'm getting a lot of pressure with the team and with my classes. We have the rest of our lives to figure us out, but I need to focus on me right now. I think we both do."

Everything he is saying really isn't sinking in, but I can't ignore the anger that I'm feeling.

"I still don't understand. How does being with me negatively affect you? First of all, we barely see each other. I'm not bringing you down. I just don't get what you are even saying right now."

"Exactly. We barely see each other because of our crazy schedules. I feel guilty all the time because I don't give you the time or attention you deserve."

"I don't complain about that. I understand that you are under a lot of pressure, Jax."

"I know you don't complain, but I hear it in your voice, Lil. I don't want you to sit around, waiting for me to call you. You wanted to go away to college to follow your dreams, and that is what you should be doing. This is your time to do what you want."

"I wanted to get a certain degree, Jax! That is all. I don't have any dreams that don't include you. You can't be serious right now. We just made love! You told me that you loved me." I pause for a moment, reining in my fury. "How could you say that to me just to crush me a minute later?"

"I do love you. Of course I do. That hasn't changed, and it won't. I'm not saying this is forever. It is just for now. I'm sorry, but I need to do this, Lily. I have too much going on. We need to focus on ourselves. We can come back to our relationship later, but right now is the time in our lives to be independent. We'll never get this time back."

"I don't want this time back. I hurt every day because I miss you. I hurt every day because I want you. I look forward to when we can be together, just the two of us. Why would I want this time back?"

"That is my point! Why are you not listening? I don't want you to hurt every day. I don't want you to miss me. I want you to be happy, to enjoy college, and to live life for yourself."

My hot tears are streaming down my face. "Don't you dare make this about me. This has nothing to do with me. This is not what I want! Yes, I miss you. So what? You breaking up with me isn't going to make me miss you any less. It will make me miss you more. I don't want to live a life without you. You are my other half, Jax, my best friend. I can't do this, any of this, without you!"

I bury my face into my sheet-covered knees. My chest aches and heaves in and out as I cry violently into my legs. I can't begin to wrap my mind around what is happening right now. Only a fraction of it has registered, and the agony of that minuscule amount is causing me the greatest pain I have ever felt in my life.

"Lily."

I feel the bed dip beside me, and Jax's hand is on my back.

"I'm sorry. I'm so sorry. I'm trying to do the right thing here for both of us. We'll be together again. I know it. I just can't give you any more of myself right now. I'm spread too thin. You deserve so much more than I can offer. You don't deserve to be the afterthought at the end of my day. You deserve to be the reason I wake up, the reason for everything. You deserve all of me, not just a tiny fraction. It's not fair to you, and it's not fair to me. I can't take the guilt anymore. I'm suffocating in it."

I wipe my drenched face on the sheet and look up. "I'm okay with that, Jax. I know you are overwhelmed. I understand. Don't you see that I would rather have a small part of you than nothing? Even the tiniest part of you is enough to make me the happiest girl in the world. But ending things? Jax, I can't. I won't be okay. We aren't supposed to end. We are forever and always, remember? I can't live without you. I can't." I cry into the soaked sheet again.

Jax scoots next to me on the bed and wraps his arm around my shoulder, pulling me toward him. "You can. You've lived without me before."

"No, I haven't," I mumble into the sheet. "I've always had you. In my earliest memory, you've been there. I don't know how to do life without you, Jax. I can't. Don't you see that? You are going to destroy me if you do this."

"Lily…" Jax's smooth voice is attempting to soothe me, but it is a failed effort. "We'll still be friends. That will not change. I will always be here for you."

How can it not change? And why does the word friend all of a sudden sound so evil? That word used to fill me with joy because it made me think of Jax, but now, when I think about it in relation to Jax, it tears me apart.

"Friends?" I ask, the word almost painful to say.

"Of course. You are my best friend, and you always will be. This isn't forever, Lily. It's just for now."

Lifting my head, I turn to look at his pained face. "You don't know what the future holds, Jax. This is a mistake. I feel it."

"You're right. I don't know what the future will bring, but I trust it. I trust us, and I believe in our destiny. I do think we'll be together, if we are meant to be, Lil. Fate brought us together from the start, and it has kept us close for twenty-one years. I have to believe that everything will work out in the end. I just know that, right now, I need a break. I can't keep going on the way I have been. I'm going to shatter under all the stress. I know it might not make sense to you and that all of this probably sounds like it is coming out of nowhere, but I've been thinking about it for a while, and it is the only solution that I can come up with. I think we both need to focus on ourselves for the next couple of years while we finish college and make plans for our future. Then, maybe we can come back together when the time is right."

"This is coming out of nowhere. Why didn't you talk to me? Why was I not included in this decision, Jax?" My heart is broken.

"Because it was something I had to work out on my own. I want you to understand, Lily. I do. But I don't think you can. You don't know what it is like to walk in my shoes, and I don't really know how to explain it."

"You could try."

"Lil, please don't make this harder than it is. You know I wouldn't make this decision lightly. I've played out all the options in my head, and this is the only way that will work at the moment. You know that I love you and want what is best for you. I'm not the best for you right now."

I press my fingers to the sides of my nose. I make a swiping motion under my eyes and over my cheekbones, catching some of my tears. "You're not the best for me? What does that mean? You want me to date other people?" The thought makes me sick.

Jax clears his throat, obviously shaken by the question. His response is clipped. "If that's what you need."

"I don't need anyone else! I need you!" I cry. "Is this about someone else? Do you want someone other than me? Have you cheated on me?" I can't even believe these words are coming out of my mouth.

"No! Of course not! I would never cheat on you. You know that."

"Apparently, I don't know much when it comes to you," I answer solemnly.

Jax's voice is softer as he says, "Yes, you do. You know me better than anyone. No, I don't want to date anyone else. No, I have not nor would I ever cheat on you. This isn't what *this* is about. Dating someone else has nothing to do with my decision. Does the thought of you being with someone else make me happy? Absolutely, not. But can I ask you not to date anyone else? No, I can't. How can I break up with you and ask you to wait? I can't."

"I will wait for you. Of course I will, Jax."

"Lily, no." He raises his hands and drags them through his hair again before dropping them to his lap. Staring down at his empty hands, he says, "You have to stop thinking in terms of what is best for me and think about yourself. If you don't date anyone because you don't find anyone who interests you and who would make you happy, that is one thing. But if you don't date because you are waiting for me or because you don't want to hurt me, then that is another thing. You can't do that."

My chin trembles. "Are you going to date someone else?"

Jax sighs. "Honestly? I don't know." His monotone answer cuts through my heart like a knife.

I wrap my arms around my front and grip my shoulders. Closing my eyes, I slowly rock back and forth, willing the calmness to come, pleading with God to make this all a dream, a nightmare. If it's not that, I pray I can withstand the upcoming agony because the pain in my chest right now is blinding.

"How do we go back to just a friendship? How does that even work?" I ask quietly. My fight is gone, drowned by the overwhelming heartache I feel.

Jax is unmoving, still against the headboard. "I'm not sure, but we'll figure it out. We have to." His voice is void of emotion.

Squeezing my eyes closed, trying to keep in the tears, I lower my chin to my chest and breathe in through my nose.

I can't believe this. I truly can't understand how this is happening to me. I still have so many questions. *How did I go from making love to the love of my life to sitting naked in his bed, covered only by a sheet, trembling with sadness and heartbreaking pain?*

This whole scenario is a page straight out of my book of worst nightmares, if I had ever written a book of nightmares. But I didn't. I didn't even think about possible nightmares because my life was amazing.

I feel as if I have nothing left. The rational part of my brain is screaming about all the wonderful aspects of my life that don't include Jax. But I can't listen to that right now because the part of my brain that knows Jax is *the one* for me is screaming so loudly in despair that everything else is blocked out. I feel nothing but pain and overwhelming sadness that physically hurts.

At this moment, I don't know how I will survive the screaming sorrow in my head.

twelve

My head hurts, pounding with a fierce intensity. My body feels like it ran several marathons, every fiber of every muscle sore. It takes me a second to remember. For a second, the pain is all physical, but the moment I remember, it intensifies. The physical soreness in my head and muscles from exhaustion and forcefully crying until I passed out doesn't compare to the emotional torture.

The grief radiating from my chest is paralyzing. I don't feel my heart beating. I know it is. I'm alive, so it has to be. But I can't feel it. The acute sting of pure anguish mutes all other feeling. I still can't wrap my head around it, yet I know it to be true.

I lost my Jax.

He's gone.

I'm alone.

I don't know how to go on from here.

I hear a light knock on the door before small footsteps close in on the bed.

"Lily," Jess says softly, her voice laced with pity.

I turn toward her. My eyes barely open from the puffiness from hours of crying.

"Oh, Lily." Jess sighs. "Let's get out of here."

I nod, but I don't move.

Jess starts going around Jax's room, collecting my clothes and stuffing them into my bag. She pulls out a pair of yoga pants, a T-shirt, and some undergarments, and she tosses them onto the bed. "Get dressed, Lil," she says kindly.

"Tylenol?" I ask, eyes squinted.

"Sure thing. Get dressed. I'll be right back."

She leaves, and I push through the pounding headache and put on my clothes. She returns just as I'm sliding on my UGGs over my pants, and she hands me a glass of water and two pills. I take them and drink the entire glass of water before handing it back to Jess. She places the empty cup down on the end table and grabs my phone and purse from Jax's dresser before tossing them into my bag. She slings my bag over her shoulder and stretches her hand out to me. I grab it, and she pulls me forward. I cling on to her hand like a lifeline as we exit Jax's room.

"The girls are bringing around the car. They should be in the parking lot by now."

"You know?"

"Yeah, Jax told us before he left," she says, leading me through the apartment to the door.

"He left?"

"Yeah, he left really early this morning or really late last night—however you want to look at it."

I sniff. "Where did he go?" My voice breaks.

Jess shakes her head. "I'm not sure."

"Should we wait for him?"

"No." Jess loses the sympathetic tone, her voice more firm now. "No, I'm pretty sure he wanted us to go."

I don't have words. Just tears. Streams of tears burn my already swollen cheeks as they fall to the floor.

As we walk down the hall of the apartment building toward the door that exits into the parking lot, I can do nothing but hold on to Jess's hand and cry as she leads us out. She pushes the door open, and I'm assaulted with a gust of cold wind, momentarily taking the breath from me. We walk down the steps toward her waiting car.

"We should never have come," Jess says aloud. "Fuck Michigan. Fuck football. Fuck Jax Porter."

I slide into the back of her car and shut the door. Molly is sitting on the other side of the seat, looking at me with pity in her eyes and a sympathetic smile on her face. I nod to acknowledge her before turning toward the closed door and leaning against it. I cover my head with my hood and rest it against the window. As Jess drives out of Ann Arbor, I stare blindly out of the window, watching as my whole world gets farther away.

"Lily, I'm serious. You need to get up. Enough is enough. I'm going to call your parents if you don't get up right now." Jess's voice is laced with concern, and I don't blame her.

I've been quite the lunatic this past week. Since getting back from Ann Arbor last Sunday, I haven't gotten out of bed more than twice a day. I've eaten a couple of bites of food at Jess's insistence. I've drunk some water when Jess was standing over me, making me. But other than that, I have done nothing but sleep. It is too agonizing to be awake, so I've decided that sleeping my life away is my best option.

Jess went around and told all my professors that I had a horrible case of the flu. It was so nice of her to look after me, and I should be grateful, but I'm not. I want to be, but I can't feel anything, except for pain.

I've only had one text from Jax. He sent it after he left his apartment the night it happened.

> Jax: I'm sorry. I think it will be easier if I'm not here to say good-bye. I love you more. Always.

I hate him. I want to punch him in the freaking face.

I'm lying. I love him. I still love him more than anything, and that is why this hurts so much. I would also be lying if I said that I haven't read his text one hundred times over the course of the week because I have, especially the last line.

I haven't told my family. I still can't believe it is real. But I know it is. I also know I can't lie in bed forever, but I want to. If it weren't for Jess, I would probably lie in bed until I died. I just don't have the energy to care anymore.

"Come on, Lily. Please get up today. I don't want to call your parents, but I will."

I ignore Jess—not because I want to be mean, but because I can't find the words. I don't have desire to do anything other than lie here.

Jess exhales loudly and leaves the room. I wouldn't say she stomped out, but it was pretty close. She was definitely taking harder steps than usual.

I close my eyes and drift off into darkness.

"Ah!" I scream, sitting up abruptly, causing my head to sway.

I'm soaked with cold water. It takes me a moment to understand what has happened.

I raise my head to see Jess standing there with her arms crossed, an empty pitcher hanging from her hand. "I'm sorry, but no more. You're getting up today."

I don't will the tears to start, but they begin to fall. They just always come whenever I'm awake. The warm tears falling down my face are such a contrast to my wet cold skin.

"That's fine. You cry. Get it out. Whatever. But you are getting up today. I will give you five minutes to cry it out and two minutes to get dressed. I'm coming back in here in seven minutes, and I want you up. Actually, you need a shower—badly. So, in seven minutes, I will be back to escort you to the shower. If you do not get out of bed to take a shower, you will get to take an ice-cold one right in your bed. I have more where this came from." She holds the pitcher up, shaking it back and forth in my view, before leaving the bedroom and closing the door behind her.

After the door shuts, I wrap my partially wet blanket around me, trying to calm my chills. I swing my legs over the side of the bed. Leaning over, I bury my face in my hands and cry, my back shaking violently through my sobs.

Minutes later—I'm assuming seven—Jess returns. She reaches her hand out, and I take it before following her to the bathroom.

"Do you need me to help you?" she asks.

"No." My voice is scratchy.

Jess reaches into the shower and turns it on, putting her hand in the water to check the temperature. She turns toward me. "Okay, I'll leave some clean clothes for you on the counter."

"Okay." I nod.

She puts her hand on my shoulder. "You're going to be okay, Lily. I know you don't see it now, but you will."

I shake my head in protest.

"You will," she says firmly, squeezing my shoulder before walking out.

I take off the clothes that I've been wearing since leaving Jax's apartment, and I get into the shower. I feel light-headed, but admittedly, the hot water makes me feel better. It's a small step in the right direction on my long path back to normal, but it's a step.

I return to my classes, and I resume eating, but besides that, I continue to spend a lot of time in bed. But Jess doesn't say anything, and I don't receive any more cold showers. I guess these two steps are enough progress for her at the moment.

Two weeks after the breakup, I get a text from Jax.

> *Jax: How are you?*

> *Me: Not good.*

> *Jax: Me neither.*

> *Jax: I miss you.*

> *Me: Me, too.*

Me: Having second thoughts?

Jax: No. I'm sorry.

I power down my phone before climbing into bed and crying myself to sleep.

The day before Thanksgiving, I call my mom. She is getting ready to come get me to bring me home for the long holiday weekend, so I plan to break out with a lie.

"Hey, sweetie. What's up?" my mom answers her phone.

"Hey, Mom. I have bad news." I work to sound tired and miserable, which actually isn't much of a stretch. "I have the flu. I'm not going to be able to come home for Thanksgiving."

"What?" my mom questions. "No, I'll come get you. You need someone to take care of you while you're sick."

"No, Mom. Really, I just want to stay here and sleep. Plus, the car ride would make me feel nauseous. I'd probably throw up the entire time. I don't want to get anyone sick either. This bug has been going around campus, and it is a nasty one. I would feel horrible if I gave it to someone. I'm sorry."

"I don't want you to be there alone. I'm coming to get you," she repeats.

"Mom, listen, I'm fine. I just want to sleep. I'll be okay. I need rest. Tell everyone that I said hello and that I will see them at Christmas. Winter break is only a few weeks away. I'll be fine."

She is silent for a moment, and I know she is deciding whether to listen to me or to come get me anyway. "Okay." She sighs. "I'm going to hate not having you here."

I can hear the heartbreak in her voice, and it is like a punch to my gut.

"I know. Me, too."

"Drink fluids, and get lots of rest. Call me to check in, too."

"I will, Mom. Thanks. I love you."

"I love you, too."

This will be my first holiday without my family, and I now feel extremely guilty. I'm almost to the point of calling her back to tell her that I've changed my mind about coming home.

But I don't.

Being home would not only be painful because everything would remind me of Jax, but my family would also know that something was wrong, and I would be forced to talk about it. I'm not yet ready for the saying-it-aloud part. Letting my family know about Jax would make it seem more real and by extension…permanent. I'm still getting by on the whole notion that this nightmare will soon end.

Jess actually stays at school for the holiday weekend as well. She doesn't go into it, but I get the feeling that she doesn't want to go home. Tabitha and Molly along with most everyone else on campus are gone, so Jess and I are in our own little world.

We spend Thanksgiving morning in our jammies, eating Frosted Flakes and watching the Macy's Thanksgiving Day Parade on TV.

"We need to go shopping," Jess declares.

"For what?"

"Ingredients for our Thanksgiving feast of course."

I shrug. "Okay."

We end up having to drive half an hour out of town because our local grocery store is closed for the holiday. We finally find a store that is open.

"The trick is going to be making the entire dinner with only our microwave," Jess states. She grabs a cart from the cart return in the parking lot and starts wheeling it toward the automatic entrance doors.

"True," I agree. "Although, we can cheat a little."

"How so?"

I grin for what seems like the first time in weeks. "Follow me." I lead Jess to the frozen food aisle, scanning the freezer cases until I spot what I'm looking for. Opening the cold glass door, I pull out two Lean Cuisine turkey dinner meals. "Ta-da!"

I wave my hand under the icy box of food-like substance. *Really, can frozen dinners qualify as real food?* I don't know how these meals are processed, but it just doesn't seem natural to me.

"See?" I say. "We have our turkey, mashed potatoes, gravy, and green beans all in one convenient microwavable container. Oh, look. It even comes with a small compartment of cranberry sauce, not that I really like the stuff anyway."

Jess smiles. "Yeah, I don't enjoy cranberry sauce either. And I have to give it to you. I don't think we could do much better in terms of a turkey dinner."

"So, what else do we need?"

"Rolls? Um, some sort of dessert. Maybe they have some premade pumpkin pies left."

"Oh, and let's get some cheddar cheese slices and a box of Ritz crackers."

"That doesn't sound very Thanksgivingy."

"Um, hello? Crackers and cheese will be our appetizer. We have to have appetizers for our Thanksgiving dinner. You know, to eat while our meals cook?"

Jess chuckles. "Totally."

We grab all our supplies, check out, and start our drive back to campus.

When we return to our room, we blast Taylor Swift's new album—once again, it's my choice in music—and we dance around while preparing our feast. Deciding we need a proper dinner table, we drag my desk from our bedroom to the living area and cover it with a sheet. I take a small jar candle from our room and put it in the center of our makeshift table. While our meals rotate in the microwave, we take turns squirting the aerosol can of whipped cream that we bought for the pie into our mouths.

"Best Thanksgiving ever," Jess declares with her cheeks full of whipped cream.

Her comment takes my mind to all the other Thanksgivings I've had. This immediately makes me think of my family and Jax's family at home, enjoying the meal without me for the first time. That thought brings the pain back to the forefront, but I push it aside, not wanting to drag the happy mood of the day down. I'm actually starting to feel semi-normal.

"It's a great day," I agree.

After we each eat our entire frozen dinner, several rolls, lots of crackers with cheese, and a large slice of pie, we decide to have a movie night. I discover that Jess has never seen *13 Going on 30* with Jennifer Garner, and I gasp. Among my sisters and me, it's a classic in my house—one of my favorite movies. Plus, it's fun and upbeat, just what I need.

Halfway through the movie, when the tears start pouring out of my eyes like waterworks, I realize that maybe this movie wasn't the best choice. I didn't even think about the fact that the story line is about childhood best friends who grow apart even though they are meant to be together. Unlike the movie, I'm not sure if I'll get my happy ending.

My phone dings, and I look down to see a text from Jax. It contains a photo of our favorite old oak tree. All the leaves have fallen, and the burnt orange sunset is glowing past the barren branches.

"I'll be back," I say to Jess.

Then, I walk swiftly to our room and close the door. I stare at the photo on my phone screen, and my heart breaks, knowing that Jax is in our spot and I'm not there with him.

My phone sounds again.

Jax: It's not the same without you.

Me: You're home?

Jax: Yeah, Thanksgiving dinner and all. I thought you would be here.

Me: I couldn't go home yet. I didn't think you were coming home today.

Jax: Those of us who live close got to drive home for the day. I'm leaving in a bit to head back. Catching a bus to Columbus tomorrow for the game.

Me: Oh. How was dinner?

Jax: Great as always. Why haven't you told your family, Lil?

Me: Because I'm not ready to talk about it. I can't yet.

Jax: Well, my family knows now. It won't be long until my mom says something to yours. I asked her not to do it today while I'm here.

Me: Wouldn't want you to be uncomfortable.

Jax: Lily, don't be like that.

Me: How am I supposed to be? Please tell me because I don't know.

Jax: I guess I really don't either.

Jax: Maybe we could start texting each other more often—as friends.

Me: I don't think I'm ready for that. Today was the first day in a long time that I started to feel human again, and that was because I was able to avoid constantly thinking about you. If we are in contact, it will make it harder for me not to think about you.

Jax: Okay. I get it. But soon though?

    Me: I hope so.

Jax: I miss you. I miss my best friend.

    Me: You don't get to miss me.

Jax: Maybe not. But I do.

    Me: Miss you, too.

Jax: Love you.

    Me: You, too.

Jax: Love you more.

    Me: I wish that were the case. Later, Jax.

Jax doesn't respond, and for some reason, it makes me feel better, knowing that my comment got to him. I read over our texts and love the bit of feistiness that I see coming from my end. I'm not an angry person, but I feel so darn angry at Jax.

I'm flipping mad at Jax for doing this, for making me feel this way, and for not loving me enough. And the fact that I'm experiencing this intense anger makes me feel better. I realize that anger is a better emotion for me than depression.

I sit cross-legged in my bed, holding my phone in my hands, and a sense of accomplishment runs through me. I'm so relieved to feel another step of the grieving process besides utter depression and despair. I can't remember in what order the stages go, so I'm not sure if anger is what I'm supposed to be feeling next or if I'm just jumping around in my stages of grief. But I'm so relieved that, at least right now, I'm experiencing something other than sadness.

So, yes to anger.

Fuck you, Jax Porter.

Fuck you for making me love you.

Fuck you for leaving me.

Fuck you for everything.

I just want to send it out into the universe that Jax Porter sucks ass.

So, there.

thirteen

jax

I lie in my bed, staring at my phone—more specifically, at my text thread with Lily. She's so mad, and I can't blame her. I can't believe she didn't come home for Thanksgiving. Not only did I fuck up her life as far as we're concerned, but now, I also fucked up her life with her family.

I don't know why I thought this break would make things better for her, but I truly did. I knew that she would be upset at first, but I was hoping that she would be back to her normal self soon. She knows it's not forever.

I have had my dad in my ear, calling her a distraction, since my freshman year of college when I refused to break up with her as he'd thought I should. He has always been so afraid that my relationship with her would hold me back, not allowing me to reach my potential, my dreams—or more accurately, his dreams.

It has been my father's goal that at least one of his sons would play for the University of Michigan and go on to play for the NFL. Landon was a decent football player in high school, but he wasn't made for the sport like I am. I have been playing football since I could walk, and I have loved every minute of it…until college. Something switched in college, and the sport became a chore when the option of not being the absolute best was taken away.

Winning isn't sufficient anymore. My father finds fault in my game, even when we win. Nothing is ever good enough. My father knows my coaches and even some of my professors personally. He is an alumnus of U of M and a generous donor to the university. He's orchestrated it so that he has eyes and ears on me at all times. I'm so tired of his visits and phone calls to check up on me and let me know that some staff member told him I wasn't at my best or that I was distracted.

He has sucked the joy out of my life, and I'm counting down the days until graduation. In less than two years, I will be finished living the life he wishes he had lived, and I will be living the life I want.

I don't know why I even care about what he thinks. More than anything, I wish that I didn't. I wish I had the balls to tell them all to fuck off before walking off of the field and out of my classes, raising my two middle fingers in the air as I go.

But the thing is, I do care. I want to do my best and see this through. It is not in my nature to quit. My father doesn't know this yet, but after I graduate, I'm done with the game. I plan to use the prestigious business degree I will have earned to get a good job that will set Lily and me up for our happily ever after.

I haven't told Lily how stressed I am. She has no idea that my father talks about her being a distraction, and I will never let her know. If I get my way, she will never be tainted by his negativity. Indirectly, I guess she already has been though.

It has all become too much this year. I've finally reached my breaking point. My inability to keep up with everything has come to the surface. Maintaining my relationship with Lily and being a good boyfriend was time-consuming, and I was failing at it. Most days, it was a struggle to fit in time to talk to her on the phone.

She finally took the step to go away to college and make her dreams come true. She deserves a fun, carefree college experience full of laughs with her friends, drunken nights at bars, and pajama parties with her roommates where they stay up half the night, watching movies and gossiping—or whatever it is that college chicks do. She doesn't deserve an experience full of missed opportunities because she is waiting around for her boyfriend to call. She doesn't need to worry about solving my problems or stress about how she could make my journey easier on me.

She has always given me everything. But I can't let her give so much that it takes away from her quality of life. It wouldn't be fair to her even though she might not see it now. Down the road, I hope she will realize that all I've ever wanted is for her to be happy.

Once the shock of our breakup wears off, I pray she sees that this is a great opportunity for her to enjoy her time away at college. I'm hoping that she believes me when I tell her that it's not forever. I hope she knows that I love her more now than I ever have and that this separation does nothing to diminish that.

I pray I haven't made a mistake. When all of this is over, if I don't end up with Lily, nothing will have been worth it. None of my hard work will have mattered.

I just have to go with my gut and do what I feel is right for Lily because she is truly all that matters.

fourteen

lily

December passes in a blur. I have one more final this afternoon, and then my parents will be arriving to get me. I have been able to catch up on all my classes, and I have rocked my exams so far.

In general, I finally feel good. I wouldn't go as far as saying great because when I let myself think of Jax, the gloom creeps back in. So, I try not to think of him.

I've been focused on my classes and my friends. Now that I'm not constantly trying to call Jax, I've been chatting with my sisters, Mom, and Kristyn from back home more often. I have wonderful people in my life who love me regardless of what happens with my love life.

I will be okay—at least, after two months of wallowing in my self-pity, that is what I tell myself.

"You sure you can't stay and go out tonight?" Molly asks from across the table.

I fork the chewy chicken in front of me, thinking about how much I'm going to enjoy my mom's cooking over the next three weeks. "No, Molls, I can't. My mom will be here tonight." I love going out with the girls, but I really am happy just to go home and chill with my family.

"Do you think you will see him?" Jess asks hesitantly.

The subject of Jax has slowly worked its way back into our conversations. The mention of his name does not initiate a sudden waterfall of tears anymore, which is always a bonus.

I slowly nod my head. "I'm assuming. Our lives are so intertwined back home. I don't know how I wouldn't."

My grandparents live in Arizona, and Jax's grandparents have passed, so our families really only have each other. Whether it is uncomfortable or not, I don't see us doing holidays with anyone else in the future. We have always celebrated with the Porters, and that's not going to change because of our relationship status.

"Yikes," Tabitha sighs. "I hope we don't get comatose Flower Child back. You're finally starting to be semi-normal again."

I raise my stare to meet Tabitha's. "I'm sorry, Tabs, that you've never loved anyone more than you love yourself. If you had, you would understand how it feels to lose that person. So, good for you for only investing in yourself. That way, you can always be *normal*."

Jess and Molly remain silent, but the uneasy tension at the table is tangible as they expectantly stare at Tabitha.

Tabitha holds our gaze, her face as still as stone. After a few beats, she exhales. "Touché." She pouts her lips, and her eyes are slanted, appraising me. Nodding, she states, "Feisty Lily—I like her."

Conversation resumes, everyone going over their holiday plans. Jess doesn't sound too enthusiastic about going home.

"I'm serious when I say, you are welcome to come home with me, Jess. My family would love to have you."

"Thanks, Lil. I have to go home though. My mom would blow a gasket if I skipped out on Christmas."

"Hey, beautiful." A tall body takes a seat in the open spot next to me.

"Hey, Trenton," I answer, resigned.

He seems to be everywhere lately, and he always makes it a point to chat with me. I have to admit, his overconfidence is growing on me. I'm finding that the whole arrogant player vibe he has going on is more for show. He's actually a pretty cool person. I've come to see him as a friend. *And really, who couldn't use another friend?*

My roommates have warmed up to him as well, mainly Molly. She and Trenton have a class together, and he has come over a few times to study. Jess, I would say, tolerates him, and Tabitha loves to be a bitch to him, but I think that is how she relates to guy friends in general. Sometimes though, I find she and Trenton exchange looks that communicate something, but I'm not sure what it is. I have a feeling that she might be starting to see him as a friend, but she is too hardheaded to say it out loud.

"So, Lil, you wanna hang out over break? Grab a coffee or something?"

Trenton's parents' house is only half an hour away from campus, so he will be close by during break.

"I can't. I'll be home the whole time."

"Bummer. Well, when you get back?"

"Maybe."

He's asked me out as friends several times over the past month, and I always turn him down—nicely, of course. I can always use another friend, but I have the feeling that Trenton is the kind of friend who I should hang out with in a large group—at least for now. I'm still unsure of his motives and sincerity when he tells me he only wants to be friends, and right now, a friendship is all I can do.

Just my mom comes to get me, and it's nice to see her. I've missed her so much.

Shortly after Thanksgiving, my mom called to discuss the breakup, but I wasn't ready. She didn't ask about it after that, knowing that I would explain everything once I was able.

We use the entire ride home catch up. I tell my mom everything—for the most part. Of course, I don't notify her about the amazing sex Jax and I had right before he crushed my soul. That information would definitely be classified in the TMI category, but other than that, I divulge it all—Jax's reasons, my reaction, the grieving I experienced over the past two months, and the few times we've texted since.

"Well, honey, you might not agree, but perhaps it is a good thing. You know that we love Jax. He is like a son to us, and we'll always care for him. But you are our little girl, and your happiness will always be the most important thing to us. I think he did the right thing here. Eventually, you'll see that. You are both still very young, and you'll probably get back together at some point. But he's correct. This is your time to figure yourself out—to be who you want to be and to do what you want to do. And I think a part of you has always known that, which is why you chose Central over U of M, right?"

I'm quiet for a moment. "Yeah, I wanted some identity for myself, and deciding to go to a different school than Jax was all my doing. I just wanted to experience a small part of life on my own, to be my own person for a while. But a breakup is not what I wanted. I was happy during the first month of school, doing my own thing but still having Jax. That's all I wanted. I didn't want to be alone."

"You are definitely not alone. You'll never have to worry about that. Promise me that you will enjoy this time. No more wasting energy being sad. Jax is still a part of your life, and I truly believe, in some capacity, he always will be. Time will tell what that capacity is, but for now, enjoy yourself and be happy. College is such a great stage in your life. You will never again have this time, so make the most of it. Everything happens for a reason, Lily. I believe that."

Does it really though? Well, I hope fate knows what it's doing.

I agree with what my mom is saying, and I want to believe that it will all turn out how it should be in the end. But something just isn't sitting right with me.

I feel like I'm walking on a tightrope toward my destiny, and if I slip or make one wrong move, I will fall, and I'll never reach my fated destination. Since I believe that Jax is waiting for me at the end of that tightrope, the risks of falling aren't ones I'm willing to take.

But I guess the choice really isn't mine.

After putting down the curling iron on my bathroom counter, I run my fingers through the ringlets I just made until the curls break up into waves. I'm wearing my favorite skinny jeans, tall boots, and a tight red sweater. It is one of the only red articles of clothing I own, and it's perfect for the holiday.

"Ready?" Amy asks from the doorway.

"I guess." I shrug.

"You are gorgeous. He's going to have a serious case of regret tonight."

"You know that's not my intention."

"I know, but admit it. It would make you feel a little better if you saw some regret in his eyes tonight." She smirks.

"No, I want him to be happy, Ames."

"Lily…" she drawls out my name, raising her eyebrow in question.

I can't stop the laugh that comes. "Maybe a little,"

The trees lining the Porters' drive are each lit with tiny white lights. Each light is twinkling with the Christmas cheer I'm trying so hard to harness. We have had Christmas Eve dinner with the Porters for as long as I can remember, and I knew that this year would be no different. Every year, we alternate between our houses, and tonight, we get to spend it on Jax's home turf. *Wonderful.*

My heart is pounding out of my chest with nervousness as we slow to a stop in front of their house.

I'm greeted with a big hug from Susie. Her embrace lingers a moment longer than normal, and I know she misses me as much as I miss her.

"So good to see you, sweetie."

"You, too," I answer, pulling back.

I smile weakly, and she smiles back as she rubs my cheek.

"Hey, Lil," Landon calls from the kitchen. He grabs an hors d'oeuvre from the island and tosses it into his mouth.

Mr. Porter pats me on the back as I make my way toward the kitchen island. "Good to see you, kiddo."

"You, too, Mr. Porter."

Where I've only called Jax's mom by her first name my whole life, I've always addressed his dad more formally. I like his dad, but he's had an intimidating air to him for as long as I can remember.

Reaching the island of food, I throw a piece of cheese into my mouth. "How's the job going?" I ask Landon.

"Good. Can't complain," he answers. "How's Central?"

"Can't complain." I smile.

Then, I feel *him*, and my smile drops. I take a deep breath and turn.

Jax is standing at the entrance of the kitchen, looking as gorgeous as always. My heart beats rapidly at the sight of him, and my body wants to run into his arms and smother him in kisses, but I stand immobile instead.

He smiles. It's not the full one that I'm used to but a small grin. I have to force it some, but I return the smile. He exhales, his broad chest moving under his form-fitting henley.

After a few forced breaths, he walks to me and pulls me into a hug. I rest my face on his chest, relishing in the familiar warmth it brings.

"Merry Christmas, Little."

"Merry Christmas," I answer.

"So?" he asks awkwardly.

I chuckle. "So?"

"Can we be friends again?"

I look around to find the family has migrated out of the kitchen, leaving Jax and I alone. "I guess," I concede. "Consider it your Christmas present."

"You mean, you didn't get me a present?"

I cross my arms in front of my chest while popping my hip to the side. I raise my eyebrow. "Really?"

"I'm kidding." He laughs.

Dinner goes well, and despite my reservations, I'm having a great time with Jax. Our friendship is so innate and natural that it shines through the awkwardness. The conversation is kept light as we chat about classes, football, and our roommates.

After dessert, as my sisters go to grab their coats, Jax says to me, "Stay."

"What?"

Jax steps toward me. "Stay for a while. You can't leave yet." Lowering his gaze, his eyes grab me, pulling me in.

"I can't?" My heart thumps wildly beneath my chest.

He is so close now that I can see the light golden specks in his emerald eyes. I can smell him. The light fragrance of his cologne is intoxicating.

He chuckles. "Not yet anyway. We haven't watched it yet."

I exhale, letting out the hopeful breath I was holding. When I breathe in again, it's the air of reality. "Right. *Elf*."

"Of course." He smiles down to me.

Jax and I love everything about Christmas, including the holiday movies. Our favorite Christmas movie is *Elf* with Will Ferrell, and we've watched it every Christmas Eve for years.

"Okay." I nod.

After I tell my parents that I will be home later, Jax and I head to the movie theater room. He opens the huge wooden cabinet full of hundreds of Blu-rays, and he pulls *Elf* out.

"The best way to spread Christmas cheer..." he starts.

"Is to sing out loud for the world to hear," I answer, reciting one of our favorite quotes from the movie.

"Do you think we'll ever tire of watching this?"

I shake my head. "No. It's a classic—timeless."

He laughs and approaches me where I stand in front of the large leather sectional. Facing me, he grabs my arms, running his thumbs along them. At this moment, I wish that I'd worn short sleeves. The desire to feel his skin rubbing against mine is deafening as the blood rushes through me, pounding in my ears. His eyes darken, and I know he feels it, too.

We played a great game of make-believe all evening, pretending that it was four years ago when we were only best friends before our bodies knew what it was like to touch in an intimate way. But the reality is that we do know what that is like, the amazing chemistry we share, and it is extremely hard to resist when it is right in front of our faces.

He sighs. Removing one of his hands from my arm, he tucks a loose strand of my hair behind my ear. We remain like this, inches apart, breathing in the same air into our cocoon of longing. I don't know what to do or say. All I know is that I don't want him to move away. My body craves this closeness and so much more.

His eyes dart to my lips before returning back to my eyes. His neck bends, and his head leans in, making its descent. I close my eyes, and a second later, I feel his lips on my forehead. Before I can register this action, the chaste kiss is over, and Jax is taking a step back, removing his other hand from my arm.

He clears his throat. "Tonight has been great. I've missed you so much. We're doing a great job at this just-friends thing, don't you think?" His voice breaks.

I simply nod, not trusting my voice to come out steady.

"We can do this, Lil. It will only get easier from here."

I nod again. Unable to stare into his eyes, I choose to focus on a piece of lint on his shirt.

"Thank you," he says.

That catches me off guard. I raise my questioning gaze to him. "For what?"

"For doing this whole friends thing when I don't deserve it. I'm not worthy of you, but I need you. I need this."

I sigh. "You deserve it. We'll always be friends. I don't think not being friends is an option."

He pulls me into a hug, and I tightly wrap my arms around him, holding on to the man I love.

He breaks the hug. "So, popcorn?"

I grin. "Sure."

"All right. Be right back."

I walk to the cabinet that holds the movies, and I run my finger over the titles. Most of them, I've watched in this room with Jax over the years. Some of them bring specific memories to mind, and I can't help but smile when I think back to all the amazing times we've shared together.

I hear a ting and look to the small table next to the cabinet where his phone lays face up. His screen is lit up with a new text. The message knocks the wind out of me, and I circle my arms around my waist, trying to stop my pending breakdown. My shallow breaths come in rapid succession. The message is two words, but they tear me apart.

Stella: Miss you.

Bending over, I hold my knees and slowly breathe in until the impending panic attack subsides. I walk over to the sofa and plop down on the very end, far from the section with the leg rest where we usually sit and cuddle.

Jax returns with a big bowl of popcorn that I'm not remotely hungry for. He looks at me concerned, obviously assessing the situation.

"You okay?" he asks.

"Yep. Fine," I say in the cheeriest voice I can muster.

I can tell he's not sure where to sit. Seeing that I'm sitting at the end of the fourteen-person sofa, it would be odd to sit all the way down here next to me. He looks around the room as if it will give him answers, and he notices his phone. After handing me the bowl of popcorn, he walks over to retrieve it. I watch him read the text, and his lips automatically curve up as he looks at the screen. He quickly types a response and then puts the phone in his back pocket.

"Ready?"

"Yep," I answer enthusiastically.

He nods before turning out the lights. He ends up sitting toward the other end of the sofa, closer to where we normally sit together. He grabs the remote and starts the movie.

I sit through the movie, holding the full bowl of untouched popcorn. I don't laugh at all the parts I usually do. I don't laugh at all. My brain can't stop thinking about the text and its implications.

Is he dating Stella? How long did he wait after breaking my heart before he jumped into bed with her? Has he been dating her while I've been lying comatose in my dorm room, overcome with debilitating sadness? Is she part of the reason he broke up with me in the first place?

I have so many questions, but ironically, I don't really want to know the answers. He and I are friends after all, so I could just ask him. But I choose not to. Somehow, I'm afraid the truth will crush me deeper than my assumptions. If I know the truth, it will become reality, one that I can't deny. Denial is my friend, and I'm going to hold on to our friendship until the time comes when the truth won't be too much to bear.

fifteen

We are having one of the coldest Januarys in history. We've had days on end where the temperature hasn't gone above zero, and with the biting winds, it feels like negative twenty degrees all the time. The winds that chill me to the bone every time I step outside are comforting in a way because they mirror the icy coldness of my heart.

If a heart could freeze from heartache, mine certainly has, yet I go on with a smile on my face. I refuse to go back to where I was in November and December. I'm not going to be that weak, miserable girl any longer. I owe myself more than that.

Jax and I are back to texting—not every day, but a couple of times a week. Our texts never consist of anything substantial. It's just a few words here or there to keep the communication going in our broken friendship. With time, I know our friendship will come more easily. But I don't think we'll ever be the same. It's not possible. You can't experience a deep love and connection with someone and then pretend you never had it. It doesn't work that way. Our romantic history will always cast a shadow over our friendship.

I'm sitting at a local coffee shop. I was lucky enough to score a table situated by the fireplace. Trenton has been hounding me daily since I returned from holiday break four weeks ago to get coffee with him, and I finally relented. So, here I am. However, he is already fifteen minutes late. If he stands me up, I'm going to lose it on him.

The bonus about Trenton's lack of timeliness is that it gives me time to chat with Kristyn for a few minutes.

She and I were able to get together over Christmas break, which was great. It had been a year prior since I last saw her. She is attending UCLA and only comes home once or twice a year. We've lost touch over the past few years, but commiserating over our lost loves over break brought our friendship back to where it had been in high school. She is one of those friends that no matter how long we go without speaking, we can pick right back up where we left off when we do get together.

She still misses Ben even though they broke it off over two years ago. She likes to get updates on him, and since he's Jax's roommate, I tend to know, for the most part, what is going on in his life. When Kristyn and I departed over break, we promised to stay in better contact, and I hope we do. One can never have too many good friends.

My cell phone vibrates.

Jax: Hey, Little.

Me: Hey, mister.

Jax: Whatcha up to?

Me: Meeting a friend for coffee. You?

Jax: Just taking a quick break from studying.

Me: What are you studying?

Jax: Business law.

Me: That doesn't sound fun.

Jax: It's not. Cheer me up.

Me: Would you rather be a billionaire and be blind or be extremely poor and be able to see?

Jax: That's kind of depressing.

Me: LOL.

Jax: A poor guy who can see.

Me: Why?

Jax: Because there are too many beautiful things in this world, and I couldn't live without being able to see them. There's one especially that I couldn't live without seeing. Plus, money isn't everything. It in itself won't bring happiness.

Me: True.

Jax: Gotta run. Stella just got here. We need to study for our test.

Any traces of the warm and fuzzies I was feeling have just been splashed with ice water.

185

Me: Okay. Bye.

Jax: Love you.

Me: Love you, too.

Jax: Love you more.

I'm staring at the dark screen of my phone as if the answers to all the world's problems will appear if I just focus long enough.

"Did the phone kill your kitten or something?"

"Huh?" I look up to see Trenton.

He chuckles. "Your evil stare is burning holes into that phone."

"Oh." I smile. "Just thinking."

"Can't be good."

"No. You know what's not good? You being twenty minutes late," I say, raising my eyebrow.

He sits down across from me, holding his hands up in surrender. "Sorry. Sorry. Something came up. It won't happen again."

"You could have at least texted me or something," I respond.

"Sorry," he says again before reaching across the table and grabbing my hand.

I look down at his hand on top of mine and then back up to him.

"Forgive me?"

I gently pull my hand out from under his and place it in my lap. "Of course. What are friends for?"

"You don't want to know all the ways I could answer that."

I laugh. "No, I probably don't."

Trenton and I sit and talk for an hour. His crude humor makes me laugh often, and the text exchange with Jax from earlier gets lost in the recesses of my mind.

I'm grateful for friends who help me forget.

February doesn't fare any better than January as far as the weather goes. I hear the expression *polar vortex* thrown around a lot, and I'd say it is a good descriptor even if maybe a little dramatic.

Words that come to mind are *bleak, windy, frigid,* and *desolate,* and now, I'm speaking to my love life, not the environment. It's ironic how the adjectives defining the coldest winter in history and my lack of romantic interactions are so interchangeable.

Yet the positive aspect is that those descriptors no longer define my mood. I wouldn't say my disposition would be synonymous with the words used to describe a tropical paradise like Aruba. But it would be fair to say I'm feeling along the lines of South Carolina. *It's warm and pleasant there, right?*

Four months post-breakup, I'm good. School is great. My friends are wonderful. Most importantly, my friendship with Jax is positive and now brings me more joy than sadness.

We are currently being pounded in what is being called the biggest snowstorm of the year, which is comical because we are barely two months into the year. I think they named this one Vulcan, which is also funny because Vulcan was the god of fire in ancient Roman mythology. When I think of fire, twelve inches of frigid snow doesn't immediately come to mind.

They should have named this storm after the god of partying, if there were such a thing, because Central is gearing up for the celebration of the year. School has already been canceled for tomorrow. Even though the college is closed, the bars are not, and the student body is taking full advantage.

I'm wrapped in a soft blanket in the living room, waiting for Molly and Tabitha to finish getting ready. I guarantee that Tabitha, along with most of the girls on campus, will be showing lots of skin tonight despite the frigid temperatures. I try to look decent when I go out, but my skinny jeans, black sweater, and boots will work just fine for me tonight.

"Here, Lil." Jess hands me a plastic cup with a straw.

"What is it?" I ask before taking a sip.

"Grape vodka and Sprite."

It is heaven. Jess knows my distaste of beer and has made it her mission to find acceptable yet yummy alternatives for our pre-party beverages.

I sigh. "OMG, Jess. You've outdone yourself. This has to be my new favorite. It tastes like a grape sucker—or better yet, a popsicle."

"Thanks. Yeah, it is pretty good. This might have to be our go-to for a while."

"I'm down with that." The fruity-tasting liquid goes down smoothly, almost too much so. This concoction could be dangerous.

I haven't spoken to Jax for a few days, so I decide to give him a call. His schedule isn't as busy now that the fall football season is over, and I've enjoyed being able to talk to him more. I dial his number.

He picks up on the second ring. "Little Love. How are you?"

"Good. You?"

"Very good. Not much going on. What are you up to?"

"Just waiting for Tabs and Molly to get ready. We're going out. Hey, have you ever tried grape vodka and Sprite? It is so delicious," I say with enthusiasm.

"No, I haven't." He chuckles.

"Well, you should. It is seriously good," I say.

Jess conveniently refills my cup after I consumed the first in record speed. "Do you have any plans tonight?"

"No. I think I'm just going to stay in. So, anything exciting going on? I'm sure you have a Tabitha story to tell," he says with warmth in his voice.

I love Tabitha and admit that her shenanigans could probably single-handedly keep me entertained in this isolated city. I think about if there is anything I haven't shared with Jax, and I'm about to respond when I hear it.

"Jax, you ready?"

The words are quiet coming through the line, but I clearly hear them. I could pick out that voice in a crowd. I've thought about the source of that voice a lot over the past two months.

Stella.

I hear a rustling and then Jax's muffled voice, "I'll be out in one minute."

The honey-sweet voice says something in response, but I can't make out her words through his hand, which I know is covering the phone. His relationship with Stella isn't something we've ever spoken about. He will mention her in passing sometimes, but he doesn't talk about her much, and I don't ask. I'm admittedly doing well with the just-friends thing, and I think that Jax and I both know that I have my limits.

His voice returns, now addressing me, "Hey, Lil. I'm going to let you go."

189

I clear my voice. "Yeah, I have to go, too. Just wanted to say hi."

"I'm glad you called. Have fun tonight. Be safe."

"I will. You, too." That's a partial lie. I don't want him to have fun with her tonight. But I do want him to be safe. "Love you," I say out of habit. I regret it the moment it comes out of my mouth, knowing he's hanging up with me to go be with her.

"Love you more. Bye."

"Bye."

I drop the phone to my lap and replay our short conversation in my head. My heart aches, and I automatically want to go into myself, let the cold take me over, and lie in bed, feeling sorry for myself.

But I won't.

I am South Carolina, warm and happy. I repeat this mantra in my head until we leave for the bar.

I open the exit door of our dorm, stepping into the freezing night air, and my face is assaulted by a powerful gush of frigid wind and snow. I feel like Storm Vulcan has physically slapped me. The force to my face is a physical reminder that I'm not in the tropics but in the polar vortex. The air is so cold that it hurts to inhale, chilling my body from the inside out.

But I breathe it in. I've been cold before, and I will be cold again. This storm will pass, just like all the others. When the heat returns, I will appreciate the sun on my face, warming my skin, more than ever before.

The Pub is standing-room only. We make our way over to the bar and stand behind the crowd of people waiting to be served. As we wait, I turn away from the bar to take in the scene. I scan the room, seeing many familiar faces, but I halt when I spot a particular face staring straight at me, his usual smirk present. I raise my hand and wave.

Trenton takes his finger and points to me as he mouths, *You.* Then, he points his finger toward his chest as he mouths, *Me,* before gesturing toward the dance floor and mouthing, *Dance.*

I laugh at his primitive communication skills and nod.

"I'm going to go dance with Trenton," I say loudly toward the girls, trying to be heard above the music, as I point to the dance floor.

Jess gives me a thumbs-up and turns back toward the bar.

I start weaving my way through the crowd of people, and Trenton does the same until we meet.

"Hi," he says, grabbing my hand. He leads me out to the dance floor.

We walk around the large square in the center of the room and stop at a spot in the back corner. We're not technically on the dance floor, but it's as close as we're going to get.

Trenton is a great dancer. I've danced with him several times over the past few months, and he always makes me feel happy and carefree. His attitude toward life is refreshing. He says what he feels, does what he wants, and really doesn't care what others think about him. Yes, he can come off as an ass at times, but I think I understand him.

He's from this city. I think his father might be the only lawyer in a sixty-mile vicinity. I'm sure there are others, but Mr. Troy, Trenton's father, is the only one I've ever heard of. Mrs. Troy is a socialite. I hear she comes from a lot of money. Her father invented and patented many items that most of us use every day. The Troys are one of the wealthiest families in Mount

Pleasant, and they are kind of a big deal here. The similarities between Trenton and Jax are not lost on me.

A slow song starts, and a sense of uncertainty comes over me. They usually play these slower dance songs closer to last call when everyone is smashed and hanging all over one another. I'm usually with the girls at that point.

Pulling away, I look to Trenton and try to read his expression, thinking he might want to head back to the bar. He simply smiles and pulls me back in. Wrapping his arms around me, he holds me tight as we move to the music.

I lay my head against his chest, feeling his firmness against my cheek. He smells good, and I'm comfortable in his arms. It's nice, being held like this, and momentarily, I feel guilty that I like it. Then, I remind myself that I'm single, and my best friend is dating a sickeningly sweet girl. Besides, dancing is innocent enough.

Trenton leans forward, positioning his mouth in the crook of my neck. He softly kisses my skin, and I freeze.

"Lily"—his husky voice vibrates against my skin, carrying to my ear—"I like you. A lot."

I'm not sure how to respond, so I just nod. His lips find my skin once more. His light kisses start at the base of my ear and work their way down my neck. I'm so confused as to how I should be reacting to this. Part of me feels I should push him away and run, yet another part of me actually likes it.

He pulls away from my neck, and his hazel eyes are dark with desire, drawing me in. I'm unable to look away as our gazes lock for a moment. Then, he breaks his stare, his eyes darting down toward my lips, before looking back to my eyes.

"Lily." My name is a question, a declaration, and a want coming from his lips.

I give a small nod, my eyes closing, and then I feel his lips on mine. His kiss is tentative at first, his lips gently massaging my own. He tugs my waist in closer to him, our bodies sharing the same space. The kiss deepens, his lips moving with more fervor, and I focus on the sensation it brings.

His tongue slides across my lips, and I sigh, parting them to give him access. He takes it, entering my mouth with soft strokes. My senses are on overload as I process my body's response to this kiss. I've been kissed thousands of times before, but it has never been like this. This kiss isn't better or worse. It's simply different and new. His groan resonates into my throat as his tongue explores the crevice of my mouth with an unfamiliar passion.

My conflicting emotions flood my body, and I gasp, pulling away from Trenton. I look up to see his concerned expression. His eyes are still dark with lust, showing his hunger for more. I give him a forced tentative smile before laying my face against his chest once more. He holds me close, and our bodies sway to the music.

Squeezing my eyes shut, I deeply breathe in through my nose and exhale. I'm such a whirlwind of emotions. A confusion that I have never known has invaded my soul, and it physically hurts. My chest is tight, and my heart is shattered with guilt, but at the same time, it is filling with hope. *How do I even process that?*

"*Jax, you ready?*"

Those words, her voice, resonate within, reminding me that it's okay to shut out the guilt.

I'm not sure what is starting here with Trenton or what I want to happen, but I sense something is beginning.

It's something new, something different, and something that doesn't include Jax.

And it's okay. It has to be.

So, I'm going to dance with this cute boy and concentrate on the hope swelling in my chest, allowing it to silence the guilt.

We leave the packed bar early. Another six inches of snow greet us when we exit the bar. The streetlights cast a golden glow on the empty streets. Trenton offers to walk us back, and the five of us amble down the center of the snow-covered road—so eerily desolate, but beautiful. It's surreal really.

It feels like we are the first people on earth to discover this cold paradise. There is something magical about the world being covered in fresh white powder. All the imperfections of our surroundings are softened with the rolling whiteness before us.

Us girls start giggling—over what, I'm not sure.

I begin to spin around with my arms out. Raising my face to the sky, I open my mouth and take in the flakes, letting the pureness fill my body and nurture my soul.

Someone calls out, "Snow angels!"

The next thing I know, the five of us are sprawled out, lying on our backs in the middle of the deserted street, making snow angels. Spreading my arms and legs wide, I move them out to the sides and back again as I stare up to the white flecks steadily falling from the dark sky. The innocent joy of the moment is healing, bringing a calmness that I've been craving. I laugh along with my friends, enjoying every second of this time.

This right here, this feeling of happiness and abandonment, is what I came to college for, and I know I will always cherish it. All the sad energy that has been weighing on me during the past few months leaves, easing the pressure on my heart. The desolation falls from my body to the ground where it is absorbed by the purity of the fallen flurries.

And just as this blizzard came in strong and fast, bringing the flurries that cover this part of the world with their innocence, so comes the overwhelming sense that I'm on the right path. I'm going to be okay, regardless of what the future brings.

From here on out, I'll live in the moment—not for the memories of the past or the dreams for the future, but for now, this space in time where I'm here. I'm happy. I'm free. I'm just me.

I'm living for the laughs with my friends. For the snow angels in an deserted street. For the stolen kisses. For the feeling of newness and discovery. For this moment in time and each one that follows.

I'll live for each and every instant, for they will never be repeated. I'm going to experience and enjoy this life right now because, really, no one knows what tomorrow will bring.

At this moment, the sky is dropping fluffy cool flakes of hope that land on my cheeks, tickling my skin, and for now, that is enough.

sixteen

I'm going on a date. A real date. I'm not going to lie. I'm freaking out a little. I'm not sure why exactly.

Trenton isn't a stranger. He's a friend whom I've known for seven months now. Yet *friend* isn't the best way to describe him. He's more than a friend, but how much more, I'm not sure.

I have to give him credit. He's been patient—like, really patient—especially over this past month. Since our steamy kiss on the dance floor a month ago, he has been a daily presence, but I've been hesitant to move our relationship to the next level.

I miss Jax, terribly. I miss everything about him. We continue to chat and text a few times a week, and we carry on our best-friend status, but it's not always authentic. I can tell we are both trying to take our relationship back to when we were seventeen before all the awkwardness that came along with a physical and romantic relationship.

Our conversations lack depth, and that's part of the issue. *What does one talk to her ex-boyfriend about?* There are so many topics that bring up hurt or uncomfortable feelings. I don't ask about Stella, and he doesn't ask about my dating life here. We try to keep our topics of conversation in the safe zone, but to be honest, those zone lines are blurry at best. So, lately, our talks have been short and dry, but I know it will get better with time.

Trenton has made his feelings for me clear. He wants a relationship. For the past month, he has been content with a touchy-feely friendship. We hold hands and snuggle up on the futon as we watch movies. We do coffee dates and study dates. He accompanies my roommates and me when we eat dinner. He's been understanding of my situation and confused feelings. He's waited and put in his time.

But I can tell he is getting impatient, and I don't blame him. I need to make a choice. *Am I going to move forward or stay stagnant?*

I know the answer. I've known it for months, but it's hard nonetheless.

Do I still hold out hope that Jax will show up here and confess his undying love, apologize for his lack of judgment, and beg for me back? Of course I do, multiple times per day.

But is that going to happen? Nope. In my heart, I know it's not—at least, not right now. Whatever has been troubling him is still there.

I haven't given up hope for a future with him, but there's no present—at least, not as a couple.

And I promised myself that I would start living for today.

So, here I am, ready for a date and anxious as crap.

Jax and I have done things as a twosome for as long as I can remember, so dating with him was more of the same with the addition of kisses.

With Trenton, it is all new. This nervous feeling in my belly, my insecurities coming to the surface is unfamiliar territory. I'm not used to insecurities—period.

"Flower Child, date's here!" Tabitha calls from our living room.

I look into the full-length mirror hanging on my closet door one more time, running my fingers through my hair. *Here goes nothing.*

"You look gorgeous, Lil, as always," Trenton says. He kisses my hand.

"Thanks," I say shyly.

We exit my dorm and make our way to his car. He opens his BMW's passenger door for me.

I slide in and take a deep breath as I fasten my seat belt. Trenton opens his door, and a gust of chilly wind hits me before he closes it.

"So, what's the plan?" I ask.

His lips turn up into a smirk. "I'm not giving you all my secrets at once, babe."

"A hint?" I ask.

"Well, we'll start with dinner. You hungry?"

"Yeah, sure," I answer.

Trenton navigates through the snowy streets to a restaurant I've never seen before. It is outside of town. A narrow winding drive takes us through a wooded area that opens to a clearing with a building that looks like a grand Southern plantation home. It has a porch that wraps around and tall columns that span from the floor of the porch to the tall roof above. I imagine that this place is even more stunning in warmer weather when the greenery surrounding it is bright. I wonder if people eat out on the deck, encircled by the gorgeous scenery.

"What a beautiful place. I've never been here."

"Yeah, one of my father's clients owns it. It caters to a more affluent clientele. I'm guessing not too many college students eat here."

Trenton opens the car door and takes my hand, gently aiding me up from the leather interior. Hand in hand, we walk up the steps to the restaurant.

The interior is utter luxury with marbled floors, wooden beams, and artwork adorning each wall. We are taken to a private room. In the center of the room is a table set for two. The room isn't bright. From the candles adorning every surface, warm flickers of light dance on the walls.

Trenton pulls out my seat, and I sit down.

Taking a seat across from me, he says to the server, "We'll start with the 2007 Gaja Barbaresco."

The server nods. "Yes, sir," he responds before exiting the room, leaving us alone.

"I have no idea what you just asked for." I chuckle.

He smiles. "It's a red wine, one of my favorites."

"Ah, I see." I nod. I feel slightly out of place.

Trenton is a senior, making him a year older than me, but at the moment, I feel a lot younger.

He moves the candles to the side, so he can take my hand in his. Rubbing his thumb across my skin, he says, "So, the beautiful and untouchable Lily finally agreed to go out on a real date with me."

"I'm not untouchable."

Trenton lowers his gaze. "Yes, you are. I've been trying to get you to go out with me since September."

I shake my head, dismissing his comment. "No, you haven't. I had a boyfriend in September."

"Oh, believe me, I know," he says dryly. "Hopefully, after tonight, you'll have one again—someone better suited for you."

I grin weakly. Trenton has no idea how perfect my previous one was, but that isn't a conversation that I want to have with him.

"And what makes you think you are suited for me?" I ask, cocking my head to the side.

Trenton laughs, squeezing my hand. "Oh, Lily. I have never had to work this hard for anyone in my life."

"Meaning?" I ask simply even though I already have an idea.

"Well, not to sound arrogant, but all the girls who have captured my attention in the past have immediately wanted to be with me. I didn't have to do the friend thing first or wait around until they were ready to be in a relationship. They were always willing and ready from the start."

My eyes go wide as I'm slightly offended with his tone.

He notices and continues, "Listen, all I'm saying is that I have wanted you from the very first time I saw you dancing with your friends in September. You are the most stunning woman I have ever seen in my life. You and me, Lily—we're great together."

Trenton looks to the ceiling and lets out a low groan before returning his serious gaze back to me. "You can't possibly know how much I want you, or you would realize how difficult these past few months have been. Imagine what it would be like to be dying of hunger, and picture the ripest and most delicious peach. Now, envision what it would feel like to have the peach dangled in your face every day. You are so hungry, and you want it so badly, but it is kept just out of your reach, taunting you. I'll tell you. It's pure fucking torture.

"Lily, I've always gotten what I wanted. That's who I am. I'm not used to waiting. But I've waited for you because you are worth it. For the first time in my life, I have found something that is. But I can't do it anymore. I need you more than you could possibly know."

I'm speechless as I'm both frightened and intrigued by his recent admission.

"Come here," Trenton commands softly. Letting go of my hand, he scoots back from the table and taps his thigh. "Please."

I stand and walk around the small table until I'm in front of him.

"Straddle me," he orders in a husky voice.

"But I have a dress on," I say, motioning to the tight black fabric that ends above my knees.

He runs his hands from my knees and up to the sides of my hips, pushing the fabric up. He stops just before exposing my behind to the air.

"Come here," he urges again.

The need in his voice makes my tummy feel weird flipping sensations.

I widen my stance and climb up on his lap, facing him. My bare legs dangle from the sides of the chair. He runs his fingers through the hair at the nape of my neck, and I close my eyes, enjoying the feeling it brings.

I sense movement and open my eyes to see the waiter walking in with our bottle of wine.

"Leave us," Trenton orders.

"Yes, sir," the waiter says, pivoting around and immediately retreating.

This Trenton is not like the one back at college who has patiently pursued me for months. He is demanding.

For reasons that escape me, I feel my body reacting to this side of him, and I find his bossy arrogance attractive. My skin warms with desire, and my blood pounds through my veins as my body craves his touch.

Using his hands entwined through my hair, he pulls me toward him until my lips meet his. I moan into his mouth at the contact, and he uses the opportunity to slide his tongue in between my lips.

I've kissed Trenton before, but this kiss is different. Last time, my senses were overwhelmed in a haze of alcohol, loud music, and bodies bumping into us on the crowded dance floor. But now, I have nothing to concentrate on but this kiss.

And I like it. A lot.

Trenton's lips continue to capture my own as his tongue dances seductively in my mouth. I feel wanted, and that is the biggest turn-on. Trenton makes me feel not only beautiful, but also sexy.

He explores the exposed skin of my thighs, arms, neck, and chest as we kiss. My skin burns with desire at his touch. It might be the out-of-control lust cheering me on in my subconscious, but for whatever reason, this feels right.

I lose track of time, lost in the lust-filled haze, as we continue to kiss. Trenton pulls away, groaning slightly. My lips feel swollen and warm from use.

"I just want to get out of here, and take you somewhere else, so I can explore every inch of your body." His raspy voice is raw with need.

My stare widens, and I study Trenton's face, his hazel eyes darkening with desire. His lips look fuller than usual, slightly parted, as he breathes deeply.

He sighs, rubbing a strand of my hair behind my ear. "But I have a whole evening planned, and you deserve the romance, too."

I can't be sure, but his tone seems contradictory to his statement.

"Hop off, baby. Let's get you something to eat."

And with that statement, I get off of his lap, push my skirt down until it is where it should be, and half-walk, half-stumble back to my seat. The whole time, I'm trying to figure out what the hell just happened.

The dinner is delicious. I enjoy every bite of my crab pasta with truffle butter cream sauce. The wine he picked is perfect as well.

Despite our high-intensity make-out session earlier, the conversation flows naturally. Trenton talks a lot about his life, but I enjoy the reprieve of not having to think about my own. Anything I could tell him about home would bring back some sweet moment or memory with my best friend, and the last thing I need on my first real date is for those recollections to capture my attention.

I thought that Jax's family had money, but I sense that the Porters' wealth isn't anything compared to the Troys'. Parts of our dialogue make me feel uneasy as Trenton speaks about their summer home in Hawaii and family trips to Paris. From his family's various homes to his time growing up in a ritzy boarding school, I start to doubt my ability to fit into his world. I'm the down-to-earth country girl who grew up in a small town.

My family is affluent for our area, but his family and mine wouldn't run in the same circles. I'm not sure I would want them to anyway. There is something superficial and shallow about that life to me. But then again, that's judgmental of me to think—just as it would be equally judgmental if Trenton thought less of me a beautiful kind of love

because I didn't come from that life. By his actions, he doesn't seem to judge me like that, so it's unfair for me to. I quiet the thoughts in my head that wonder what type of an individual could be raised in such a life.

A part I don't understand is why Trenton chose Central instead of an Ivy League school. I love it here, but it's certainly not known for its prestige.

"What made you pick Central?" I ask.

"Not sure exactly. I guess it is comforting to be close to home. This is just a stepping-stone to law school for me. I'm guaranteed a job at my dad's firm when I get my degree, so I just figured that there wasn't a real point in going somewhere else. Why work harder for something you're already guaranteed, you know?"

I nod slowly, taking in his statement. I suppose that makes sense. Maybe? I don't think I've ever heard anyone put it like that before.

Jax has always strived to be the best at everything, regardless of the outcome. He wanted to go to the best school with the best business program despite the fact that it is a lot tougher than other programs.

I'm thrown off by Trenton's way of thinking, but I have to stop comparing him to Jax. Trenton isn't anything like Jax, and I have to be okay with that. I will never move on if I compare every guy to Jax.

After dinner, Trenton starts heading back toward campus, but before we reach the school, he pulls off to the side of the street and parks. Looking across the street, I see two beautiful large white horses attached to a sleigh fit for Cinderella. I gasp and turn to Trenton to find his wide smile.

"Is that for us?" I ask, pointing to the sleigh.

He runs his hand down my cheek. "That's for you."

Trenton comes around the front of his car and opens my door. He takes my hand as our feet crunch across the snow, and we make our way toward the other side of the road.

A soft large blanket is folded neatly on the leather seat of the sleigh.

Trenton shakes it out and lays it over the back of the seat. "Have a seat, baby."

I sit, and Trenton sits next to me, wrapping the blanket around the both of us. In front of me are two silver travel mugs sitting in the cup holders. Trenton reaches for them and hands one to me.

"What's this?"

"Hot chocolate, of course." He winks.

"Wow. This is quite the date. I think you've thought of everything."

After setting his mug back into its cup holder, he sweeps my hair to the side and places a warm kiss on my neck beneath my ear, making me shiver.

"I sure hope so." He gently kisses my neck.

I close my eyes, reveling in the sensation his soft kisses bring. "Not sure how a date could get better than this," I say softly.

His lips tug on my earlobe. Huskily, he whispers, "Oh, I'd like to prove you wrong on that one later tonight."

My body shudders. Whether it's from the chill of the night air, anticipation of what is to come, or the fear that my life is about to change forever, I don't know.

We circle the park once. The man holding the horses' reins looks to Trenton in question, and some sort of nonverbal communication is exchanged. He nods at Trenton before pulling the sleigh over to the side, parking it where we started only a few moments ago. I get the feeling that Trenton is cutting the ride short.

Trenton takes my hand and helps me from the sleigh. We walk back across the street toward his car. I start to slow when we reach the passenger side, but Trenton pulls my hand, urging me to walk beyond the car. Past the sidewalk is a line of new town houses designed to look classic. Each one has a dark roof, tan stucco exterior, and beautiful stonework along the bottom of the outer wall. We stop at a mission-styled wooden entry door.

"This is where I live," Trenton states as he reaches in his pocket before pulling out a key.

"It is?" I ask in confusion.

I was under the impression that he lived with some of his fraternity brothers in a house just off-campus because he always heads there after a night out at a bar.

"Yeah, I have a room with the guys, too, and I crash there most nights, but my parents bought me this house about a year ago, so I would have my own place when I needed it," he says matter-of-factly.

"Oh, wow. Do you stay here often?"

"Not too often really. I come here if I need to study or if I want a night away, but it gets boring by myself."

The interior looks like something out of a magazine. I scan the open living space that includes a kitchen fit for a chef, a formal dining area, and a posh living room, but I don't see any personal effects. The clean lines and warm feel of the space was most likely created by an interior designer.

Trenton takes my coat and hangs it in the foyer. I make my way across the dark wood floors, looking around the space for some hints into Trenton's life. But still, nothing personal stands out. This could be a show home. It's stylish but simple enough to appeal to anyone.

I feel his presence behind me, and I stop walking. His arms circle me from behind, and he buries his face in my hair, sighing with contentment.

"Lily, Lily, Lily," he chants in an almost whisper.

I turn in his embrace to look at him. "Yes?" I question.

He studies my face for a beat longer than is comfortable. Then, he blinks and asks, "So, what do you think?" He gestures toward the room.

"It's nice, really nice. I like it."

His eyes darken. "Good, because I've been wanting to spend more time here."

"Yeah?" I ask.

"Yes, and now, I have you to spend it with."

"You do?" I ask playfully.

Trenton's face is serious. "I have another room that I really want you to see."

"Which one is that?" Nervous energy courses through me.

"My bedroom. Are you ready to see it?" His gaze locks with mine.

Am I? My heart begins to race, beating in an anxious pace. I look down, contemplating.

Trenton places his finger underneath my chin and lifts it up. The moment my eyes connect with his again, his mouth is on mine. The kiss is urgent and pleading. His tongue enters my mouth, licking and twirling around mine, in an attempt to coax out my answer. It sends my emotions into a tailspin and my hormones into overdrive.

My body wants this. My body wants him. It is hard to know what my heart wants because the carnal desire running through me is so loud that I can't think through it.

I can't speak, so I nod. It isn't a sure movement. It is tentative and questioning, but it is enough for Trenton. He picks me up, and I wrap my legs around his waist. He doesn't remove his mouth from mine as he carries me into his bedroom.

He releases me, and I slide down until my feet hit the floor. He makes quick work of my clothes, and before I can catch my breath, I'm standing bare in front of him.

He scans me from top to bottom. "Fuck, Lily," he growls before tearing off his own clothes.

He pushes me back onto the bed, and his mouth and hands are everywhere. The foreplay isn't long, but it is skilled. I can tell that Trenton knows what he is doing, and if the rumors are right, he's had plenty of practice. I push that thought out of my head as puts on a condom and enters me.

I gasp as my body is pushed upward, and I reach my hands up to the headboard, steadying myself, as he continues to pound into me with an intense force and speed. He holds on to one of my breasts, squeezing it with each thrust. My mind is running on full speed, trying to process all the sensations, both mental and physical. My body is reeling with such a contradictory mix of emotions.

Trenton pulls one of my nipples to the point of pain, and I cry out.

"Say you're mine, Lily," he demands. "Say. You're. Mine."

He continues to tug on my nipple as his already relentless pace intensifies. I feel my orgasm coming, and I close my eyes, bracing for the tremors that will wreck me.

"Say it!" he yells.

I gasp for air. "I'm yours! I'm yours!" I scream. I see colors beneath my eyelids, and an intense orgasm rips through me.

I'm coming down from my high when I feel Trenton's body tightening in release. He collapses on me, and we are quiet as we catch our breaths.

After a few moments, Trenton rolls off of me and removes his condom before tying it off and tossing it into the trash can next to the bed.

We lie side by side, both facing the ceiling.

"Fuck, Lily," Trenton breathes. "I knew your tight little cunt would be perfect. Fucking perfect."

We remain in silence for a few beats before he says, "Night, baby."

Then, he rolls to his side, facing away from me. I lie still, studying the shadows on the ceiling, as I listen to his breathing even out. When he is asleep, I roll out of bed and exit the bedroom.

It doesn't take long to find the guest bathroom. Entering the bathroom, I close the door and lock it behind me. I turn on the shower, making the water as hot as I can bear, and I step in. I close my eyes, letting the hot water cover me, scorching my skin in its descent.

Leaning against the tile, I slide to the floor of the shower and cry. My body shakes with grief as I sob into the steam-filled space. The tears continue to fall until my skin is wrinkled and red from the prolonged onslaught of the burning water.

When I have no more tears, I drag myself out of the shower. After drying off, I head back to the bedroom. I find Trenton asleep in the same position I left him in. Using the limited light from the moon shining in through the bedroom window, I go through his dresser drawers to find a pair of boxers and a T-shirt.

After slipping them on, I slide into bed and tightly wrap the comforter around my body. The warmth and pressure of the blanket enveloped securely around me bring a sense of contentment. My mind and body are exhausted. I'm not sure what to feel anymore, but at this moment, I don't have the energy to figure it out.

My eyelids close, blocking out the confusion within me, and I fall into a fitful sleep full of dreams of the emerald eyes that I've loved my whole life. The beautiful greens flash with disappointment and hurt. They radiate heartache, and that vision will haunt me always.

seventeen

I bolt upright, gasping. It takes me a second to remember where I am, but when I see Trenton's toned back next to me, it all returns at rapid speed. I bend my knees resting under the blanket and hold them to my chest. I rock faintly, burying my face into the soft comforter, as I try to calm down.

My dream about losing my virginity with Jax at his lake house was so vivid, bringing back all the raw emotions that I've been working so hard to bury over the past several months. With the visions of the dream so fresh in my mind, waking up next to a naked man who isn't Jax is enough to make me vomit. I have to work hard to keep my composure.

This reaction is natural. It was bound to happen. Moving on sucks, but it is a part of life. Jax wanted this break and his subsequent relationship with Stella. It wasn't my choice. I didn't want this, any of it, yet here I am. I have to move on.

I refuse to let myself wallow in sadness anymore.

Trenton makes me laugh. I feel beautiful when I'm with him. He really likes me, and I feel the same for him. *Do I think that he and I could be in it for the long run? I don't know.* My emotions with Jax are still all over the map, so it's difficult for me to get an adequate read on my feelings. But I know I want to try.

It is hard to figure out my thoughts about last night. Trenton physically pleased me, but emotionally, I felt guilty the entire time. Jax has obviously been having an easier time with moving on, but he slept with many girls before me, whereas he was my one and only prior to last night. Now, he's not, and that is something I can never change. Jax will never again be my only lover, and that breaks my heart.

The bed shifts next to me.

"Baby." Trenton's voice is rough from sleep.

I lift my head and turn toward him. "Hey," I answer tentatively.

"Come here." Trenton motions to the crook of his outstretched arm.

I lie down against his skin, and he pulls me into him.

"You okay?"

"Yeah, I'm fine," I lie.

"Last night was awesome, baby," he says as the palm of his free hand runs up and down my arm.

He slides his hand onto my waist and under the T-shirt, warming my skin. His touch makes its way to my breast, and I suck in air.

"Only one thing could be better than a night of sex with my hot-ass girl." He pauses a moment, and when I don't respond, he continues, "A morning fuck with my hot-ass girl."

He rolls so that he is on top of me. Then, his lips cover mine, and he groans. I feel his excitement as it presses into me through the boxers that I'm wearing.

"First things first, you need to be naked and now." He makes quick work of removing his clothes from my body. "God, Lily," he says as his gaze scans my exposed flesh. "Fucking amazing."

The sex isn't earth-shattering, but it is good. I am now two times removed from having Jax as my only partner. I have to quiet the regret in my head as I lie here in post-orgasmic glow with Trenton.

Unfortunately, regret is one persistent bitch.

Over the next month, Trenton continues to sweep me off my feet—in more ways than one. Every day holds some new adventure or gesture that makes me feel cherished and adored. If he isn't having flowers or other sweet gifts delivered to my dorm room, he's taking me on romantic dates. The days usually end in some very satisfying physical activities, and that is getting easier, too. I don't feel as guilty as I used to. The reality of my new relationship status is becoming less painful to handle.

It's not like Jax wasn't romantic because he was, but part of the excitement of Trenton is the newness and the anticipation. I'm still learning about Trenton. It was hard to feel like this with Jax because we knew each other so well. It is difficult to be spontaneous when your partner can predict what you are about to do. Jax and I had a lifetime of knowledge and experiences embedded into our relationship. I don't remember what it was like discovering new things about Jax because it just seems like I always knew him.

Again, it is unfair to compare Trenton and Jax. The two relationships I've had in my life aren't even like comparing apples and oranges. It would be more like comparing apples to cars. These relationships aren't even in the same category. They are simply not comparable. Yet I find myself comparing them often to justify my life, if anything.

Having Trenton in my life in this way for over a solid month now is making it less difficult for me to accept my loss of Jax and move on. The underlying sadness is still there, but I'm trying to completely extinguish it, so I can officially get on with my life.

Jax continues to be a constant presence. We are still friends and communicate often, but I'm keeping him at a distance, and it's working. Little by little, I'm finding a new normal, a life I can live with. I haven't told Jax about Trenton yet, and that doesn't sit right with me, but to be fair, he hasn't told me about Stella either.

My phone buzzes in my lap. I look down to see a text from Jax, and my lips automatically turn up. In the text is a photo of Jerome, Jax's roommate. He's sitting in a booth with a girl leaning adoringly on his arm. The girl looks smitten, but Jerome looks annoyed.

> *Jax: At breakfast with the guys and Jerome's conquest from last night. Apparently, she is going to stay around for a while. LOL. You can see he's happy about it!*

Me: Nice. Well, serves him right. ;-)

Jax: Yes, it does.

Me: Keep me informed! Hopefully, she stays all day and drives him crazy! LOL.

Jax: I will! What are you up to?

Me: Heading to a friend's parents' house for brunch.

I immediately feel guilty for failing to mention that my friend is now my boyfriend. *Omitting the truth isn't exactly lying, right?*

Jax: Awesome. Well, have fun. Miss you, Little!

Me: Me, too! But summer break is only a couple of weeks away!

My finals finish up during the last week in April, so I will be home by May.

Jax: Can't wait.

Me: Love you. Bye.

Jax: Love you more.

"Who are you texting?" Trenton asks from the driver's seat.

"Jax," I reply truthfully.

It is silent in the car, and I can sense the tension rolling off of Trenton. He hates my relationship with Jax, but I was very clear with him that my friendship with Jax was nonnegotiable.

"What's *Jax* up to?" Trenton huffs out.

Not acknowledging the distaste in his voice, I respond cheerfully, "He's at breakfast with the guys. One of his roommates, Jerome, is stuck with his one-night stand from last night. Jax sent me a picture of the two of them, and Jerome's expression is hilarious."

"I don't like it, Lily."

Staring out the passenger window, I roll my eyes. I really don't want to get into this again. I understand his reservations. I would hate it if he had a girl best friend whom he chatted with on a daily basis. But I chose to be with Trenton, and I'm not going to screw him over. I'm not that type of person. He needs to trust me, especially where Jax is concerned because my best friend isn't going anywhere.

"I know." I'm not going to get sucked into an argument about this right now.

I've said what I have to say many times. Now, he needs to accept it. Hopefully, with time, he will.

Trenton's parents are not my favorite people in the world. They carry themselves with such an air of superiority, and to be honest, I feel inadequate around them. They are courteous enough and attempt polite conversations, but nothing with them seems genuine. There are people in life who are sugary sweet to your face, and the moment you turn your back, they will say vile things about you. That is the impression I get with the Troys. I would bet money that they talk about me when I'm not present, but I let it go. They have been nothing but pleasant with me, and perhaps my insecurities are getting the best of me.

"Oh, Lily, dear. So wonderful to see you," Mrs. Troy's shrill voice greets me.

"Thank you for having me, Mrs. Troy."

"You're welcome." She nods toward me before turning her admiring gaze to Trenton. Her voice is sincerely happy when she addresses him, "Trenton, dear, how have you been, sweetheart?" She places her palm on the side of his face.

"Fine, Mother."

"Well, please do come in. Isabel has created the most impressive spread. I hope you brought your appetites." Her heels clang against the marble floor as she descends to the dining area.

I've had Isabel's cooking many times, and I agree with Mrs. Troy. It is pretty amazing.

The brunch goes as I knew it would. Trenton and his father go over the recent cases at the firm, talking about different strategies and angles. They use a lot of law words that cause me to zone out.

Mrs. Troy tells Trenton all the gossip about the affluent families who run in their circle. "Can you believe that Veronica dropped out of Harvard to tour with her drummer boyfriend in that low-life band? It is truly deplorable! Her poor parents are so embarrassed. They had to miss last week's dinner at the country club," she chimes in.

Isn't it astonishing the tragedies that people can live through? I hope Veronica's parents can make it through this. Gag me.

Trenton slides into the driver's side and shuts his door. He laughs loudly. "Oh, Lily, your face is priceless. Good thing you aren't going into acting!"

"What?" I ask innocently.

"It wasn't that bad, was it?" he asks with laughter in his voice.

"Define *that bad*," I tease.

"I know my parents are a bit much, but you will get used to them. They mean well."

Sure they do.

I want to tell him that his parents are stuck-up jerks, but I don't.

"I know. I'm just not used to being around them. I have nothing to add to their conversations, and it makes me feel stupid." Not that his parents have ever tried to ask anything about me or talk about something I could contribute to.

"I know, but the longer we are together, the more familiar you will become with my life, and it will be more natural for you. You'll get there."

I nod in affirmation, but I hope I will never have anything in common with the Troys—except for Trenton, that is. Trenton has a cockiness to him, but he isn't like his parents. He fits into their world, no doubt, but when he is not with them, he is a different person. He can be crude and bossy at times, but he does it in a way that I find attractive. He isn't always an ass. He is fun, smart, loving, and carefree, too. He is a walking contradiction of attributes, and maybe that is why I find him so interesting.

"So, what do you want to do for the rest of the day?" he asks.

Tomorrow starts the last full week of school before preparing for finals, and I have a ton of papers due. "I have some schoolwork I need to do tonight."

Trenton drives with his left hand on the wheel, and his right hand is holding mine, his thumb circling over my skin. "All right. How about we go get your stuff and head back to my house? We can stop at your favorite coffee shop on the way. Plus"—his voice changes, sounding like trouble—"my place is really accommodating when it comes to study breaks."

I laugh. "Oh, believe me, I know, but I wouldn't call them *breaks*. I usually don't get much rest during them."

"Very true."

We reach my dorm room a few moments later.

"Go get what your things, including what you need for tomorrow, and I'll be back to get you in a few. There are some things I have to do."

"Okay, but it's fine if I return here tonight. I have to be back on campus by eight thirty tomorrow morning."

"No problem. I have a long day tomorrow, too. I can drop you off."

"Okay, I'll see you in a few. Text me when you get back, and I'll head down." I lean over the middle console to give him a quick peck.

"I will. Love you, baby."

My eyes flicker to his before I quickly drop my gaze. "See you soon," I say before rapidly exiting his car.

"Seriously, Lil? Can't you come back tonight? It's karaoke night. Come out with us," Tabitha whines.

"Sorry, Tabs. I already told Trenton I would stay at his house. Plus, I really do have to study."

"Fine," Tabitha huffs. "But we never see you anymore."

"I'm sorry. I promise we'll get some good girls' nights in before I head home for the summer."

My phone buzzes in my pocket. Pulling it out, I swipe the screen to read the message. It is Trenton letting me know that he's waiting outside.

I look back up to Tabitha. "After the craziness of these final two weeks is finished, we'll have some serious nights out, okay?" I smile reassuringly.

"Okay, Miss Responsible. Go forth and study." Tabitha waves me off with a pout.

I chuckle.

I direct my attention toward the futon where Jess and Molly are both sitting with bowls of cereal. "Bye, girls." I wave before leaving the dorm room.

I feel mildly guilty about all the time that I have been spending with Trenton because I don't want to feel like I'm missing out on any girl time. As my mom told me a few months back, this is the only period in my life when I will have this experience, and I need to live it up while I'm here at college. A small part in the back recesses of my mind worries that I'm replacing my need for Jax with Trenton, yet I don't completely buy that.

Do I love feeling needed and wanted? Yes, absolutely.

Trenton makes it clear how much he wants me. But what I have with Trenton is so different than what I had with Jax. I'm not fully invested in the relationship yet, and I'm not sure if I ever will be. Trenton's good for me right now, but it is impossible to know if he will be good for me in the future, and I'm fine with the unknown, for now.

Unlike Jax where I felt our future had been written for us from the moment we were born, my feelings for Trenton are a complete mystery to me. We might go the distance and reach a happily ever after, or we might last until tomorrow. I'm not concerning myself with either scenario. I'm living for today.

eighteen

Finals are over. Tonight is my last hurrah as a junior. Tomorrow will be my last day living in the dorms. The girls and I have signed a lease on an apartment near to campus for next school year. I feel happy, and it has nothing to do with the strawberry margaritas flowing through my veins.

"Now, Lil, phone on the table," Jess instructs, sitting across the booth from me at our favorite Mexican restaurant.

I sigh and place my cell facedown on the four-phone tower we have going on in the center of the table.

"There. Now, whoever checks her phone first pays the tab," Jess reminds us.

She saw some meme on Facebook about placing all the phones on the table like this to allow us to better concentrate on our real-life friends and not our social media ones.

"This is stupid." Tabitha pouts.

It's a rare occurrence, but I actually agree with her. This is very stupid.

I feel almost panicked without direct access to my phone. My finger is itching to press my screen to see if any red notification numbers are popping up on any of my icons, showing that people out there has said something that they want me to see. More than anything, I'm freaked that I might miss some message from Jax.

What if he texts me? What if needs something?

I rapidly bounce my knee up and down under the table and put my focus on taking little bites of the tortilla chip in my hand. Then, to further grab my attention from my phone anxiety, I decide to play a little game with myself to see if I can eat the chip using only my four front teeth, like a squirrel.

It is unlikely that Jax will text anyway. Our communication isn't what it used to be. Our messages have been more spaced out. I suppose it is healthier this way. I shouldn't be obsessed with hearing from my friend anyway. *Texting each other twice a week is more normal, right?*

"Oh my God, you are all insane. You can go an hour without checking your phones. Plus, this is our last roommate dinner until the fall. So, don't you think it would be best to focus on each other instead of on some random dude from high school who you haven't spoken to since graduation is tweeting? I mean, seriously. You all are crazy and need to get a grip," Jess says.

"You're right," Molly concedes.

Tabitha lets out an exaggerated breath. "Like anyone would be contacting you anyway." She directs her comment toward Molly.

"Hey, knock it off, Tabs," Jess warns with an air of authority.

Tabitha huffs, "Fine." She turns her attention toward me. "Lily, what the hell are you doing? You look like a rodent."

Pulling the chip away from my mouth, I say, "Just chewing." I shrug my shoulders.

Tabitha shakes her head.

Our entrees and another pitcher of margaritas arrives, and the conversation starts to flow. We all laugh as we reminisce over some of our favorite roommate moments of the past year.

"Okay, number one favorite memory or event of the year," I say.

"Getting a B-plus in statistics," Molly pipes up first.

"So lame." Tabitha shakes her head.

"No, it's not. That was the third time I took that freaking class. Me and stats are not friends. I needed to pass it. That grade is a huge accomplishment for me."

"That's awesome, Molly." I smile.

Statistics was one of the classes that she and Trenton had together. They spent a good chunk of the year studying for this class, and I can't help but feel proud of my boyfriend for helping my friend understand something that was difficult for her.

"My favorite was going to the U of M versus Michigan State game." Jess clears her throat and apologetically looks at me. "Before Saturday night, of course."

I smile wide, not wanting her to feel bad. I know what a huge U of M football fan she is. I realize it meant a lot to her to be at such a great game where they beat a huge rival.

"I agree, Jess. That was a fantastic game." And it was.

Jax and the whole team played their hearts out and beat State for the first time in several years. The energy of the crowd at the U of M's Big House was something I will never forget either.

"I think mine was walking home from the bar during Storm Vulcan." I'm immediately filled with a sense of gratitude for being able to experience that beautiful night. It is a memory I will always cherish. I continue, "Remember how beautiful everything all covered in white looked? The snowflakes were huge and fluffy as they fell. I loved doing snow angels in the abandoned street."

Everyone is silent as they think back to that night.

"Yeah, that was definitely a highlight," Molly says.

Jess and Tabs nod their heads in agreement.

Tabitha hits her hand on the table to bring us all back out of our snowstorm remembrance. Then, she leans in, commanding our attention with a gleam in her eye. "My favorite event of the year was…" She pauses for dramatic effect. "Finally fucking Travis Peters."

I lean back.

"What?" we all say in disappointment, expecting something more profound.

"What?" she questions innocently. "I've been trying to get my hands on that boy since Freshman year."

"But you only slept with him the one time," Jess points out.

Tabitha waves her hand through the air in dismissal. "Well, yeah. After I got him, I realized I didn't want to date him. He's kind of a tool." She looks off in the distance with a satisfied smile on her face. "He wanted me bad though. Such a great feeling."

Jess shakes her head, taking a drink of her margarita. "Tabs, you need therapy," she states bluntly.

Tabitha chuckles. "Whatever. You all wanted to know what I loved about this year, and I told you. I'm fucking proud of catching Travis. I had to work for that."

Then, one of the phones tings loudly in the center of the table. We all look to Tabitha, knowing the sound her phone makes.

Jess looks to Tabitha. "I said to turn off all sounds, Tabs."

Tabitha looks to the pile of phones.

"Don't you dare," Jess warns.

Tabitha bites her lip, her eyes darting from her phone and then back to us. After a mere three seconds of what I'm sure was a huge internal struggle for her, she reaches for the phone.

"Tabs!" we exclaim in unison.

She ignores us and looks to her phone. Her fingers rapidly move over the screen before she plops her phone in her purse, and then she proceeds to dig around in it. She throws three twenties on the table. "Dinner's on me, bitches. I gotta run."

"What?" I ask.

She grins. "Yeah, something came up. I have to go. I'll meet you all at the bar in a few, okay?" she says sweetly.

She hops up from her seat and all but skips out of the restaurant, her hips swaying from side to side as she sashays through the exit.

"Well, cheers to a free dinner." Jess holds up her margarita glass.

"Cheers," Molly and I say, clinking our glasses together.

The bar is packed as students are fitting in one last celebratory night of partying before heading home for the summer.

My feet ache from dancing, but I don't let it bother me. I feel such a sense of accomplishment. I made it through this school year, which was chock-full of new experiences, unknowns, and heartbreak, and I'm ending it by dancing with my friends, a giant smile on my face.

Trenton knows I need this night with the girls, and he has been very gracious to stand off to the side with some of his friends to let me enjoy it even though I know he would rather be dancing with me. Speaking of, it would feel nice right about now to dance with him. Being wrapped up in Trenton would take some of the pounding pressure off my feet.

I turn around to face the table where he has been sitting all night with his friends. I scan the area a few times, but I don't see him anywhere. Shrugging, I turn back to my friends.

Jess has her eyes closed, and she's shaking her hands in front of her. Her index fingers on both hands are pointed out, like she's shooting a gun. It is her signature drunken dance move, and every time I see it, it makes me happy.

Molly, too, is in her own little world. Her hands are raised, and her hips are swaying to their own beat.

Tabitha isn't in our dance circle anymore. I briefly wonder where she is. I don't remember her leaving. If she were here, she would be thrusting her pelvis back and forth with her arms in front of her, her fingers spread out as if she were doing rapid air push-ups.

I know I have a signature drunken dance move, too. I'm not exactly sure how to describe it, but it does include sexy finger snapping.

"Hey, where's Tabs?" I call out to Jess.

"Not sure. Restroom?" she yells back.

I nod, still scanning the crowd for Trenton. Even though tonight was about the girls, I would like to have one dance with him. I heard it was last call a few minutes ago, so there aren't many songs left.

Right before the last song, Trenton wraps his arms around me from behind.

"Hey, I was looking for you," I say.

He leans down to my ear, so he doesn't have to shout over the music. "Sorry, baby. I got caught up talking to an old buddy of mine across the bar."

"Well, I'm glad I get one dance with you." I turn and wrap my arms around his neck.

"I'll make it up to you tonight, babe."

I nod, my cheek against his chest.

"Well, that's it," I say as Jess puts the last of my boxes into my car. "Can you believe the year is over already? It was both the longest and fastest year of my life."

"Yeah, it sucks to be going home." Jess has made it clear that she doesn't particularly enjoy her parents' company.

I pull her into a hug. "It's only a few months, and then we'll be back."

"I'm gonna miss you," she says, returning my hug.

"Me, too," I agree.

I say my good-byes to Molly, and then I text Tabitha to say that I'm leaving.

Tabitha is the biggest mystery to me. She has been either hot or cold with me all year long. She's either whining because I'm with my boyfriend too much, or she's absent, not showing up to our scheduled plans. She left this morning when I got home from Trenton's, and apparently, she isn't going to make it back to say good-bye to me. I don't take it personally though. Besides, I will be living with her again in a few months.

I stop off at Trenton's on my way out of town. I use the key he gave me to get into his house. He's in the shower when I arrive, so I wait on the sofa. Leaning my head back against the soft cushions, I close my eyes. I'm anxious to get home. I have so much catching up to do with my family. I'm hoping my friendship with Jax will get less uncomfortable and start feeling more normal as we spend time together over the next couple of months.

"Hey, baby." Trenton's bare feet pad over the wooden floors. He is wearing a pair of worn jeans and a tight-fitting T-shirt. His hair appears more brown than blonde, still wet from the shower. He climbs onto the sofa next to me and pulls me into him. "Don't go. Stay here with me this summer."

This conversation has been on repeat for the past month. "We've already talked about this. I have to go spend time with my family. I want to."

"But I want you here with me." He kisses the top of my head.

"Yes, I know, and I also know that you are used to getting what you want but not this time." I sigh. "Come on. Let's just enjoy each other's company for a few minutes before I have to go. I don't want to rehash all of this again."

"Fine. But I will get you back here this summer." His hand moves up and down my back. His voice gets dark as he says, "What do you have in mind? I can think of several activities that would help me enjoy your company."

I suppress a smile and shake my head. "No way. I only have a few minutes. I need to get on the road."

"Lily." His tone sounds like my father's when I did something wrong as a child.

"Trenton." I imitate his tone.

"Come on, baby." His voice softens.

"I can't. Besides, we enjoyed each other's company several times last night. You'll survive." I mockingly pat him on the chest.

Trenton lives for sex. Maybe most men do. But I'm not in the mood. I'm too excited to get home and see everyone.

"Fine," he says grumpily.

I laugh at his pouting face. "Is this the face you want me to remember when I'm at home this summer?"

"I don't know. Do you find it attractive? Will it make you miss me?" His eyebrow quirks up in question.

"Hmm." I think for a moment. "No, I don't think so. I find it cute, like puppy-dog cute, but not attractive, like I-want-to-do-you attractive."

"Then, no." He is adamant. "Do not remember that face this summer. What about this one?"

He purses his lips out and squints his eyes in what I'm thinking is an attempt to look sexy.

I shake my head, laughing. "Definitely no. You look constipated."

He lets out a scared yell. "Okay, wipe that look from your memory." Then, he busts out laughing, too.

I reach up to cup his smiling face. "I'll remember this one." I lean in and give him a chaste kiss on the mouth. "I do have to get going though," I say in an apologetic tone.

"Okay," he says as he stands to walk me out. "I will see you soon."

"Sounds good. We'll only be a couple of hours away from each other. I think I can find some time to get up here this summer." I wink.

"You'd better."

"I will. I will. Stop pouting. I gotta run." I squeeze his hand before hopping down the steps toward my car, my excitement to get home filling me with giddiness.

nineteen

I lean back against the hard bark of my favorite tree, my favorite place on earth. I set my Kindle down on my lap, my legs outstretched before me, as I sit on a blanket in the shade of my—or rather, our—old oak tree that resides in the field behind my house.

I've been home from school for a couple of weeks now. I haven't seen Jax yet. He had to stay at school for spring conditioning. It's been good for me to have some time for myself—away from school, my friends, Trenton, and Jax. I've enjoyed these past two weeks filled with downtime and quality time with my family.

I'm in a good place. I'm content. I'm happy with my relationship with Trenton. I'm looking forward to my summer off before my senior year of college. I'm thrilled to be renting an apartment with my roommates in the fall. Through all the changes, I've been able to maintain my friendship with my best friend, and that makes me happiest of all.

I take in the hilly fields before me. The tall grass in its varying shades of green, gray, and brown are swaying in the gentle wind. The woods beyond the field are full of tall trees topped with vibrant green leaves that cast dancing shadows on the grass. A quiet noise fills the air. It is the white noise of nature, the sound of nothing but so much at the same time.

Leaning my head against the tree behind me, I listen, taking in the gentle hum of tranquility surrounding me. I look toward the horizon. The sky is strikingly blue with the most perfect type of clouds, the kind that looks so fluffy and soft that it seems like I could reach up and feel their softness. I love the clouds that appear as if I could get up there and skip across them, eventually stopping to hang out in Care Bear village. I love staring at each cloud until a clear shape forms. The one directly above me looks like a ballerina.

A crack sounds, alerting me to someone's presence in my surroundings. I turn my head. Even before I see him, I know he's here. Our innate connection comes to life, and my heart pounds in my chest in anticipation. I know it's probably in my head, but the air around me feels different with his presence. It's alive, dancing with his energy.

Jax stands next to me, just out of reach. Looking down, his green eyes sparkle with joy. "Little."

His husky voice sends chills down my spine. The peacefulness that surrounded me moments ago is replaced with nervous but heated energy.

"Hey, you," I reply, my voice coming out tentative.

Setting my Kindle on the blanket, I anchor my hands on either side of my hips, preparing to push myself up. Before I have a chance, Jax's arm extends toward me, his hand outstretched. I place my hand in his. His fingers wrap around mine, and he pulls me up and into him. Wrapping his arms around my middle, he hugs me tight, bending so that his face rests against my neck. I return his hug, leaning my face flush with his chest.

As we hold each other in this embrace, I hear his heart pounding beneath his chest. He smells like Jax, delicious and sexy. I close my eyes, pushing back all my urges that want me to cross out of the friend zone and make me a cheater.

Jax breaks our contact first, and I open my eyes to meet his stare.

"God, I've missed you," he says, his gaze alternating between my eyes and my mouth.

"I've missed you, too. I didn't know you were coming home today."

He grins. "I didn't tell you. I wanted it to be a surprise. What are you reading?" He nods toward the Kindle lying on the blanket.

"Some cheesy romance novel. You wouldn't be interested."

He chuckles. "Probably not. Can I join you anyway?"

"Of course."

We sit down on the blanket, side by side, with our backs against the tree. Our inner legs lean against one another.

"So, talk to me," Jax states.

"About?"

"Anything. Tell me anything. How did your finals go? How was your last few months of school? What have you been up to since you've been home? Just talk."

"Well, you know a lot of those answers already," I tease.

We have been regularly communicating through calls or texts.

"I know, but it's not the same as talking to you in person. I just want to hear you talk. I've missed it. I've missed you." His voice gets quiet with the last statement.

So, I talk. I tell Jax all about my classes. My junior year at Central exceeded my expectations. I finished all my basic classes and ended up getting all As. My senior year will be great because I will only be taking photography classes. My friends are awesome. I got really lucky to get such different yet fun roommates.

I continue to ramble on for what seems like an hour, telling Jax everything I can think of from the horribly fitting toupee that my communications professor, Dr. Liles, wore to my favorite shot called Benny's Farewell at the little bar down the road from our dorm. After a year of trying, the girls and I still haven't figured out what exactly is in the shot that was named after a previous bartender who had created it right before he moved away.

I turn to Jax. His head is resting against the tree, and his eyes are closed.

"Hey, are you sleeping?" I ask.

"Nope," he says, a smile gracing his face as his eyes remain closed. "Just enjoying the sound of your voice."

"Are you listening to me or just letting my rambling put you to sleep?"

"I heard every word you said, Little Love."

"Okay, you're lucky, mister," I say playfully, poking his side.

He wraps his arm around my shoulder and pulls me in. I lay my cheek against his chest. We lie there in silence for a moment, absorbing the peacefulness surrounding us.

"Jax?" I say quietly.

"Yeah?"

"I haven't told you something about my time at Central."

"Oh, yeah? What's that?"

I feel sick to my stomach as I rest against his side. I don't know why I'm so nervous to tell him. I haven't done anything wrong, but I'm terrified to tell him nonetheless.

"Well, I have a boyfriend," I say quickly, ripping off the Band-Aid, like saying the words faster will make it less painful.

Jax immediately tenses. I feel his firm muscles turn solid beneath my cheek as he hardens and removes his arm that was draped around my shoulder.

I sit up and face him. The carefree, dreamy smile that graced his face moments ago is gone.

"What do you mean?" he asks curtly.

I clear my throat, wiping the palms of my hands against my shorts. "I have a boyfriend. His name is Trenton."

Jax looks at me like he has no idea who I am. His muscles are visibly tense, and his posture is now rigid. "Trenton?" he says as if the name is a disease.

I drop my chin, nodding slightly.

He brings his knees up, resting his elbows on them, as he runs his fingers through his hair. "I can't believe this," he says so quietly that I think he is talking to himself. "I can't fucking believe this."

My eyes widen, watching him shake his head between his hands. My brows furrow before I respond, "I don't understand. This is what you wanted. You moved on. Why don't you want me to? You told me that I should date someone else."

Jax looks at me, his pupils dilated. "I never told you to date someone else."

239

"Yes, you did."

He takes a step further back. "No. What I said was that if you needed to date someone else, then you could. I never said that you should. I just...I...can't believe you wanted someone else." His mouth opens again, but no words form. He slowly shakes his head, looking down.

I feel my face redden as I glare at him. "I didn't want someone else! I wanted you! You know that! I begged you not to break up with me! I begged you. You just wanted to be friends. You wanted me to move on! It was hard, and I was a wreck for a long time, but I moved on. You moved on. Why wouldn't you want that for me? Don't you want me to be happy?"

"Of course I do, Lil. I just didn't think you would want another guy to make you happy. I thought you would always want me."

"I do—did. I *did* want you. You didn't want me!" All the feelings I felt last fall when he broke my heart rush back to me, and my frustration continues to grow. "This is what you wanted, Jax! Why are you so upset?"

He shakes his head. "No, I didn't want this. I wanted us to take some time to focus on our education. I was stressed and needed to put my energy into football and school. I didn't think it was fair to always put you last. I wanted to take a break until I could put you first, like you deserve."

"Well, I don't deserve your anger right now or you making me feel bad about a decision that I didn't want to make in the first place. You moved on with someone else. So, I did, too. I didn't want to, but I did."

"What are you talking about...me moving on with someone else?"

"Jax, don't think I don't know about Stella," I huff out.

He is standing now, pacing. I stand, too.

He turns to face me, his features emitting confusion. "Stella?"

"Yes, Stella. I know that you are dating her."

"I am not."

"Come on, Jax. I'm not stupid."

"Is that what this is all about? Stella?" He clenches his jaw before sighing heavily. "I'm not dating her," he says with sadness in his voice. "She's just my friend, Lil. I promise you. She likes me, yes. But I've never done anything to lead her to believe that we'll ever be more than just friends."

"You've never kissed her?"

"No. Never."

A plethora of emotions assault me, almost knocking me down. Anger, sadness, regret, and confusion resonate the loudest in my jumbled mind. "I just thought you two were together."

"I wish you had asked me. I never told you I was dating her. Don't you think I would have told you if that were the case?"

"I guess I thought that it would be uncomfortable for you to talk to your ex about your current girlfriend. So, I thought you were avoiding the topic." I shrug.

"An ex," he asks. "You are not my ex. You are my best friend, my soul mate, my everything. I would never keep something like that from you."

I sigh. "Well, I'm sorry. I don't know how all this works. I've never been broken up with before. I didn't know the protocol. I just took the information I had and made the best decisions I could. You didn't want to be with me. I did what I could to move on. I'm sorry."

"How long have you been dating him?"

I think back. "Officially, four months, I guess."

"Do you love him?"

I take a deep breath. "Yes, I think so. It's different than the way I loved you, but I really care for him. He treats me well and makes me happy." *He does, right?*

Jax runs his hands through his hair, looking up to the sky. He drops his gaze to meet mine. He bites his bottom lip before asking, "Have you slept with him?"

My eyes fill with tears, and my lips press together in a hard line.

"Fuck!" he yells. He starts to walk away from me.

"Wait!" I call out.

He stops and turns to face me. He looks lost, sad. His voice breaks as he says, "I gotta go. I can't...I just can't." He turns away once more and leaves without looking back.

My knees give way, and I let my body fall to the blanket. I lie on my side, curled up, as the tears stream down my face. I don't know what I'm feeling, but I'm miserable. He is upset that I'm dating someone else, but not once did he say that he wanted us to be back together.

If he had, would it have mattered? I have Trenton now, and I'm happy.

I think.

I feel sick to my stomach because I read the Stella thing wrong. *Would it have made a difference anyway?* He ended things. Maybe he didn't suggest that I move on, but he didn't ask me to wait either. *What would I have been waiting for anyway? Waiting for a time when he could put me first? Who knows when or if that would have ever happened?*

I didn't do anything wrong here. My heart was broken. Someone else wanted me, and I liked him. I moved on. That's the way it goes.

What did Jax expect? I have nothing to feel guilty for. I tell myself this over and over as guilt continues to invade my senses, seeping its way through my body, tainting my every cell with its presence.

Only one other emotion is radiating as loudly as the guilt, and that's remorse.

As I lie here, I mourn everything that was, everything that could have been, and everything that is. This is not how my life should be, yet here I am.

An hour ago, I was content, happy even. Now, I have to begin the journey to find that happiness again, and I hate it. I just wish the state of joy were a permanent one and not the destination of a never-ending battle. Right now, I simply don't have the energy to fight.

twenty

"You should just go talk to him. I don't like this silence thing you two have going on. It's not normal. It makes things weird," Amy says as she turns from her back to her front on the deck chair by our pool. She unties the back of her bikini strap, letting the strings fall to the sides. She folds her arms under her chin, positioning them so that she can prop up her face to see me.

I am sitting up on a deck chair, a large table umbrella casting shade over me. I don't even attempt to get a tan anymore. I simply burn and then go back to being a pale white. I figure there is no point in putting my skin through the pain of burning if I'm not going to get the benefits of a tan.

"Yeah, tell me about it, Ames."

Obviously, the silent treatment with Jax is extremely uncomfortable for me, too. It's been a little over two weeks since I told Jax about Trenton. I've sent Jax a few texts, but I haven't gotten a response. I hate not being on speaking terms with him, but I don't know what else to do or say. I feel horrible that he is hurting, but at the same time, I'm hurting, too. And I can't help but think that all of this is his doing.

"I've sent him texts. He knows where to find me when he's ready."

"Are you going over to the Porters' for the barbeque tomorrow?" she asks.

"I guess so. I wouldn't feel right not going. I can't avoid the whole family just because Jax and I aren't talking." I think for a moment. "It will be weird though, and I'm sure I will feel uncomfortable the entire time."

"I can imagine," she agrees.

"I wish you could go. You could be my buffer."

"Me, too. Damn work." Amy has been home, visiting, for the past two days, but she has to head back tonight. She is scheduled to work at the hospital this weekend. "Have you talked to Trenton about everything?"

I shake my head. "No. He hates everything to do with Jax. He's very jealous of the relationship we have. I can't really blame Trenton. If the roles were reversed, it would bother me, too. I just don't want to worry him or upset him."

"Yeah, you're probably right. Have you thought any more about the job offer? It's a sweet deal, Lil."

I nod, chewing on my bottom lip. I take a second to think.

Trenton's father offered me a freelance job at the firm this summer. He wants to put out a series of various ads, billboards, and promotional material over the next year, and he asked me to be the photographer who will take all the shots for these ads. It is a huge opportunity, one that I'm not really qualified for. I know that Trenton had something to do with this. He has adamantly been trying to get me to come back for the remainder of the summer. The job pays very well and would be an awesome resume builder. It would be silly to turn it down. But taking the job would mean going back to school over a month early, and because our lease doesn't start until late August, I would have to stay with Trenton.

"I know. I'll end up taking the job. It would be dumb not to. It is just hard to think about it right now with everything going on with Jax. I hate being at odds with him. The whole ordeal is consuming my thoughts, making it hard to think about the job offer."

"I get it," Amy states. "But you can't live your life based on other people, even Jax. Things will work themselves out. For now, you need to focus on yourself."

"I know. It's not just Jax though. I was really looking forward to being here the whole summer. Mom is going to be sad if I leave early."

"She'll understand, and she'll get over it. Plus, you'll only be a couple of hours away. You can come home on weekends if you want."

I sigh. "True. I should probably call Mr. Troy to let him know that I'm interested in the job before he gives it away to someone else."

"Yep, I think that's a good idea," Amy agrees.

As I'm walking up to the Porters' house, my hands quiver while holding my mom's bowl of potato salad. My entire body feels jittery, and I have a faint queasiness in the pit of my stomach. We have dinner with the Porters weekly, and Jax has been absent the last two times. By the fact that his car is in the driveway, I'm assuming that he is here today, and I'm extremely nervous to see him.

Susie greets us and takes the bowl from my hands. My mom follows her onto the deck where she places the other salad she brought on the table with the rest of the food. The two of them are all smiles, chatting away. With a grin on my face, I'm watching our mothers laughing when he comes up next to me.

"Hey," he says quietly.

"Hey," I respond without looking at him.

"Can we talk?"

"Sure."

"Walk with me?" he asks.

I turn and follow him. We stroll silently around his massive backyard for several minutes before Jax stops at the wooden swing and sits down. Lifting my legs up and crossing them beneath me, I take a seat next to him. His feet press against the grass, allowing the swing to move in a steady rhythm.

He exhales. "I'm sorry."

"Me, too," I answer.

He shakes his head. "No, you have nothing to be sorry for. This is all me." I listen as he continues, "You're right. This breakup was my choice, and now, I have to live with the consequences. I don't blame you for wanting to date someone else."

"I didn't want—"

Jax cuts me off, "I know. You didn't want any of it. It is my fault that we aren't together, and that makes it my fault that you are with someone else. I don't have the right to be mad at you. Why wouldn't you date someone else?"

"I didn't want to, and I didn't for a long time. I was just so sad and lonely. You broke my heart, Jax, and to be honest…I still don't completely understand why."

He nods. "I know."

"I was so tired of being sad. Trenton came along and made me feel happy again. He wasn't you, but he was someone who wanted me, and…it felt good to be wanted." My chin trembles, and the honesty coming from my lips is making me feel more vulnerable.

"Oh, Little…come here." He wraps his arm around my shoulder and pulls me to him.

I tilt my head to the side, resting it on his shoulder.

"I'm so sorry I made you feel that way. I truly am. I'm sorry for everything. I'm sorry that I fucked this all up."

We swing in silence for several beats.

"Are you saying that you wish we didn't break up?" I ask, trying to hide the hope in my voice.

His hand squeezes my shoulder. He lets out a long sigh. "No. I still think it is what's best for us—for now. I can't be who you deserve right now. I can't give you what you need. There's just so much…shit that is stressing me out, and I don't want you to be a part of it."

My instinct wants to argue, to fight for us…but there isn't an *us* anymore, and I'm tired of fighting. Not to mention, I'm part of another *us* now.

He continues, "I want you to be happy, Lil, and if this Trenton dude makes you happy, then I have to accept it. I didn't ask you to wait for me, and it would have been selfish of me to ask anyway. This whole breakup was my attempt at not being selfish. I was trying to put you first."

Jax has said this before, and I disagree with him now just as I did then. But he seems pretty set on his decision. *What is the point in arguing?* So, I just nod.

"So, let's just go back to focusing on our friendship. The other stuff will work itself out in time, or it won't. Regardless of what happens in this lifetime, no matter what paths we follow or detours we take...you, Lily Anne Madison, are my best friend. I'm a whole lot of messed up right now, but the one thing I know for certain is that I need you in my life, and I'll need you forever...in one way or another." He takes my hand with his free one, squeezing gently. "Friends?"

"Always," I whisper, tilting my head to meet his gaze. "Love you."

He lets out an exhale, relief filling his expression. "Love you more."

As we swing, the sky begins to turn colors in the distance while the sun starts its descent. Distant laughter from the back deck fills the air around us.

"So, what are your plans for the rest of the summer?" he asks.

I sigh. "Well, I actually only have a couple of weeks of summer left."

His eyebrow lifts in question.

I continue, "I got offered a freelance photography job, and it's kinda a big deal. I can't turn it down."

I tell Jax about the job and the timeline that the lawyer has given me to get it done. I fail to let him know that this lawyer is Mr. Troy or that I will be staying with Trenton until school starts back up.

"That sounds amazing, Lil. Truly, I'm so proud of you."

"Thanks."

"I mean it. You are so talented, and others are starting to recognize it. You are going to be a hotshot photographer someday. I just know it. I have to go back soon as well. Practice is starting up."

His lips turn down into an exaggerated sad face, and it makes me laugh.

"How soon?"

"A week."

I nod. "Okay," I say firmly. "So, we have to pack everything into this week. We'll have to prioritize. What is the most important thing on your to-do list?"

"The lake house," he answers immediately.

"I agree. What else?"

"Well, we have to spend a day at our spot. Maybe a picnic and a wicked game of Would You Rather but no fighting this time." He winks.

I'm grateful that my carefree Jax is back.

"Those are my top two as well," I say. "Anything else?"

He shakes his head. "Nope. I just want to hang with my BFF."

I can't stop the giggle that erupts. This whole situation is so not funny, but it is hilarious at the same time.

"So, how about this? Since we have limited time, we need to skip straight to our must-dos, right? So, let's leave for the beach tomorrow. We'll stay there for five days or so and come back. Then, we'll spend your last day here, just chilling at the tree."

"Sounds like a perfect plan," he agrees.

"Should we go join the fam? Eat something?" I ask.

"Not just yet. This right here, swinging with you, is on my must-do list, too. I forgot to mention that." His smile is warm and mischievous.

It makes me so happy.

"Okay," I say, chuckling.

"So, Miss Lily, would you rather have no one show up at your wedding or no one show up at your funeral?"

"Wow. I'm a real loser if either of those is a possibility. But definitely funeral. I'll be dead. I won't know the difference. If no one shows up to my wedding, it might put a damper on my big day." I laugh. "Would you rather be immersed in the world of your favorite book for a day or have your favorite character from a book live in your world for a week?"

"Neither. I don't read."

I playfully slap him on the leg. "Yes, you do. You read all the time."

"Not for enjoyment. Only to gain knowledge. I read business journals and shit about stock market trends. Nothing exciting. What about you?"

"Duh. Obviously, I'd go to Harry Potter land. I'd be a kick-ass wizard."

"Yeah, you would. You'd go all Avada Kedavra on some Death Eaters' asses."

I laugh. "It sounds like you read to me."

"Well, back in the day, I had this girlfriend who was a crazy Harry Potter fan. She used to swear that going to see the Harry Potter movies were so much more enjoyable after one had read the books. So, I read the books to make her happy."

"She sounds awesome."

"Oh, she is. She's the most amazing person I know."

Our gazes lock, and I give Jax a faint smile. My heart hurts, and my thoughts get lost in his deep emerald eyes.

He clears his throat, breaking my stare.

I close my eyes, blocking out the torrent of emotions threatening to erupt. I ignore the fear in the pit of my stomach. I'm terrified of what the future will bring, but I can't let the worry consume me.

Opening my eyes, I smile. "Well, Mr. Porter, you didn't technically answer the last question, and as you know, that is breaking the rules. So, it's still my turn to ask a question, and you have to answer."

"Got it, boss," he answers playfully.

We swing and talk for hours, enjoying the warm evening. Everything feels right in the world. Right now, I'm just a girl hanging out with my best friend. I let our laughter fill me with hope as the summer night sky darkens around us.

twenty-one

"These are really great, Miss Madison." Mr. Troy flips through the images that I shot. "You really captured the essence of what I wanted to portray." He holds up a picture of a family. "Take this one here. When I see this, I think these people look happy, secure, and satisfied. That's exactly how I want people to feel after choosing us. Well done."

"Thank you so much for the opportunity to work with your firm, Mr. Troy. I really appreciate it."

"The thanks is all mine, Miss Madison. Trenton told me you were great. Good to see he was correct." He places the photos down before him. "I will give these to our marketing team. I'd like you to sit down with them, if you don't mind. I think it would be beneficial for you to contribute to the brainstorming session."

"I don't really have any experience with that," I reply.

He waves me off. "No worries, dear. I simply think it would be helpful for you to go over the emotions that

ELLIE WADE

each picture represents. It might spark some ideas for the marketing team, that's all."

"Oh, okay. No problem. I can do that."

"Great. I will email you with the time and date of the first meeting. I assume you want to get going now?"

I look to him in question.

"Don't you have plans with Trenton since it's his last night here and all?"

Oh, yes. Plans. "Oh, yes. Thank you again, sir," I stammer out before awkwardly exiting Mr. Troy's office.

My heels click against the tile floor of the office building as I make my way toward the exit door leading to the parking structure.

Tonight is Trenton's last night here in Mount Pleasant. Fall semester starts on Monday, and he is leaving for law school at the University of Michigan.

Of course.

He didn't want to go out of state, and U of M has the best law school in the state and ranks in the top ten in the country. So, it was his top choice.

Ann Arbor's a big place, so I'm not too worried about him and Jax running into each other. The bright side is that Trenton will only be a two-hour drive away, so I should be able to see him a few times a month.

"Babe, I'm back," I call out into Trenton's foyer as I kick off my heels. I drop my purse and keys onto the small table against the wall and enter the house. Scanning the living area, I don't see him, so I make my way upstairs. "Trenton?" I shout out again.

"In here, baby!" he calls from one of the guest rooms that he has turned into an office.

I open the heavy wooden door and see him sitting at his desk, his fingers typing quickly against his laptop keys. "What are you up to?" I ask, walking toward his desk.

He looks up for a second and gives me a brief smile before returning his attention to the screen. "Just finishing up an email. Give me one second, beautiful."

I walk around his office, looking at the pictures hanging on the wall—some of him with his fraternity brothers and others with his family. I focus on a photo of him and his father with a few other men whom I don't know. They're standing in front of a golf cart, and Trenton is wearing the most absurd white golf outfit. It makes me smile.

I hear a few loud clicks and the sound of his laptop closing.

"All done. Come here, baby."

I walk toward him, and when I'm within reach, he grabs me by the hand and pulls me onto his lap, pushing my tight pencil skirt up my thighs in the process.

"How did it go?"

I wrap my arms around his neck. "It was so great. Your dad loved my photos. He even wants me to meet with the marketing team to go over my vision of each photo and help them out with ideas." I'm beaming with excitement.

Trenton pulls me in for a quick kiss. "That's great, baby. I knew you would do an amazing job. I'm so proud of you."

Trenton's eyes are smiling with pride, and it makes me feel happy. We have had such an amazing summer together. At first, I thought it was going to be weird and awkward, like we would be playing house, but it really wasn't. It has seemed so natural, so right. We've created a happy little routine while living together in our own private world. I'm really sad that he's leaving. Once I'm living with the girls again, I know it will be great, but right now, I'm focused on how much I will miss my time with him.

"Thank you." I lean in and give him another kiss. "What are our plans tonight?"

I'm assuming Trenton has some extravagant date planned. He likes to go big when it comes to dates. He has taken me on many over the course of the summer.

"Well"—he pulls my silk blouse out from under the waist of my skirt and runs the palms of his hands over my back, causing goose bumps to erupt across my skin— "since this is our last night together for a while, I was thinking that we could just stay in."

Surprised, I pull my head back to look at him. "Really?"

He chuckles. "Yeah. Is that okay?"

I laugh. "Of course! It's great. I just figured you'd have some fancy night lined up."

"Well, I thought about it, but then I realized that all I really want to do is be here with you."

"That sounds perfect to me. That's exactly what I want, too." I pull him in for a hug.

"Good. Now, for starters, I would like to spend time with you right here on this desk. Then, I'm thinking we should order some take-out, and while we wait, we can spend time together on the kitchen island. After we eat, we should spend time together in the shower. We should end the night spending time together in bed…maybe a few times."

I throw my head back in laughter. "You really have the night planned out, don't you?" I bite my lip.

"That sounds like a lot of spending time together. Can you handle it?"

I squeal as Trenton abruptly stands from his chair. He pushes his paperwork and laptop aside with one hand and holds my arms above my head with the other. My skirt is pushed up, resting around my waist.

Trenton takes his free hand and pulls down my thong. He looks at me, intensity radiating from his stare. His voice is deep and gravelly as he says, "Oh, I can handle it."

"Flower Child," Tabitha whines, "make me a coffee with that yummy creamer you bought."

I put down my Kindle, lowering my gaze at her. Raising my eyebrow, I give her the evil eye.

"Please," she offers halfheartedly.

"You're something else," I say as I stand from the couch before heading to the kitchen.

"I know, but you love me," she says flippantly.

"Something like that," I respond in a bored tone, knowing it will irk her.

"Hey!" she complains.

I smile as I grab a K-Cup.

"Kidding, Tabs!" I call from the kitchen. "You know I love you."

I return to the living room and hand Tabitha her coffee. She takes it, not looking up from her textbook. I clear my throat and cross my arms.

She lifts her face, meeting my gaze. "Oh, sorry. Thanks."

"You're unbelievable." I chuckle.

"Sorry. You know I don't like studying. This is hard."

"Yes, life is hard." I shake my head, rolling my eyes.

I turn to Molly and Jess who are both sitting at the table with their textbooks open. Molly is frantically writing on a piece of lined paper.

"Can I get you guys coffee?"

Jess looks up from her book. "No, thanks."

"Molly?" I ask.

"I'm good. Thanks, Lil."

"No problem," I reply before plopping back down on the couch.

My roommates all have intense class loads this year as they're trying to fit everything in before graduation. I, on the other hand, had hard class loads my first three years of college, so all I have left are my photography classes, and there isn't a lot of homework assigned in those.

I pick up my iPhone and see a text from Trenton.

Trenton: Come see me this weekend?

Me: Sure!

We've been back in school for a month, and I've only visited him once. He has been busier than he anticipated.

"Hey, girls. I'm going to Ann Arbor this weekend. Do you want to come? I think it's a home game. Jax could get us tickets."

My roommates look up from their work.

Jess's face lights up. "Hell yes, I'm in!"

Molly and Tabitha both agree to come also.

I text Trenton.

Me: My roommates are coming, too.

His reply is immediate.

Trenton: Fucking-A, Lily. I don't want to spend time with them. I only want you to come. Tell them no.

Me: I can't take back my invite. That would be rude. It will be fine. We'll have alone time. I promise.

Trenton: No, I don't want them staying here.

He can be so difficult sometimes.

Me: Okay, fine. I will text Jax and see if they can stay with him.

Trenton: Whatever, but they aren't staying here.

Me: Okay...heard ya loud and clear.

I take in a deep breath. I don't want my roommates to know that he is being such an asshole and then feel bad about coming along.

Me: I'm going to text Jax and see if he can get us tickets. Do you want me to get any for you or your friends?

Trenton: I'm a student here, too, you know. If I want to go to the football game, I will get my own damn tickets.

Me: You know what? I really don't appreciate your attitude. Maybe I will come another time.

Trenton: I'm sorry, baby. I just don't want to share you. Please come. I need you.

I sigh.

Me: Okay, I'll be there.

Trenton: Love you, baby.

Me: Love you, too.

I try to let my annoyance with Trenton go. I know he is stressed, and long-distance relationships make everything more tense.

I text Jax.

Me: We're coming down this weekend.

Jax: Awesome!

Me: Can the girls stay at your place?

Jax: Of course!

Me: Can you get us tickets to the game?

Jax: Yes!

Me: Thank you!

Jax: Anytime!

The girls are so excited for a weekend away, and to be honest, I am, too. I love Michigan's campus. It really is a gorgeous school and has such a fun environment. I've been here so much over the past four years that it feels like another home.

We stop at Jax's apartment first. We ring up and are immediately buzzed in without anyone checking to see who we are. Standing outside of his apartment door, we can hear loud music and voices coming from within. I knock a few times, but when no one comes to the door, we decide to let ourselves in.

The first thing I notice is Stella and Jax standing in the corner of the room. Their conversation seems intense. They both have stern looks on their faces as they talk adamantly.

Jerome notices us first. "Ladies!" he calls out. He makes his way over to us and gives us each a hug.

I release Jerome from my hug and notice Jax walking toward us. Jax gives each of my roommates a hug and then pulls me into him. He hugs and lifts me off the ground at the same time.

I wrap my arms around his neck to steady myself. "Good to see you, too!"

"It's so great to have you here," he says. He kisses me on the top of my head as he puts me down.

I look around the apartment. "I thought you weren't supposed to have parties the night before a game. You slacking off your senior year?"

He chuckles. "This isn't a party." He pauses for a moment. "Just a small gathering of friends who like to listen to music loudly."

I laugh.

"And we're drinking water, not beer. So, you know that in itself means this is definitely not a party."

I squint at him in question.

He laughs. "I'm serious. Everyone will be kicked out shortly, so we can get our beauty rest for tomorrow's game. Happy?"

I raise my hands in surrender. "Hey, it's not my football career on the line."

He shakes his head, smiling. "Not a party, okay?"

The girls have already started mingling.

"Thanks so much for letting the girls stay here."

"Anytime." He grabs my hand and leads me toward his bedroom.

I stop abruptly. "What are you doing?" I ask, pulling my hand from his.

He looks at me, confused. Raising his hand, he rubs the back of his neck. "I just thought we could go to my room where it isn't as loud. You know, so we can catch up and talk? I haven't seen you in forever."

"Oh, right," I answer, feeling silly. "I would love to, Jax. I really would. I just can't right now. I promised Trenton that I would come over as soon as I dropped off the girls." I lower my gaze to the ground, afraid of seeing the disappointment in his face.

But it doesn't matter because I hear it in his voice as he says, "Oh. Okay. Yeah."

"I'm sorry," I offer.

Jax waves me off. "No, I get it. No worries. I'll see you tomorrow?"

"Yes. I will be at the game, and I'm sure we can catch up after."

"Great. Well, have a good night."

"Yeah, you, too, mister. Don't party too hard." I wink.

"Not a party, Little Love. Not a party."

I laugh as I turn toward the living room. I find the girls and say good-bye. Then, I make my way back to my car. I've only been to Trenton's apartment once, and I definitely don't know how to get to it from Jax's, so I plug the address into my GPS. It turns out that Jax and Trenton live less than a mile away from each other, only a two-minute drive with all the Stop signs.

"Don't go, baby." Trenton's arm wraps around me.

We're lying side by side with my cheek resting against his chest, our legs entwined beneath the sheet.

"I have to. I would feel horrible being here when there is a home game and not going."

"First of all, you've been to many of his games. Hell, you watch the games every Saturday. You came here to see me, not him. I don't think that I'm asking too much for you to spend your only full day here with me." Trenton's voice is controlled, but I can sense he's on the verge of anger. "Listen, baby, I have missed you so much. I hate being away from you. Can we please spend the weekend together, just the two of us?"

I take in what he's said and see his point. "Okay."

"Okay?" he asks happily. "You'll stay here with me all day?"

I lay a quick kiss on his chest. "Yes, I will stay here with you all day. Happy?"

"Very."

I squeal as he grabs my waist and twists me, so I'm lying beneath him. He starts peppering rapid kisses over my face and neck, and I laugh.

"I'll only be a few minutes. I promise." Trenton chastely kisses me.

"I can come with you and keep you company," I offer again.

"No, baby. I just have to do a few boring things for school. You stay here and shower and relax. I'll be back before you know it. Then, we can pick up where we left off." He winks.

I take a long hot shower, and it feels great on my tired muscles.

I get dressed, eat a bowl of cereal, brush my teeth, and text my friends.

I check the time on my phone. Trenton has been gone for over an hour.

I run my hands along my face and sigh deeply as I plop down on the couch. Grabbing the remote, I turn on the game. I watch the kick-off and settle into the comfortable leather sofa. Time passes quickly as I watch Jax play on the big screen in front of me. I text him frequently, commenting on his great passes and plays. He won't receive the texts until later, but I've always texted him my thoughts and compliments as I watch the game. I don't want to forget to mention something about the game to him later.

Halfway through the third quarter, I hear the rustling of the door. I stay focused on the TV screen as Trenton's footsteps get closer.

"Hey, baby."

"Hi." My greeting is clipped.

He sits down next to me, pulling me into his arms. My body is stiff beneath his embrace.

"Sorry that took longer than I thought."

"Yeah, apparently."

"Aw, baby, don't be mad. I'm sorry." He leans in, giving me a kiss on the cheek. "I'm going to go take a shower, and I'll make it up to you."

I let my annoyance go. I'm sure whatever it was that Trenton had to do wasn't what he wanted to be doing. I know he'd rather be here with me. I don't want to waste our weekend together being annoyed. So, when he returns from his shower, I resume my upbeat attitude.

The rest of the weekend is wonderful. The girls have been hanging out with Ben and the Three Js, and Trenton and I haven't left his apartment. We've soaked in as much time together as we can before I have to head back.

I stop off at Jax's apartment building to pick up the girls. By the looks of them, I missed a good party last night. They all look rough. Jax walks out behind them, holding Tabitha's suitcase. Either he didn't party with them or a hangover looks really good on him because he radiates handsome perfection as always. A smile spreads across his face when he sees me. The girls fall into my car with little more than a grunted greeting toward me.

Jax meets me at the trunk and sets the suitcase inside.

I close the trunk and turn to him. "Looks like you all had a exciting evening."

He chuckles. "Yeah, I think they had fun."

"A little too much apparently."

"Maybe," he agrees with a smile.

"Good thing I didn't come out with you all. We wouldn't have anyone to drive home."

His smile fades fractionally, but he recovers. "Yeah. Well, drive safe. See you at Christmas."

"Will do."

I lean in, and he pulls me in for a hug. We separate from the hug, and he steps back from the car. I walk around to the driver's door.

Before I open it, I look back to Jax. "Bye. Love you." I give him a small smile.

"Love you more," he answers before turning.

With his hands in his pockets, he walks back to his apartment building, and I watch him go.

twenty-two

jax

"A Bloody Brain, Statutory Grape, Nuts and Berries, and a Dirty Girl Scout." Josh quickly scans the menu. "Yep, that will do it for this round."

"Don't think I'm holding your golden locks back if you spew all that shit later." Jerome shakes his head.

"That's a lot of mixing, man," Ben agrees.

"I'm good," Josh answers, not pulling his eyes away from Brittany, our waitress.

Her ample chest is displayed nicely in her shirt that is shrink-wrapped to her body.

The rest of us order a beer, and Brittany breaks away from Josh's advances to go put in our order.

Good Time Charley's, a popular local bar, is always packed, and tonight is no different. It is a rare Friday night during the fall semester when we've been able to go out. We had our last game of the season this past

Saturday, and now, we have three weeks before the bowl game at the end of December.

Several beers in, my attention is pulled from the guys when I hear my name.

"If it isn't Jax Porter," a male voice says from beside me.

I look over to my side where a typical college preppy guy stands in his designer jeans and button-up. Every time I go out, I'm approached multiple times, but it's usually by chicks who want to take a selfie with me or dudes who want to discuss the game. This guy is sporting what appears to be a scowl on his face, which is different than normal.

Great, he's probably pissed about some play I made this season. This should be fun.

"Yeah?" I answer.

"Just wanted to see you up close to see what all the fuss is about. Still don't get it." He shakes his head, narrowing his eyes at me.

"Dude, go away," Jerome pipes up.

"Gladly," he snarls. "I have no idea what she saw in you."

My irritation with this asshole is wearing thin. "What the fuck are you talking about?"

"Lily," he answers, getting my full attention.

I stand up. "What about Lily?" I ask, annoyance radiating from me.

The guy chuckles, a fake display of nonchalance. "Oh, yeah. I guess I should introduce myself. I'm Trenton, her boyfriend."

What the fuck?

My fists clench to my side, and my lips press together as I search for the words I want this asshole to hear.

All six feet four of Josh stands next to me as he speaks to Trenton, "Man, I think you need to step away—now."

Trenton holds his hands up in mock surrender. "I have no intention of fighting with you." He shakes his head, forcing out a laugh. "I don't need to fight for her. She's already mine."

"Not for long, asshole," I bark out.

"The rock I picked out for her would beg to differ. Too bad you didn't know what you had when you had her. But I'm not complaining. I loved comforting her after you broke it off. Actually, maybe I should be thanking you."

Any semblance of composure I had evaporates, and I feel my body moving toward him of its own accord. Jerome and Josh each grab one of my arms, holding me in place.

"Not worth it, man," Jerome says.

"Go away, motherfucker!" Ben yells. "You're about to have the four of us pounding your face in. You're not very fucking bright, are you?"

Trenton smirks again, backing away. The normal sounds of the crowded bar around me fades. All I hear is my deep breathing and a pounding in my ears. My arms shake beneath Josh's and Jerome's grasp.

"Keep walking," Jerome calls out.

I work to steady by breaths, my chest heaving in fury.

Trenton turns, but before he is out of earshot, he says, "Oh, one more thing. You need to move on. Stop calling her. Stop texting her. It's pathetic. She's more than satisfied with what I have to offer, and you're just embarrassing yourself."

I lunge toward him, but he turns on his heel and walks away.

"Jax! Stop!"

My name registers as I struggle to pull away from the hands binding me.

Ben steps in front of me. "Dude, so not worth it. That dick will press charges, and your career will be over. He's trying to get to you. Don't let him."

Closing my eyes, I take in some calming breaths. My arms are released, and I bring my hands up, running them through my hair. "Fuck! Fuck! Fuck!" I yell.

"Come on, man." Jerome pats me on the back. "Let's sit back down."

I fall into my seat and stare at my half-full glass of beer.

"What does she see in that asshole?" Ben asks, his question mirroring my own thoughts.

"Hey, Brit!" Josh calls. When she is in earshot, he shouts, "A round of Ninja Turtles!"

She nods and walks toward the bar.

"Ninja Turtles?" Ben asks, referring to the shots that Josh just ordered.

This place is known for their extensive shot menu.

"Fuck yeah. Heroes in a half shell," Josh answers.

"Turtle power," Jerome chimes in.

Josh smacks his hand on the table, startling me from my dark thoughts. "Yes!" he shouts, holding his fist out to Jerome, waiting for the return bump. "Great idea, J. Great idea."

"What?" Jerome asks, bumping Josh's outstretched fist, confused.

"Turtle Power," Josh says. When we all look at him with blank stares, he continues, "We need to order a round of Turtle Power."

"Which is?" I ask.

"Four Ninja Turtles stacked on top of each other for each of us."

"So, like sixteen shots," Ben clarifies.

"Well, yeah, but only four each—plus, the Ninja Turtle we already have coming." He nods his head in approval. "I think this evening really calls for some Turtle Power."

"You're an idiot," I say. But I can't stop the grin that crosses my face. "Fuck it. Why not?"

We take our Turtle shots, all five of them.

"So, in our group, who would be who?" Josh questions.

"What are you talking about?" Jerome asks.

"Who would be which turtle?" he explains. "I mean, obviously, Jax would be Donatello."

"Why's that?" I ask.

"Because you're a genius and a badass, just like Donny." Josh shrugs. "Obvious." He continues, "I would be Raphael."

Ben shakes his head, laughing. "No. If there is an obvious matchup, it is you and Michelangelo."

"I agree," I say, "You're definitely the jokester of the group. I'd go with Jerome as Raph."

"You think Jerome is the toughest?" Josh asks.

I shrug. "He's pretty tough."

Jerome places his hand on mine and looks me in the eyes. In a serious voice, he says, "Thanks, man. That means a lot."

We all laugh loudly.

"So, that would leave Ben as Leonardo," I say.

"Well, it makes sense that I would be the leader. After all, I am *the* Ben in the awesome group Ben and the Three Js."

The alcohol goes to our heads, and we order a few more shots before closing down the bar.

It was great to be out with the guys, and for once, my brain wasn't worrying about everything. It is rare that I get this smashed. I can't afford not to be at my best, and getting wasted doesn't fit into my regimen. But lately, I'm finding it hard to care.

A while ago, I decided that I was going to get Lily back when I see her over Christmas. Now, after meeting the douche who I forced her toward, I'm even more anxious to get home and make things right between us.

I have worked my whole life to be everything that my father, my coaches, and my professors want me to be. And I'm done. I'm done living my life for others. I'm done with the stress. I'm over the expectations. I couldn't give a rat's ass what others think of me. None of it fucking matters.

There is only one person in this world whose approval I need, and in a few weeks, I'm going to beg for her forgiveness. I'm going to implore her to take me back and convince her of how wrong I was. I can only hope that I'm not too late.

twenty-three

lily

I toss my bikinis, all eight of them, into my suitcase. I can't decide which ones to bring. It's not like they take much space anyway, so I opt to bring them all.

Keeley walks in, tossing a pickle wrapped in ham and cream cheese into her mouth.

"No way! Mom made my pickles?"

"Yep, and you'd better get down there before they are all gone!" she exclaims before licking her fingers.

"I still can't figure out why those things are so darn delicious."

"I know, right? But they are." Keeley walks over to my bed and visually peruses the contents of my suitcase. "So, Fiji, huh?"

I grin, looking down. "Yeah, I know. It's crazy."

"This Trenton guy must really like you."

"Yeah."

"You've been together for ten months, and he buys you a trip to Fiji for Christmas. That's just…wow. I don't know."

"I know. It seems insane, but that's how he is. He doesn't do anything small. He's taken me on tons of extravagant dates. Our first official date included a horse-drawn sleigh ride, for goodness sake."

She shakes her head, chuckling. "Well, we're all definitely excited to meet him. That's for sure."

I pick up my cell phone off my dresser and check the time. "He should be here any minute," I say excitedly.

"Do you think it's going to be weird, having Trenton and Jax sitting at the same table?" she asks, a smirk appearing on her face.

I exhale loudly. "Um…yes, very."

Trenton insisted on coming to our Christmas Eve dinner, and I agreed that it would be a good idea. I want my family to get to know him.

"But Jax is always going to be in my life. If I'm with someone else, he's going to have to be around Jax. Maybe they will hit it off and become friends?" My voice raises an octave.

Keeley lets out a dry laugh. "Maybe."

I shake out my hands at my sides. "I'm getting nervous though," I admit.

"Um, yeah," she agrees.

"So, tell me about your first semester of college, all the dirty info you didn't tell me on the phone," I suggest, needing something to take my mind off of the impending awkwardness.

She laughs. "Later. I'm thinking we should chat downstairs and help Mom."

"Oh, yeah. Good idea. Plus, I need to chow on some pickles right about now."

"If there are any left." Keeley starts toward my door.

We make our way downstairs and see Mom, Amy, and Susie in the kitchen, organizing dishes of food on the bar. Our dads, Landon, and Jax are sitting in the living room, talking. Jax's face lights up when he sees me, and he stands before shortening the distance between us.

He pulls me into a big hug. "Little Love." He plants a big kiss on my forehead. "I've missed you."

"I've missed you, too." I hug him tight, taking in all that is Jax.

"So, the boyfriend's coming, huh?" he asks with a hint of something representing anger in his voice.

"Yep." I smack my lips. "The boyfriend's coming."

"This should be fun," he deadpans.

"It's going to be something. Not sure if *fun* is the operative word." I release my grip from around his neck and pull away from our embrace.

"Lily," my mom calls from the kitchen.

I walk over to her.

"Honey, do you know when Trenton is going to be arriving?"

I scan the full spread of steaming dishes lining the bar.

"He should be here already, Mom. But let's just go ahead and get started. He'll understand."

"Are you sure? We can wait a little longer."

My mom is too sweet, but having everyone eat cold food because one person is late would be silly.

"No, really. Let's eat." Grabbing my phone, I type out a quick text to Trenton, asking where he is.

My mom nods and calls everyone in to eat. We fill our plates and take a seat at our large dining room table. Jax sits to my right, and the seat to my left is empty.

"It's been a while since we've all been together," my dad says.

My mom nods in agreement. "Yes, it has. This is great. Everyone, raise your glass for a toast."

I take my glass of wine, lifting it from the table, and hold it out in front of me.

My mom continues, "This has been a wonderful year full of many blessings. We are so grateful that everyone could make it home to celebrate with us. We have the best family anyone could ask for. To family."

"To family," we all say in unison before taking a drink of our wine.

"So, Landon, what's your new project at work?" Mr. Porter asks his eldest son.

Landon begins talking about his work projects, and my phone buzzes from my back pocket. I remove it and see a text from Trenton.

> Trenton: Hey, baby. Not going to make it tonight. Sorry. Something came up. I'll see you at the airport. I hope you have a wonderful Christmas with your family, and I look forward to showering you with my gifts many times while we're away. ;-) I love you.

I read his text a few times. When I look up, everyone's eyes are on me.

I clear my throat. "Oh. That was Trenton. He can't make it. Something came up." I look down at my phone and click the top button, making the screen go black, before sliding it into my back pocket.

"Oh. Well, that's too bad. Hope everything is okay. We look forward to meeting him another time." My mom's lips turn up in a reassuring grin.

Everyone gives me sympathetic smiles, and the side conversations around the table resume.

"Bummer," Jax whispers into my ear.

I can't stop the smile that spreads across my face.

"Stop," I whisper, bumping my knee into his under the table.

He takes his leg and bumps mine back. He leaves his leg against mine, and the contact makes my heart beat faster. He leans closer, his lips an exhale away from my ear. His warm breath tickles the delicate skin on my lobe. I run my hands over my jeans, down my thighs. I hold on to my knees that are quivering underneath the crimson tablecloth.

He whispers in my ear, "So, Little, would you rather I lick you till you come or fuck you till you come?"

I gasp, sucking the moisture in my mouth into my windpipe, and I start coughing. My eyes water as I take a drink of my water.

"You okay, Lil?" my mom asks from across the table.

Clearing my throat, I cough out, "Wrong pipe," and give her a thumbs-up, letting her know I'm fine.

Jax's hand rubs across my back. His fingers stealthily work beneath my bra strap through my thin sweater.

"Stop," I say under my breath.

He leans in again. My eyes dart around the table, and I exhale a sigh of relief when I see everyone is involved in their own conversations.

"But you haven't answered the question." His husky whisper vibrates through my ear.

Stop, I mouth, my eyes widening in warning.

His paralyzing whispers continue, "Okay. Would you rather spend your time with the love of your life or a stuck-up douche bag?"

What the hell? Where is all of this coming from?

"Please stop. You're being mean. This isn't the time or place for this conversation." My eyes begin to water. I stand and quietly address the table in the cheeriest voice I can muster, "Excuse me. I have to use the bathroom." I turn and force my body to casually walk up the stairs toward my bathroom.

I close my bathroom door behind me and grip the counter before me. I breathe in deeply, focusing on getting air into my lungs and calming the sensation of blood pounding beneath my skull.

What in the hell is going on tonight?

My head jerks up when there is a soft knock at my door. I cautiously swing it open to find Jax standing there, his hands in his pockets. At least he is attempting to appear remorseful.

"Lily."

"No," I say in a hushed tone. "I don't know what crap you are trying to pull down there, but it is not okay."

"Listen," he says gently.

"No, I'm not going to listen to you. You obviously have some things you want to get off your chest, but you are choosing a horrible time to talk about it. We are not going to argue upstairs on Christmas Eve when our families are sitting downstairs." I hold four fingers of both hands up to my temples and rub in a circular motion. "You are making me insane right now. Go." I wave toward the door.

"I want to talk—"

I cut him off, "Yeah, I get that. But not right now." I suck in a calming breath. "I will talk to you in private after dinner. We don't do drama, Jax Porter. Knock it off." I purse my lips and glare toward his beautiful face that is struggling not to laugh.

His eyes shine with humor. "So, you want to talk later then?"

"Go." I hold out my arm, directing my finger toward the door.

He chuckles. "I'm going. I'm going." He turns to leave, but he quickly spins back around and plants a kiss on my cheek. "I love feisty Lily."

"Jax," I warn.

He raises his hands in surrender and backs out of my room with an adorable smirk on his face. I hear his steps retreating down the stairs.

I take a minute to compose myself before returning to the dinner table with a smile that radiates calmness and normalcy—or at least I hope that's what my face is showing. I've never been much of an actress.

The rest of dinner goes somewhat normally, and I'm grateful. I immerse myself in everyone else's conversations, asking lots of questions. I figure if someone else is always talking to me, then Jax won't have an opportunity to use his voodoo husky whisper voice to get me all worked up.

After we clear the table of our dessert dishes, Amy gets out the Left, Center, Right dice game. We all refill our wine glasses and each toss ten dollars into the center of the table. The dice game is so simple and very fun. There is lots of cheering and yelling as we pass our chips around the table.

We lose, gain, and pass chips for about twenty minutes until Jax and I are the last two with chips. I roll my last dice, and it lands on Center, forcing me to throw my last chip in the pot.

"Ah, man!" I complain.

Jax hollers next to me, "Winner, winner, chicken dinner!" He reaches for the ninety dollars in the center of the table. He does his money dance, which is a combination of the moonwalk and the "Stayin' Alive" finger-pointing gestures.

"Boo!" we yell obnoxiously through our laughter.

"Stick to football, man!" Landon hits Jax on the back, shaking his head in laughter.

"Hey, he's actually a great dancer when he wants to be," I say, smiling at Jax. My internal need to be Jax's biggest supporter shines through.

He stops his comic show of movement and stands looking at me, studying me, remembering. All the times I've danced with Jax through the years flash through my mind like a black-and-white movie. Still shots of us dancing rapidly pass through my brain. I take them in, each little detail—from our expressions as we stare into each other's eyes to the way his hands held my body with reverence, like I was precious, to our smiles radiating pure love and joy.

Shaking the thoughts from my head, I give Jax a sad smile and walk past him to the kitchen where I make myself useful and help my mom clean up.

When Jax's family has left and my family has retired to their rooms, Jax and I head downstairs to the den.

He takes my hand in his. "I'm sorry."

"You should be," I answer.

"I don't want to fight."

I sigh. "Me neither."

"Dance with me?"

"Jax." I shake my head.

"It's just a dance, Little. Innocent."

I cock out my hip, placing my hand on my waist. "You. Innocent?"

"I promise. Just dance with me."

"Okay."

Jax takes his phone out of his pocket and scrolls through his music. Picking a song, he turns his speaker volume up and places the phone on the table. A familiar melody permeates the room, and my eyes fill with tears.

"Jax." My voice breaks as my lip trembles.

I shake my head as Jax pulls me into him, securing his hold around me. His voice is filled with so much emotion as he begins to sing quietly against my cheek, his face bent down to mine, "Wise men say, only fools rush in..."

Tears course down my face as the melody to our life surrounds us, sending so many emotions rushing through me. My body moves against Jax on instinct and memory. Amazing memories saturate my mind. I think of a boy and a girl who spent seventeen years of their lives falling in love and not just ordinary love but a beautiful kind of love. This kind is unique. It's special. It's a love that gives, a love that sacrifices, a love that cherishes. It is never taken for granted, and it is never to be duplicated. But unfortunately, this love can be lost but not forgotten. It's just missing under layers of uncertainty and fear.

Jax's heart beats against his chest, a painful rhythm that matches my own. His breath hovers over my sensitive skin as he sings softly to the music. Elvis's deep voice permeates the air around us, and for the first time in my life, it sounds sad. This song has always been so beautiful to me, a man confessing his unwavering love for a woman. But tonight, his voice sounds pained, like the voice of a man whose heart is broken. It's surreal how something I've seen the same way my whole life can all of a sudden change to mean something drastically different.

The song ends, and I pull away from Jax. The room is silent now, except for the quiet echoes of our deep breaths. I stare into his eyes, my own wide with confusion. Bringing his hand up to my face, he wipes a tear-soaked strand of hair off my cheek and places it behind my ear.

"I want to be together again, Lily."

I swallow. "Why now?" I ask, my voice coming out quiet, tentative.

"Because I can't stand not being with you any longer. Because you are the love of my life. Because it's time." His dark green eyes shine with moisture from the contained emotions he must be feeling, too.

I shake my head. "I don't understand. Why is now the time, but last fall, when you broke my heart, it wasn't the time?"

"Lily, I know you don't understand my reasoning, and fuck, I don't know if I understand it myself, but in my mind, at the time, I thought I was doing the right thing. I was stressed, just wiped. I had nothing else to give. I was putting everything I had into school and football, and it wasn't enough. I was never enough. I was angry and bitter. I wanted to be better. You don't know what I was like because I tried to hide it from you, but I was miserable. I was mad all the time—at my dad, at my coaches, at myself. I was fading, and I didn't want to bring you down with me. I wasn't in a good place, and I didn't want to drag you down. Don't you see that I did what I did because I love you?"

"No. I don't know." I lift my hands and run them through my hair. I let out a frustrated groan. "No, I don't understand it, Jax. I get that you were stressed, but why would you want to push away the person in this world who loves and supports you the most? I would do anything for you. You know that. I would have helped. I would have understood. Why didn't you let me in?" I plead.

"Because I was protecting you! I wanted you to be happy. I wanted you to enjoy your time at Central, to have a life of your own, to reach your potential and discover your dreams. You couldn't have done all of that if I was dragging you down."

"You make me happy! Being with you makes me happy! You could never drag me down, Jax. You don't understand how love works. I didn't want you to go through your struggles on your own. I wanted to be there for you because I loved you, and helping you, loving you, supporting you...made me happy. You made me happy."

I find myself struggling with talking in present versus past tense. Even now, as friends, Jax makes me happy. He has never been my past tense. He's always been my present, regardless of the manner in which he participates. But I feel like talking about my love for him in the present tense would not only be unfair to Trenton, but it would also confuse things with Jax.

I sigh. "So, what? You're not stressed anymore? I don't get it."

"No, I'm not in the clear yet, but it's getting better. I have the bowl game next week, which is my last football game ever. I have one more semester of school, and then I'm done. This last semester will be a lighter load than the rest. It's all manageable now. Plus, I feel like I'm losing you. I can't lose you."

"Jax, I've been dating Trenton for almost a year. We're going away together in a day. What do you want me to do?"

"I want you to break up with him. I want you to come back to me."

I press my lips together as a sad tear trails down my face. I slightly shake my head, dropping my gaze to the floor. "It doesn't work like that."

Jax grabs my hands in his, forcing my gaze to meet his once more. "Why not?"

I shake my hands from his, the physical touch too much. "Because it doesn't! I can't just drop Trenton like he means nothing. He has done nothing wrong. He doesn't deserve this. He has been there for me this year when you weren't. He has loved me when you didn't."

An emotion close to anger passes through Jax's eyes. "I have never stopped loving you," he says firmly.

"But you left me, Jax. You left me. You broke my heart and left me wondering why I wasn't enough for you. Now, I've moved on, and you suddenly decide that you want me back now. You expect me to drop everything and run back to you because you have determined that now is a good time for you? I love you. You know that. I will always love you, but I can't."

"Lily, please…"

The hurt in his voice causes me physical pain. I take the palm of my hand and rub it against my chest, trying to alleviate the pressure. "No. You hurt me. So much. You were the person who was supposed to protect and love me forever, and you hurt me. Pain like that isn't just forgotten. It doesn't just go away because you're jealous that I've found happiness with someone else."

Jax forcefully runs his hands through his hair, grabbing handfuls. "Ah! You aren't listening to me. I let you go *because* I love you, *because* I was protecting you."

"Well, I'm sorry. I'm sure you feel that is the case, but that's not how it felt to me. I felt broken, abandoned, and alone. I fought my way through the depression and found happiness within myself. Then, Trenton came along and brought more joy to my life. I don't know what is going to happen with him and me. I'm not sure if what we have is something that will last forever. It's too soon for me to tell, and I'm still so confused. But I'm going to see where it leads. I have to. I owe it to myself and to him to see this out."

"No, you don't!" Jax clenches his fists at his sides. "Listen to you. Listen to what you are saying. It doesn't make any sense." He stops and takes a deep breath, composing himself. "Did I do the right thing in taking a break from us last year? I don't know. Apparently, in your mind...no. But I still feel it was the right thing to do."

I open my mouth to speak, but he holds a hand up and continues, "Lily, I love you more than anything else in this world. You are my love, my beautiful love. There will never be another woman in this world who is more perfect for me than you. I would do anything for you even if it killed me. Not being together for over a year now has been torture for me, but I did it because I feel, with every cell of my body, that it was what was right for you. Maybe you disagree, but I had to do what I felt was right. I loved you too much to drag you down with me. I had to get to a place where I had enough light in my life that I wouldn't dim your light with my darkness."

I shake my head, trying to process his words, but I still don't understand. "Jax"—my voice breaks—"I don't know what you mean. You've never had darkness. You've always been happy and great at everything. You were the same you when I went to see you last fall."

"Being great at everything comes with a price, Lily. In high school, it was easy to be the best. I had less competition. Out in the real world, it's not so easy. In fact, it's really fucking hard. Giving more of myself to everything else left nothing for me to give to you. I fought it for a long time. For your sake, I pretended that everything was great. But even the pretending became too much, took more energy than I had. I did the only thing left I could do. I let you go. It wasn't going to be forever. It was just supposed to be until I could finish the commitments I made and get to a happier place, a place worthy of your presence. I couldn't ask you to wait for me." His voice drips with sadness. "But I thought you would."

All the energy has drained from my body. I'm physically and mentally exhausted. "You should have told me all of this. You should have been clearer. You should have let me in."

"I'm sorry."

"It's too late, Jax. Don't you see that?" My tone is angry, causing the words to sound harsher than I intended.

He adamantly shakes his head. "It's not too late. It will never be too late for us. We all have choices to make, Lily. Sometimes, we make the right ones, and sometimes, we don't. But you have a choice." He pauses. "Every choice you make in this life has a consequence, and regardless of what you choose…you need to be prepared for the effect it will have on your life." His voice gets quiet. "Believe me, I know."

My voice cracks, and tears continue to fall. "I can't. Not right now."

His shoulders fall and he lets out an audible exhale. "Then, I can't either."

I look to him in question.

"I need time, Lily. I can't do the friends thing with you anymore, not right now. It hurts too much. It kills me to stand by while you share the most intimate parts of yourself with another man. I don't blame you. I don't. I know it is my fault that all of this is happening. I wish I could fix it all and turn everything back to the way it was."

My body shakes with sobs as I take in his words.

He continues, "I will always be here for you, Lily. And if you don't find your way back to me, I will learn to accept it. You're not losing me forever. I just need time. I need time to figure out how to live in a world where you aren't mine."

"I'm so sorry," I choke out.

Jax pulls me into his arms, and I sob into his chest. As I lay my tear-soaked face against him, I can hear the pounding of his broken heart. He continues to hold me, and no more words are spoken as the air around us saturates with grief.

When no more tears will come and my heartache has drowned me in exhaustion, Jax pulls away. Leaning in, he kisses me on the forehead. His lips linger for several heartbeats until he pulls away.

"Be happy, Little Love." He turns and walks away.

"Jax!" I call before he ascends the stairs.

He turns to face me.

"I love you."

A sad smile graces his pained face. "Love you more." With that phrase that he has said to me thousands of times, he walks up the stairs and out of my life.

twenty-four

jax

It's the Saturday before my final semester of college. I've played my last televised football game ever. I'm getting ready to finish up my degree with the lightest load of classes I've ever had. I should be celebrating. This is the moment I've been waiting for. I can see the finish line, and it is a few easy steps away.

But none of it matters without Lily. Not a damn fucking thing.

I should be holding Lily in my arms right now. I should be hugging her, kissing her, and making love to her again and again.

But I'm not, and maybe I never will again.

A myriad of emotions flashes through me before devastation settles down in my core, drowning me in sorrow.

I might have lost her forever...and for what?

My football career is over. *Am I a better, more fulfilled person because of it? Hardly.*

Over Christmas break, I broke the news to my father that I would not be going into the draft. I have no intention of playing professional ball. He screamed at me for hours, trying to change my mind, but I wouldn't budge. I am no longer living the life he deems important. He's currently not speaking to me. But he'll get over it...or he won't. I can't find it in me to care either way.

I've maintained my 4.0 thus far. I have met some influential connections in the business world, and I have job offers coming in already. *But what will a great job bring me if I don't have Lily? Not a damn thing.*

I briefly let my mind wander to dark places where it shouldn't go. I wonder if Lily had fun in Fiji. *Did douche face propose during a tropical sunset on the beach? Did Lily say yes? Are they back yet? Is she thinking about me? Will I ever kiss her again?*

"Fuck!" I yell, throwing an empty beer bottle across the room. I watch it shatter against the wall.

I faintly register a noise behind me.

"Oh my God...Jax. What's going on?" Stella walks around the couch to where I'm sitting in my boxers, unshaven, too many bottles of beer in to count.

"Jax." Her voice is soft as she bends down, getting eye-level with me. "Hey." She reaches up and rubs my scruffy cheek with the palm of her hand.

I lean into her hand. She smells so good.

"I knocked. You must not have heard me. I hope you don't mind that I came in. I heard something break. Your door was unlocked," she explains. "Tell me. Did something happen over break. Are you okay?" She looks around. "Where are the guys?"

My throat is dry. My voice comes out in a hoarse whisper as I say, "Out. Home. I don't know."

"Come on," she pleads, gently holding out her hand.

I place my hand in hers as she helps to pull me up.

Her thumb caresses the top my hand. "You need a shower. It will help you feel better." She scans the room. "I'll just clean up a bit out here."

She releases my hand, and I walk, void of emotion, to the bathroom.

The scalding shower feels good. I stand under the hot stream, hoping it will carry the last year of regrets down the drain with it.

After my shower, I put on a pair of boxers, track pants, and a T-shirt. The least I can do for my guest is get dressed. There is a soft knock on my door.

"Come in," I call out.

Stella walks in with a glass of water and two white pills. "Here. These will make you feel better." She places the medicine in my hand. "Also, I think it might be time to switch to water."

We sit side by side on my bed.

"Do you want to talk about it?" Her soft voice is comforting.

"There's not much to talk about, Stell. I've lost her," I reply, defeated.

"You don't know that."

I expel a long breath. "No, I think I do." I pause, staring down at my hands. "I'm just so damn tired of it all. Do you know what I mean?" My voice cracks. I raise my head to find her kind gaze locked on me.

"Yeah, I do." She nods. She scoots back on my bed and lies down, patting the spot next to her. "Come here."

I questioningly look at her.

She grins. "I won't take advantage of you. I promise. Just come lie down."

I pause for a moment before lying down next to her. I turn in toward her, and she sprawls her arm out under my neck. I lay my head on the flat soft part between her shoulder and collarbone. She wraps her arm around my back and melodically drags her fingers up and down my arm.

We lie in silence. I close my eyes and let her soft touch soothe me. It has been so long since another person's touch has comforted me, and I didn't realize how much I missed it. Her rhythmic heartbeat thumps beneath her chest, a comforting lullaby.

I fall asleep to visions of sun-kissed skin, tiny little freckles, plump smiling lips, and bright blue eyes. I let the warmth of these visions pull me under, hoping they will stay dreams but afraid that they'll morph into a nightmare.

twenty-five

three months later

lily

I lie on my back and stare at the ceiling. I'm trying to find an imperfection in it somewhere, but so far, I haven't been able to. Of course the Troys would hire a painter so good that his work is flawless.

In my bedroom at home, there is a patch about half a foot by two feet on the ceiling that somehow wasn't painted. I'm not sure how a spot that big could have been missed, but it was. It is a yellowish-cream color compared to the white ceiling around it. It was probably the original color of the ceiling, yellowing slightly through the years. I haven't told my mom about the patch because she would insist on fixing it, but I like it. Depending on the lighting and angle, it can look like different things—a submarine, a hammock, a skateboard, and at a very precise angle that I can't always find, a person diving into water.

I can't explain why I love that little imperfection on my ceiling, but I do. Somehow, in a weird way, it brings me comfort. I love how the same thing can be seen in many different ways simply by minutely changing the manner in which it is looked at. Life is the same way. The same thing can be seen in many different ways by many different people, depending on how they are looking at it. In actuality, people see things in life in multiple lights, their viewpoints varying with their moods.

I've always tried to look at life through rose-colored glasses and see the positive in everything. I lost that mentality for a few months last year, but I got it back. I still don't know if Jax and I being apart is the right thing, but I don't regret it. I have learned so much about myself and had so many great experiences over the past year and a half that I might not have had if I'd been with Jax. A moment in time where one learns something is never something to regret, and I've learned a lot.

Feeling a chill, I wrap Trenton's blanket up around my bare shoulders. He is breathing steadily next to me. His breaths are a melodic rhythm that should have lulled me back to sleep, but instead, I find myself focusing on and comparing the different breathy sounds coming from his mouth.

Instead of falling back to sleep on this Sunday morning, I scan his bedroom, looking for some imperfection. I'm having a hard time locating one though, and I don't like it. It's hard to trust something that appears to be perfect because nothing and no one is. When people carry themselves with an air of perfection, I don't usually stick around. Those pretending to be the most perfect are the ones who have the most to hide. They are the type of people who can ruin lives with their hidden darkness, but nothing can stay hidden forever.

I let out a sigh and quietly climb out of bed. I make my way to Trenton's guest shower, so I don't wake him. I can't place the source of my unease, but I've been feeling my share of apprehension lately.

I'm probably still annoyed over our dinner with the Troys yesterday. I never leave them feeling more optimistic about the world around me. His parents, especially his mother, are certified joy killers. After a year, I would think that his mother would have warmed to me by now, but she hasn't. She still talks over me, ignores me, and basically treats me like Trenton's inconvenient little sidekick, but it's all done with a smile on her face. Trenton doesn't seem to notice it, and the few times I've brought it up, he has reassured me that his parents love me and that it's my own insecurities coming out. I'm not making it up. That's for sure. He just probably doesn't see it because he's been around that behavior his whole life.

I won't fail to mention that I spent the entire evening at the Troys' home without finding a flaw. There wasn't a chip or dent in any of the walls, and not a dust bunny could be found in any of the corners. It was a home straight out of a magazine, a picture of airbrushed perfection.

Coincidence? I think not.

I could still be jet-lagged, too. That's a real possibility. Trenton took me, Jess, Tabitha, and Molly to Las Vegas for spring break. I was surprised that he insisted on paying for my roommates to go, but he reassured me that he did it simply because he thought it would make me happy to have them there.

We spent six days in Vegas. Anyone who has ever been to Vegas knows that is a very long time to be there. Vegas is extremely fun and even more exhausting. We stayed up partying, dancing, and gambling until four or five in the morning every day, which is the equivalent of not going to sleep until seven or eight in the morning Michigan time. The trip wiped me out.

As soon as we got back yesterday, we went to Trenton's parents' house. So, it makes sense that my exhaustion is off the charts, but unfortunately, my mind is working on overtime.

I stay in the hot shower, enjoying the feel of the jetted water massaging my skin, until my fingers start to resemble raisins. I put on one of the robes that Trenton has in the closet of the guest bedroom instead of retrieving my clothes from his room. *Someone should be able to sleep in this morning.*

I make my way downstairs to the kitchen and plop a K-Cup into the Keurig. Spotting my phone on the kitchen island, I grab it and my steaming cup of goodness, and I get comfortable on the couch.

Before I slide my thumb across the screen to unlock my phone, I close my eyes, hoping that there will be a message, a missed call, or something from Jax. When my eyes find the screen, I'm not surprised that there isn't. Jax hasn't contacted me since he left my house in December. After he poured his soul out to me and begged for me back, I don't blame him. Some days, I'm mad at myself, too. But I miss him.

I promised myself that I would give him this time to find his new normal. However, I'm only going to give him another couple of months. There is giving him time to process, and then there is insanity. Continuing on this path of non-communication for longer than six months falls into the insanity category. So, I'll give him until June to contact me, or I will be contacting him.

Seeing no messages, I flip through the shared Vegas photo thread where the five of us put all our photos from this past week. I haven't had a moment to really look at each one. There are a lot of great shots and even more hilarious shots. I laugh out loud, looking at some of the photos I don't even remember us taking. In fact, I'm staring at a picture of us now, and I have no idea where we were—some club apparently. It is fun to watch the progression of our eyes. The photos taken at the beginning of each night capture us with enthusiastic expressions, our eyes wide open. As the night progresses and turns into morning, our eyes begin to squint, our drunken lids too heavy to hold open.

Each late-night photo session includes pictures of Tabitha hanging all over random men. There are also several photos of her with her eye openings as mere slits while she's draped all over Trenton. She is something else.

I laugh out loud again.

"What's so funny?" Trenton's voice, still full of sleep, asks from behind me.

"Hey. Morning. Hope I didn't wake you. I was just looking at our photos from Vegas. Look at this one." I hand my phone to Trenton. "I don't think Tabitha knew who she was hanging all over. She can't even keep her eyes open."

"Too funny," he says with little conviction, his voice still sounding tired. "I feel like death. I'm going to go take a shower."

"Okay. Yeah, getting your body back on Michigan time is no fun."

"No, definitely not." He hands me my phone. "Hey, baby. After I get out of the shower, let's go get some breakfast, and then I'm going to head back to school. I have a few assignments to finish up before class tomorrow."

"Okay, sounds good." I'm looking forward to going back to my apartment and taking a long nap. Luckily, I don't have anything due tomorrow. My last semester of classes has been a breeze.

Trenton retreats to the bedroom, and I decide I should get dressed, so I will be ready to go when he gets out. Once in his bedroom, I locate all my clothes, except for my bra. I've lost many pairs of underwear over here, which is never a big deal. I can go commando until I get home to get new ones. But going without a bra, especially when we are going to a restaurant, is not going to fly.

Trenton removed my clothes from me last night when we got back from his parents' house. I'm sure he threw it somewhere in his hasty mission to get off my clothing. *But where?* I scan the room.

Getting on my hands and knees, I peer under the bed. Turning on my flashlight app from my phone, I shine it under the bed. I don't see it, but I stop when I see the blue Tiffany bag all the way back in the corner.

Holy crap.

I debate on what I should do. I know I should leave it. It's not my place to go digging packages out from under his bed. This isn't my house. But the curiosity is killing me. It is the only thing under his bed. Of course, a house with perfect everything wouldn't have anything haphazardly out of place under the bed. Because the area under the bed is so clean, the bright bag almost shines, like a lighthouse calling me in from sea. I have to look. If it was thrown about among some other stuff—like random shoeboxes, stray socks, or the occasional food wrapper—maybe I wouldn't be so compelled to look. But it is the only thing under the bed. *How can I not look?*

Listening for a moment, I hear the shower running in the bathroom. I quickly do my version of the Army crawl

300

under the bed until I'm far enough in to reach the package. I grab it and slither back out.

Sitting up on my knees, I open the bag and reach in for the small Tiffany's box. Inside the box is another box, and it isn't just an ordinary box. It's a ring box. My heart begins to beat faster, and my hands feel clammy. *A promise ring maybe?*

I take a deep breath and flip the box open. I gasp when I see the ring inside. It's not a promise ring. That's for sure. I'm one hundred percent sure that I'm staring at an engagement ring. Sitting atop a platinum band that is adorned with shiny diamonds is a very large—at minimum, two carat—cushion-cut diamond.

Crap. Crap. Crap.

The ring is breathtaking. It is absolutely gorgeous. In fact, it's perfect, and that thought makes me feel as if I'm going to be ill. I hear the shower shut off, and I snap the lid of the ring box closed, tossing it in the bag before putting it back exactly where I found it.

Screw my bra.

I throw on my shirt and exit Trenton's room like it's on fire. Sitting on the living room couch, I try to make sense of what I just saw. *Trenton has a freaking engagement ring under his bed. Trenton is planning on proposing. Holy crap.*

I did not see this coming. I hope he plans on waiting—at least until I can come up with a way out of this that won't break his heart, but I won't end up with the ring on my finger either.

A few minutes later, Trenton comes into the living room. "Missing this?" he asks, holding my bra up by a finger.

"Oh, thanks," I answer on autopilot. "I couldn't find it," I say as I take my bra from him.

"You okay?" he asks, concern etching his brow.

"Yeah, I'm fine. Just tired." I smile weakly.

"Yeah, spring break will do that to you. Let's go get some food, and then when I leave, you can go back and take a nap."

He reaches his hand down to me, and I grab it, letting him pull me off of the couch.

A nap is exactly what I have planned, but waking up in my bed right about now and realizing that this was all a dream sounds even better.

Unfortunately, as we exit Trenton's place, I pinch my arm, and it stings.

twenty-six

The weighted down green bags pull at my skin as I carry them up to Trenton's front door.

I went shopping for ingredients to make chicken fettuccini and homemade double chocolate brownies. It isn't his favorite meal, but it is his favorite from the meals I'm capable of making. I also splurged to pick up one of his favorite wines, which cost me over a hundred dollars. He told me he would be back in town later tonight. He's supposed to give me a call when he gets back. But I decided I would be here to surprise him with a yummy dinner and dessert. I can't wait to see him. I've missed him.

We had our graduation ceremony yesterday. I'm officially a graduate! Trenton needed some time to wrap things up after his last exam on Friday, so he wasn't able to make it back for the ceremony.

I'm looking forward to spending another great summer with him. He has asked me to stay with him this summer until he has to go back to school. I'm not sure if I will stay the entire summer, but I'll stay for May and June for sure. I'm thinking by July, I should be on my way to having a job. A two-month hiatus after graduation seems sufficient. Any more than that, and I might be entering the slacker realm. *Maybe I can find some local work?*

I'm not sure if I'm going to address it tonight, but I have to bring up marriage. I don't know when he is planning on proposing, but I'm assuming it is going to be soon since he has the ring. I can't risk him proposing, especially considering the fallout when I tell him no. It will be much easier if I can casually slip the fact that I'm not close to being ready to get engaged into one of our chats. I still haven't figured out how exactly I'm going to fit that into a conversation and make it seem natural, but I'm hoping the right time will present itself.

I don't know when I'm going to be ready to be engaged, but I'm positive that now is not the right time. I love Trenton. *But is it forever love? Not too sure on that one.*

A part of me is still so confused over my feelings for Jax. Without a doubt, I know that I will love Jax Porter for the rest of my life. *But in what capacity?* Currently, I think that I still have the type of feelings for him that I shouldn't when I'm in a relationship with another man. But it's proven impossible to let go of Jax completely. I haven't been able to, and I'm not sure if I ever will.

Is it fair to marry someone else when I'm still in love with Jax? Of course not. But what if my feelings for Jax never diminish? Or do I just continue on with my life and push my feelings down?

It is only normal that I still have such strong feelings for Jax. I have loved him my whole life. That isn't likely to go away anytime soon.

I shake my head and clear out thoughts of Jax. Tonight is about Trenton and welcoming him home for the summer.

I just need to conquer one thing at a time, and first on the agenda is chicken fettuccini. I unlock the front door and close it behind me. After kicking off my shoes, I carry the cloth grocery bags into the kitchen and drop them on the counter. My arms immediately feel relieved with the weight is gone.

I start unloading the bags, and a knocking sound startles me. I look around, listening. The noise isn't coming from the front door. The sound gets louder, and I jump, bringing my hand to my chest when I hear a scream. I look up to the ceiling, toward the direction of the sound.

The screaming comes again, but this time, it is more of a moan.

No. No. No. No. I put my hands over my ears and shake my head, blocking out the sounds of pleasure coming from upstairs. *It can't be. It's not him. He wouldn't.*

I want to run. I want to leave, but I have to know. I take a deep breath. I feel the rapid rhythm of my heart pounding against my chest. I exhale again, deeply, and shake my hands out to my sides.

I have to do this.

I start walking quietly up the stairs until I'm standing outside his bedroom door.

Now, I can hear a male voice coming from behind the door.

"Fuck! So good. You're always so good. Fuck. Yes! Just like that."

A tear escapes and trails down my cheek. It's not just a male voice. It's Trenton's.

I turn to walk away, but I have to see it. There can't be any doubt in my mind. I need proof that the man who claims to love me and is planning on proposing is betraying me. I need to be smacked in the face with the reality because I'm finding it hard to believe it as I stand here.

I turn back toward the bedroom door and gently push it open. My mouth falls open, and my hands cover it as I gasp. Solid streams of tears leave my eyes and pour down my face. The moans, grunts, and lust-filled words continue in the bedroom as the couple in the bed is unaware of my presence. I try to turn away. I want to run. But I'm frozen to this spot. I'm so shocked that my brain can't function enough to tell my legs to move.

My heart is overcome with sadness. I've never felt like this. I've never experienced such utter betrayal, and it hurts. It burns. The pain is the most intense in my chest as my heart breaks into a thousand pieces. Although broken, my heart continues to work, pumping the immense pain throughout my body. I continue to stand and stare at the couple as I'm crippled with agony, wanting to leave but not able to.

Trenton thrusts into her at a feverish pace before finding his release, yelling into the air. He collapses on her, both of their bodies glistening with sweat.

"Fuck, I love your cunt. I fucking love it, Tabitha," he says.

"I love your cock. I crave it. I will never get enough. We have time for a few more rounds before I have to go," she says, her voice deep with lust.

I stand in the doorway, broken. My hands still covering my mouth as the tears continue to cascade down my face.

Trenton kisses Tabitha on the mouth and turns to grab a towel lying on the nightstand. He stops, and his eyes go wide as he notices me. The eye contact is what startles me, breaking my trance, and I turn and run down the steps.

"Wait, baby! Wait! I can explain!" Trenton calls after me.

I pass the kitchen island and grab the bottle of wine that I bought for Trenton. I turn toward him. He is on the bottom step. He looks like a wild man. His hair is disheveled, and his eyes are wide as he holds the towel around his waist.

"Wait. Please let me explain," he pleads.

I chuck the bottle of wine with all my strength. His eyes bulge before he shields his face as the red wine and glass shards explode against the wall next to his head. He jumps to the side, startled.

"Fuck you, Trenton Troy. Don't you ever contact me again, you fucking piece of shit."

I run around the kitchen island and into the foyer. I slide into my shoes and grab my purse before running out the front door. I don't look back as I peel out of his driveway.

I pull off to the side of the street once I get a good distance away from his house. I lay my head against my arms resting on the steering wheel, and I sob. I sit in my car, crying, until my body is exhausted, and no more tears will come.

I text Jess.

Me: Is Tabitha at the apartment?

Jess: No.

Me: Can you text her and tell her not to come back to the apartment for a few hours? Please?

Jess: Sure. What's going on?

Me: I'll tell you when I get there.

Jess gasps when she sees my tear-streaked puffy face. "What's wrong?"

I don't have the energy to talk about it, but I tell her anyway. She deserves to know why I'm leaving. I let her know everything, every disgusting detail. She covers her mouth and slowly shakes her head as I talk.

"Oh my God. I can't believe this, Lily. I'm so sorry. I can't believe Tabitha would do that to you."

"I know. Me neither," I say sadly. "I can't stay here, Jess. I'm sorry. I have to go home."

She nods. "I understand. I wish Tabitha would leave though."

"Yeah, well, knowing her, she won't. She apparently only cares about herself." My tone softens as I ask, "Can you help me pack up my car really quick?"

"Of course."

We pack everything I can fit into my car. I don't have room for any of the furniture I brought, but I don't need that stuff right now anyway. I might have my parents come help me bring it home later this summer. Or maybe I won't. I'm not sure yet. But I have everything that matters—my clothes, pictures, and other personal items—all packed in my car, ready to go.

"I wish you didn't have to leave, especially like this," Jess says sadly.

"I know. Me neither. You know you are welcome to visit anytime. My mom loves company. You can stay with us for as long as you want."

"Thanks. I'll remember that." She pulls me into a hug. "I love you."

"Love you, too. Can you please tell Molly what happened and why I had to leave? Can you tell her good-bye for me?"

"Yeah, will do."

I get into my car and begin the drive home. I'm leaving Mount Pleasant with much different emotions than I came here with two years ago. I idly wonder if I will ever be back here. If I opt to leave my furniture, I will never have a reason to come back. This place where I've spent two years making great memories, where the course of my life changed dramatically, will only be a distant memory. Unfortunately, because of the actions of two very selfish people, this town will always leave a sour taste in my mouth.

As I drive out of the city limits of Mount Pleasant, I don't look back.

twenty-seven

The house before me looks so...grown-up. I click the screen on my phone, looking at Susie's text one more time. *Yep, 325.*

Staring back at the house, I see the copper-plated *325* on the side of the front door, but I still can't believe Jax owns this. It's not that he doesn't deserve it, but I'm just surprised.

The house has a classic mission-style feel to it. The wooden siding is painted a deep blue. There is a stunning front wraparound porch compiled of gorgeous woodwork. It is like a home right out of a magazine. It's still shocking that Jax bought this. I shake my head in disbelief.

After everything happened with Trenton and Tabitha, I came home. I've been home for over a month now, licking my wounds and trying to get back to a good place.

So much has happened in the past two years. It has been a bit of a hot mess in actuality. I had a better handle on my life at seventeen than I do now at two months shy of twenty-three.

I haven't spoken to Jax since last Christmas Eve. He asked for time, and I gave it to him. I vowed to myself that I wouldn't be the one to contact him as long as I was still dating Trenton—for six months anyway. Then, when everything fell apart with that relationship, I couldn't just run back to Jax in that state. He hadn't wanted to bring me down when he was at his lowest, so I couldn't do that to him.

In reality, the whole ordeal with Trenton didn't take me long to get over. I think the hardest part was allowing my wounded ego to heal. I felt so betrayed and stupid. I was naive when it came to him. Looking back, I see it all now. He was an asshole from the beginning. He only put me first when it was convenient. He spoke of love and commitment, but they were simply empty words. He thought if he threw enough pretty words and money at me, then he could fool me forever. I admit, he had me fooled for a while.

In hindsight, I was never in love with Trenton. He never owned my heart, not even a sliver of it.

My heart has always belonged to Jax, and it always will. I don't know why I didn't go back to Jax in December when he begged me to. I've searched for the reasons, and I'm still no closer to having an answer. Part of me wonders if that was my ego, too. Subconsciously, maybe I wanted to hurt Jax for the pain he'd caused me. He'd broken my heart, so I was determined to ride out the thing I had going with Trenton to prove my point. I'm not sure. It doesn't sound like me or something I would do, but I have wondered. I can't think of any other reason I would have stayed with Trenton when the love of my life was begging for me to come back to him. Like they say, hurt people hurt people.

Or maybe I was protecting myself from losing Jax again. By staying with Trenton, who I thought was a sure thing, I had someone who wouldn't leave me. Perhaps I always knew that I would go back to Jax, but I wanted to do it on my timeline. Maybe I wanted the control—unlike the helplessness I'd felt when Jax broke it off and didn't give me a say.

There are so many possibilities as to why I made the choice to stay with Trenton, but I don't know if any of them are correct. The only thing I can say is that, at the time, I felt it was the best choice for me, reasons unknown. Also, if it were my ego, my pride, whatever I should call it that kept me away from Jax, it wasn't a conscious decision. I would never purposely hurt Jax to be vindictive.

What it's come down to though, regardless of why I made the choices I made, is that I'm now in a place where I'm once again one hundred percent happy with myself. I've waited to go to Jax until I could confidently tell him that I want him back—not because I'm alone, but because he is the only man on this earth made for me. I've waited until I could be the whole woman that Jax deserves. It wasn't easy. I've wanted to come to Jax almost every second of every day since driving out of Mount Pleasant, but I know that he deserves a whole me, not a broken one.

I've spent all of the last two months having quality time with my family. I've passed my days spending warm afternoons lying on a blanket under our tree, reading. I've written a lot in my journal, reflecting on these past two years and my role in the failure of them. I've had a handful of freelance photography jobs, and I'm starting to build up a nice resume. I've let go of all my disappointment in the choices that Jax made, knowing that he did what he felt was right.

I'm ready to face Jax and offer him all of me without the baggage of our mistakes weighing me down. I'm happier than I've ever been, especially since I'm standing at Jax's door, ready to resume the rest of our lives together.

My mom doesn't seem to have any information on what Jax has been up to this past six months. When I've spent time with the Porters, they haven't spoken to me about Jax's happenings either. There has been this awkward dynamic between our families where no one discusses Jax around me anyway. Come to think of it, I can't remember the last time Jax went home. I believe it was Christmas. So, apparently, he has been keeping his distance from us all. I'm excited to put all of that behind us and get back to the normalcy I crave.

Other than his address, Susie didn't give me any information about Jax. I know that Jax just bought this house, but I'm the first person from home to see it. Standing at this beautiful home that wasn't cheap in Ann Arbor, I can only assume that he has landed an amazing job. I'm so proud of him.

I inhale deeply, filling my lungs with air. When I exhale, I push all my nervous energy out with it. I'm moments away from my happily ever after. I knock twice on the thick wooden door. I wait for an eternity that fits into the space of several heartbeats, and finally, the door opens.

Jax stands before me, looking even more beautiful than ever. Although only six months older than the last time I saw him, he looks so much more mature somehow. He appears thicker, stronger, and his jaw is more defined.

His stunning emerald eyes go wide when he sees me. "Lily...what are you...Lil." He pulls me into a hug and firmly holds me to his chest.

I inhale deeply, squeezing my arms around his back. He smells of Jax, of happiness, of home. He grabs my shoulders, pushing me away enough so that he can see me. His eyes travel from my toes to my face, and I watch as he takes me in.

"Hi," I say quietly with a grin across my face.

"I can't believe you are here. Oh my God. It's so good to see you. Come in." His words are rushed.

I enter the house, which is beautifully decorated. It is bright from the sunlight shining in through the windows, illuminating the dark wooden floors spanning the house as far as I can see. I follow him into a formal living room area and take a seat on a plush tan sofa.

"Jax, your house is so gorgeous. I can't even get over it. It's stunning." My face turns to take it all in.

I notice a hole in the drywall. I'm assuming a table leg or something went through it when moving. I'm sure there is a story behind the hole, and I can't wait to hear it. *What a perfect little imperfection.*

I smile, but I stop frozen when my gaze connects with Jax. He is standing with his arms crossed, leaning against a wooden column that connects this room with the next. His eyes glisten, and he's just staring at me. Behind his stare are so many emotions, so many words that he wants to say.

I don't like the uncomfortable air between us. I want us back, and I want it now.

I pat the sofa cushion next to me. "Come sit. You're too far away."

Q

Jax walks toward me, slowly, his expression calculating. He lowers himself onto the cushion and pivots so that our knees touch as we continue to look at one another. I take his hands in mine, and beneath my fingers, I don't miss the minor flinch I feel coming from him. Despite his body's reservations, it is so good to feel him again. I run my thumb across the warm skin of his strong hands, and I want to cry.

"I've missed you." I bite my bottom lip to stop it from quivering.

"I've missed you, too." His voice is soft, comforting.

"I don't even know where to start. I guess I need to start by saying I'm sorry. I'm sorry for everything, Jax."

He shakes his head. "Don't. You have nothing to be sorry for."

"No, I do. I'm so sorry that I wasted these past six months. It was always you, Jax. You know that. You are the love of my life. It has always been and will always be only you."

"Little—"

"No, let me finish. Please," I plead. "These past two years have been a total waste. I can't figure out how we went from where we were to where we are now, but I can't go on without you anymore."

"Lily—" Jax's voice is persistent.

"No, please. I have a lot more that I need to say. I don't know why I didn't take you up on your offer in December. I still can't figure that out myself, but it had nothing to do with my feelings for you. I have always loved you and only you. The way I felt about Trenton never compared to the way I've felt about you. I wanted to come to you the second things ended with him, but I didn't want to come to you like that." I pause, taking a deep breath. "I've spent the past two months healing. I worked on myself until I could be the woman that you deserve. I'm coming to you now, one hundred percent whole, one hundred percent happy, and I'm ready to give you all of me. Life is too short to spend any more time apart. You are it for me, Jax Porter. You are the only man I will ever love."

I stop talking and smile. I've laid my heart out on the line. I study Jax's expression and realize he looks so sad, almost pained.

His eyes fill with unshed tears.

"What is it?" I ask, the panic rising in my voice.

He looks down, and he closes his eyes.

"Jax, tell me. What is it?"

He lifts his gaze, and his eyes scan my face, darting from my eyes to my mouth. He shakes his head. "I…"

I nod, urging him to continue.

"It's just that so much has happened. I…" He lets out an audible exhale and blinks hard. "Lily, I'm engaged."

I pull my hands back, releasing them from his touch. I scoot back until the arm of the sofa is against my backside. His words send terror through me. I slowly shake my head back and forth, unable to believe him.

He lowers his stare. "I'm sorry. It all happened kind of fast. I didn't know how to tell you. We haven't spoken in so long, and I couldn't just drop something like this on you out of the blue."

"I can't believe this. I can't believe this. I can't believe this." Hot tears break free, and I cup my face in my hands. Holding my face, I rock back and forth, desperately trying to process what is going on.

"I'm sorry," Jax says again.

I lift my head. "How could you do this? It's been six months! How do you move on from a lifetime of love in six months? How is this even possible?" My body shakes as I cry, unable to hold in the sadness.

"I know. I know this must seem unbelievable. I wanted to tell you, Lil. I did. It's just..." His voice breaks.

"What? It's just, everything you said to me was a lie?"

He reaches for my hand, but I pull it back.

"No, never. Listen to me when I tell you this. I love you. I will love you forever. This isn't something I planned. It kind of just happened. Everything I have ever said to you is the truth. You are the love of my life. That will never change."

"I'm the love of your life, so you decide to marry someone else? That makes no sense, Jax! I can't believe this!" I lay my face in my hands once more and cry. It's not a dainty sob but the uninhibited ugly cry that I know is turning my face into a blotchy mess and spreading my mascara over my skin like war paint. Yet I can't find it in me to care.

Everything I have ever wanted and every dream that I've had for my life have just died. I don't know how I'm going to recover from this.

He clears his throat. "Lily, I wish I could make you understand, let you see. I never meant to hurt you. God, I fucking love you. I'm just trying to do the right thing here. Please understand."

I lift my head and shake it from side to side. "I will never understand this." Each word coming out is laced with so much anger. "I will never get over this. I will never be okay again."

A tear slips down Jax's face. "Please don't say that. You will. You're strong and brave. You will find happiness again. Please find happiness again," he begs.

I stare into the face of the man I love, my future...but he's not my future anymore. He's someone else's.

Hearing the front door open, my face snaps toward it.

Stella enters, her shiny chestnut hair swaying as she walks. Her head is tilted down as she flips through a stack of mail. Her sweet voice echoes through the room. "Baby, do you know where I put the receipt for that lamp we're going to take back?" She lifts her face, and her eyes momentarily go wide when she sees me, but she quickly composes herself. "Lily." She gracefully ignores my tear-soaked face. "It's so good to see you." Her eyes dart between Jax and me. "I'm going to go make some lemonade. Would either of you like a glass?"

I clear my throat. "No, thank you. I was just leaving."

Stella looks around the room as if she's misplaced something before continuing in her trademark sweetness, "Okay, well, I'll be in the kitchen if anyone needs anything. I'm glad you could stop by, Lily." Her heels click on the rich wood as she retreats to the kitchen.

"Don't go. Not like this. Let's talk about this," Jax pleads.

I sigh. The last two years have drained me. From fighting to hold on to my relationship with Jax when he was determined to let it go to fighting the guilt I felt when I chose Trenton…I have nothing left. "There's nothing to talk about," I say sadly.

"I want you in my life, Lily. Maybe our friendship won't be like it was before, but I still need you." His eyes are sad.

Despite the fact that he has asked another woman to spend the rest of her life with him, I see the love he still has for me behind his beautiful green eyes that have captivated me for as long as I can remember. It is that love still shining for me that breaks me even more.

"You don't need me. You have her." I stand up and smooth down the nonexistent wrinkles on my black capris.

"No, I need you. I love you. I can't lose you completely." Jax sounds panicked as he rises from the sofa.

I stand before Jax and take him in. We remain in silence as I commit his features to memory. My heart cries with pain. The fierce love for this man before me beats through my veins, burning me with sorrow.

I raise the palm of my hand to his cheek, and he leans into my touch. The feel of his skin against my hand almost renders me speechless.

I swallow the lump in my throat. "You already lost me. I just didn't know it."

I drop my hand and walk out his front door, away from the only man I have ever loved.

twenty-eight

I run my thumb along the silver embossed letters, feeling the words beneath my skin. The texture makes it more real somehow. It is one thing to read the words and another to feel them. I can't simply close my eyes and pretend they aren't there. Their pressure against my skin is a reminder of their existence.

This is real. It is happening.

The paper itself is the most sophisticated delicate pink that I have ever seen with glimmers of real rose-hued flowers throughout. The silk ribbon that expertly tied the package of stationery together lies discarded at my feet. The presentation, every detail, is stunning.

Of course, his wedding invitations are perfection. *Why wouldn't they be? Especially with someone like Stella planning it all. She's Miss Walking Perfection herself.*

My body sways, my balance teetering. Feeling my bed against the back of my legs, I sit. Still holding the invitation in my hand, I close my eyes and let my head fall back. I breathe in deeply, sucking as much air into my lungs as I can, before I let it out in a long breath.

A lone traitorous tear escapes and slides down my cheek before falling to my lap. I'm done crying for Jax Porter. I promised myself that I wouldn't shed another tear for him, and I won't from here on out—save for any random defectors that make a stealth escape without my permission. I've given him more tears this past two years than anyone deserves in a lifetime.

It's been a month and a half since I walked out of their home. According to the date on this invitation, it will be just shy of two months before they are married. I've always dreamed that Jax and I would get married in October. I've always wanted a fall wedding. There is nothing more beautiful than autumn in Michigan. He's getting the grand fall wedding, but I'm not the bride.

I still can't wrap my mind around the rush to all of this. They will be married before they have been together a year. I'm not exactly sure when they got together, but I know they weren't a couple over Christmas last year, a mere eight months ago. I don't know if I will ever understand, but I've come to terms with the fact that it's not my place to. It's not a requirement that I comprehend their actions, but it is my responsibility to accept it.

For months now, I've been playing the what-if game in my head. *What if I'd gotten back together with Jax over Christmas? What if I'd never dated Trenton? What if I'd gone to the University of Michigan in the first place?* There are endless ways in which these past two years could have played out. I will never know what decision was the one that ultimately made it impossible for Jax and me to find our way back to each other.

For all I know, we would have ended up here anyway even if we had made different choices. I'm not sure why it worked out this way, but it did. Life is kind of crazy like that. There are no absolutes. In fact, the only thing in life that is guaranteed is that there are no guarantees.

I always thought that Jax was my golden ticket to happiness, but I was wrong. There is joy without Jax, and in actuality, there always has been. In all my happy memories, he was there, and I let myself think that he was the reason. But now, I know that he was just along for the ride, just as I was on his roller coaster through life. He was a passenger on my ride, the one I created.

I have the choice to live my life with regret or to live it with gratitude, and I'm choosing the latter. I still don't understand everything that has happened, and maybe I never will. But I know that this isn't the end for me. I'm not on the downward slide of life at almost twenty-three. Bigger and better things are out there.

A smile warms my face as I focus on the full suitcase sitting next to my bedroom door. I leave tomorrow for New York City. I still can't wrap my mind around that one either. While looking for photography jobs online this summer, I came across an internship at a huge advertising firm, and I applied on a whim. I knew that the competition would be fierce, and the chances of me getting it would be slim, but I applied nonetheless. I was thrilled when I made it far enough to have a phone interview with three separate higher-ups at the company, but I still didn't think I had a chance. My head felt like it would explode from excitement when I got the call that I had been chosen.

I know that the shots I took for Mr. Troy's promotional campaign helped me get the position, and for that and that alone, I feel gratitude toward Trenton. The woman who called me from HR to offer me the position seemed impressed with my whole portfolio, and I've never felt prouder.

It's hard to pinpoint, but I have this huge sense of hope blossoming inside me. I feel that this move is going to be great for me. It just feels right.

I've never felt more afraid and exhilarated at the same time. This is my time, my time to figure out my place in the world and to find my destiny. I'm not going to focus on anything but myself and living each day with hope and happiness in my heart.

I stand and place the invitation on the dresser. Wide smiles from the innocent faces of Jax and me as fourteen-year-olds grin up to me from a cheap plastic frame that Jax got me for my fourteenth birthday. I pick up the photo and smile at the pair of wide-eyed kids. We were the perfect pair.

I hug the photo to my chest before turning and walking to my suitcase. Unzipping the top, I slip the photo in between my clothes before closing the suitcase back up. I haven't spoken to Jax since June when I walked out of his house, but I think it's been long enough. I'm ready to move on. There have been way too many periods of silence between us this past year.

I have loved Jax for as far back as I can remember. I loved him before I could pronounce my L sounds when I would say I "yuved" him. I loved him when I made him mud pies from my driveway when the only thing more fun than cooking with mud was rolling around in it until only our eyes weren't caked with brown sludge. I loved him on our hour-long bike rides when we played Would You Rather until we had to pull off to the side of the road because we were laughing so hard. I loved him through high school when he was the obsession of almost every girl at our school, but he always put me first. I loved him when he became my first boyfriend and showed me what it felt like to be cherished. I loved him over our long-distance relationship when receiving his text messages would make my day. And I love him now as he gets ready to commit his life to another woman.

I will love him forever, and no amount of time or varying circumstances are going to change that. Jax is my best friend. He will always hold the other half of my heart in the figurative BFF necklace that we share. He will be my friend forever.

I hop onto my bed and lie back as I click my phone screen, pulling up my Favorites list. My thumb hovers over his name. I take a deep breath and touch his name. My heart thrums wildly as his phone rings twice on the other end.

His voice comes through my earpiece, and I almost cry from happiness. I can move to New York tomorrow with no regrets because the world is right as long as Jax and I are friends again.

"Little Love."

His voice sounds anxious, hesitant.

"Hey, mister." Another rogue tear escapes, but this tear is full of happiness.

"I've missed hearing your voice."

I pause. "Me, too."

"So, how are you?"

I tell him the truth, "I'm good. I'm really good."

The relief in his voice is palpable. He exhales. "That makes me so happy to hear."

"How have you been?" I ask, not afraid of his answer.

"Really good, too. Great now that you've called."

"I know. It's been quite the year, hasn't it? Where do we even go from here?"

"We talk. Let's start off with you telling me everything."

I laugh. "Everything, huh? That could take a while."

"I've got time."

I can hear the grin in his voice.

My last slivers of unease fade away as our conversation goes on for hours, and it's such therapy for my soul. My heart is happy as I know that I can leave for New York tomorrow with everything I need to start this new chapter of my life, including the one thing I've always had—my best friend.

The End

Find out how Jax and Lily's story ends in
A Forever Kind of Love,
book two in the Choices series,
releasing May 2015.

about the author

Ellie Wade resides in southwest Michigan with her husband, three young children, and two dogs. She has a master's in education from Eastern Michigan University, and she is a huge University of Michigan sports fan. She loves the beauty of her home state, especially the lakes and the gorgeous autumn weather. When she is not writing, she is reading, snuggled up with her kids, or spending time with family and friends. She loves traveling and exploring new places with her family.

acknowledgments

I still can't believe that this is my third book! Someone, please pinch me now! I truly can't emphasize enough how very grateful I am for everything that I have experienced this year. I have met so many amazing people in this book world, and I am overwhelmed by the kindness of this community. This has been a dream come true for me, and if you are reading this, thank you for being a part of this journey. My cup runneth over. ♥

To my family—I am so blessed to have a large family, full of wonderful people who have supported me my whole life. One of my wishes is that my children will grow up to love each other as much as I love my siblings. I wouldn't be who I am today without my brothers and sisters. I love you all so much.

Mom, thank you for loving and encouraging me always. I love you to the moon and back.

To my mother-in-law—I hit the jackpot with you. You are the best. I love you.

There is a core group of women who have immensely helped me. It still boggles my mind that these wonderful women take time out of their lives to help me, and many of them didn't know me prior to reading my books.

To my beta readers and proofreaders—Gayla, Nicole, Jen, Amy, Robert, Tammi, Dena, Jaime, Heather, Janice, Kristyn, Lauren, and Angela—You all are so awesome. Seriously, each of you is a gift, and you have helped me in valuable different ways. I love you all so much. XOXO

Gayla—You are the most brutal beta I have. I appreciate the time you take to make my books the best they can be. You are a blessing, and I love you more than I could ever express.

Lauren—I've said it before, and I will say it again. The day you were born, I was given one of the greatest gifts this life has to offer. I love you regardless of whether you help with the book or not. LOL.

Jen—You are one of the most beautiful souls I have ever or will ever know. My life is infinitely better with you in it. Love you always.

Nicole, my BBWFL—You are my biggest supporter and ally in this crazy book world. You are one of those people who makes everyone feel loved and important. Your friendship means the world to me. Love you forever.

Janice—You keep life exciting. I love you. Thank you for supporting me always.

Kristyn—Thank you for always fitting in my last-minute proofreads! We'll be friends until the day we die. I love you. #putasforlife

Robert—You are the best male beta reader out there! Your support is epic. Love you more always. Thanks for the most disgusting Would You Rather question ever. XO

Tammi—Your feedback brought tears to my eyes and made me feel amazing. If everyone could see this book and these characters the way you did, I'd be a bestseller. ;-) Thank you for truly getting my words. XO

Amy, my BBFFL—Thank you for your support from commenting on all my blog takeovers so that I'm not alone in promoting my books to being the best beta in the world. I am so very grateful for you. Every wall sex scene will infinitely be dedicated to you. I heart you big time. ♥

Heather—Thank you for getting my characters! You are my angst soul sister! I loved your feedback and am so grateful for you. XO

Dena—Thank you for supporting me since *Forever Baby*. I am so grateful for your pimping, messaging, and our laughs. #TMI #soulsisters XO

Jaime—You are the newest addition to this posse and already one of my favorites! Thank you for loving Jax! You are also my TMI soul sister! XO

Angela—Thank you for your enthusiasm, your teasers, and your endless support! You're awesome! XO

To the bloggers—Oh my God! I love you! Since releasing *Forever Baby*, I have gotten to know many of you through Facebook. Out of the kindness of your hearts, so many of you have reached out and helped me promote my books. There are seriously great people in this blogger community, and I am humbled by your support. Truly, thank you! Because of you, indie authors get their stories out. Thank you for supporting all authors and the great stories they write.

To Ena from Enticing Journey Book Promotions— Thank you for all your hard work in promoting *A Beautiful Kind of Love*. You're awesome!

To my cover artist, Regina Wamba from Mae I Design and Photography—Thank you! Your work inspires me. You are extremely talented at what you do, and I am so grateful to now have four of your covers. I love this cover so much. It is perfection—Everything you do is!

To my editor and interior designer, Jovana Shirley from Unforeseen Editing—Thank you so much for the amazing work you did! You are seriously the best! Thank you for fitting me in and for the quality work you do. I am so grateful for you and everything you have done to make this book the best it can be. You are truly talented. XOXO

Finally and most importantly, to the readers—If you are reading this, thank you! From the bottom of my heart, thank you for helping my dream come true! I truly hope you enjoyed reading *A Beautiful Kind of Love*. I am so grateful for your support!

You can connect with me on several places, and I would love to hear from you.

Find me on Facebook: www.facebook.com/EllieWadeAuthor

Find me on Twitter: @authorelliewade

Visit my website: www.elliewade.com

Remember, the greatest gift you can give an author is a review. If you feel so inclined, please leave a review on the various sites. It doesn't have to be fancy. A couple of sentences would be awesome!

I could honestly write a whole book about everyone in this world whom I am thankful for. I am blessed in so many ways, and I am beyond grateful for this beautiful life. XOXO

Forever,

Ellie ♥